Elizabeth Tudor:
Ancestry of Sorcery

By Theresa Pocock

12 Twelve, young person's themes suitable only for readers of twelve years and older.

Big World Network
Utah

Elizabeth Tudor
Elizabeth Tudor: Ancestry of Sorcery

Managing editor – Erica Mills
Associate Editor – Wendy Herman
Interior Formatting – FireDrake Designs www.firedrakedesigns.com

A Big Network World Book Published by Big World Network
363 E. Woodlake Dr. | 232 | Salt Lake City, UT | 84107 |
www.bigworldnetwork.com

ISBN-13: 978-0692176344
ISBN-10: 0692176349

First U.S. Edition: August 2016 Printed in the United States of America
Second U.S. Edition: August 2018 Printed in the United States of America

For those who have supported me.
You know who you are.
Thank you for helping me be brave.

Theresa

I wonder, now that I am dying and am able to look back upon what I have done, if at times I did what I should? Did I choose evil more than good? I guess I shall know when I stand at the judgement bar of God.

— FROM FILLIOS DA MENTE E DA LÚA

Elizabeth Tudor:
Ancestry of Sorcery

TABLE OF CONTENTS

DISCOVERY
SEASON 1*

*Chapters=Episodes. There are 12 Episodes per Season.
Much like television...only in book form.

OF MOON AND MIND
SEASON 2

SEASON OF TEMPTATION
SEASON 3

DISCOVERY

EPISODE 1

January 1536
Hatfield House, Hertfordshire

Lightning flashed and thunder clapped, illuminating the stone hall and sending vibrations strong enough to nearly shatter the glass panes. Those fragile frames rattled as they stood between Anne and her comeuppance. Rather shoddy defenses, unfortunately. The dark tempest outside was like a herald, and there was nothing, despite all her talent, that she could do to silence it now.

As she hurried away from the wailing of rain and wind, her body ached. It rebelled against her wishes, and the pain of that rebellion hunching her over. She closed her eyes to fight back the sting and immediately saw the face of her lifeless son behind her lids. His motionless body had come from inside her less than a week before, and the sadness, pain, and fear that surrounded the event clawed at her focus.

Henry would kill her for the death of his son, and he would do it soon. She absentmindedly lifted her ringed fingers to her small, pale neck. When it started throbbing—

she realized that she was desperately caressing herself—she forced the hand slowly down, and sped up her flight.

Lightning again broke the darkness that surrounded her. The thunder that immediately followed sent a jolt through her body that made the small hairs on her neck and arms stand up. It refocused her and she whispered, as if to the night sky, "I know, I know!" Her legs moved as swiftly as her sore body, and the decorum expected from a queen of England, would allow. Urgency drove her to consider lifting her skirts and running, but years of prudence forced the thought from her mind.

The storm was silent for a moment. As if by the power of her renewed vigor, nature's rage was temporarily quailed. In that silence, Anne heard only the clicking of her leather-soled riding boots on the hard granite stones and the swish of her silk skirts. Finally, she rounded a corner that would thankfully take her away from the windows and into the candlelit interior of Hatfield.

A door up ahead opened, and Anne instantly slowed her pace and calmed her features. It was only a servant who exited the door. He bowed very low as she passed, likely wondering why the queen was not at Hampton, still in her birthing bed. Feeling the servant's presence following her forced her to continue her measured speed. The slowness infuriated her, so she closed her eyes and felt the pull of the moon. It was already In the right spot in the heavens and, if she did not hurry, she would miss her one and only opportunity.

Concentrating, she took the power that lay in her mind and pulled it around her like a thick, shining blanket of brightness. Instantly the glow of moonlight surrounded her. She normally did not have to think about the process. It was instinctual after so many years. However, at this moment, she carefully savored every detail of what she did. This would be the last time she would ever use her power. Of course, the servant would not be able to see it in all its celestial glory. Only Anne could see the beautiful gift God had given to her.

With the power caressing her skin and the light blending with the strength of her mind, she wrapped the thought of the servant's face with the desire for something basic, something that would shift his focus from her. Then she directed the power she held in her mind at him as she whispered, "Quickly! You need to find a privy!"

She closed her eyes and willed the small orb of light to leave her and go to the man, then released the power. Her skin instantly felt cold and her steps heavy. Knowing that the orb would only take a moment to have its way with the man's mind, she lifted her skirts and began to run just as his steps behind her quickened and turned down another hallway.

She took the first corner slowly, but then scrambled up the steps that lay before her. The door she was heading for was not far now. Finally, the candlelight revealed the tall, thick wood that separated her from her only living child—from Elizabeth.

Without pausing, she forcefully pushed the door aside and entered the quiet chamber where her three-year-old daughter slept. Hoping not to wake the nursemaid, Lady Bryan, Anne hastened across the floor and pulled back the bed curtains and blankets. Gently, she gathered up Elizabeth's small body and stepped back to the door.

Eventually she wound around enough corners to bring her to a window facing the moon. Anne's black eyes glanced hopefully to the round light in the sky, surrounded by stormy clouds. As she looked down at her child, she was surprised to see Elizabeth's dark eyes staring back at her.

"Mama," Elizabeth said with a quiet voice, and Anne

smiled and embraced her, emotions finally overflowing. Her cheeks were soaked before she realized she was crying. As she squeezed Elizabeth to her chest, she did not hold back a single tear.

Suddenly, thunder clapped, and Anne's eyes shot angrily to the night sky, but then she pulled back and looked into her child's face. Ever obedient to her will, the moonlight encircled both her and Elizabeth.

"We have only moments, my love. This is not the way I would have liked to give you the most valuable gift I have to offer, but I fear this will be the last chance I have." Anne pressed her forehead to her daughter's, and, in a shaky voice, whispered the words she had never uttered aloud, but knew as well as she knew she was the Queen of England. "I willingly pass to thee, my chosen daughter, that gift which my mother gave to me and her mother gave to her. By the power of the moon and the mind, let it be given."

Just then, lightning choked the light of the moon out of discernment. The momentary light plunged them both into a deep darkness and allowed Anne to notice a glow coming from deep within her chest. There in the dark, cold, stormy night, the power that had been with Anne as long as she could remember—in her thoughts, radiating throughout her body— that power departed. It revealed itself as a small glowing orb, which parted Anne's lips as it left and entered Elizabeth's mouth in the same manner. Anne found herself wondering during this transfer what this small mystical sphere could be, but she felt its absence as soon as it was gone and was distracted by the void.

Elizabeth's eyes lit as the gift entered her mind. Anne knew the small child instantly felt the pull of the moon, for her head moved toward the heavenly yellow object which, as Anne saw now, was almost completely covered in clouds. She could no longer feel its eminence in her mind and panic struck, for she knew that not having the power would assure her fate.

September 1542
Royal Hunting Lodge, Pyrgo Park

"The fact that your mother truly was a whore should not have any bearing on whether you are restored to the succession, Elizabeth. Father has made it clear that he considers all of our mothers whores." Mary gave an unceremonious snort before continuing. "Whores he can dispose of at his royal whim, so it makes sense that he would treat his children similarly."

Her resonant voice filled the small, finely furnished chamber where we lounged, waiting for our father, King Henry VIII of England, and his escort to arrive.

"You are fortunate that he is even willing to see you today after how dreadfully disrespectful you have been in the past." Mary refined her snort to a sniff and smoothed her hair. "I certainly would make you grovel for a few more years." She paused again and turned to look at me with a tight smile. Flipping her hand nonchalantly, she moved toward the window.

"Never mind. None of this matters. It is only formality. Father's health is such that Edward is going to rule us all soon enough. You will see. All this ceremony is a result of father's pathetic and guilt-ridden attitude in his old age—though I know *I* would not feel bad for chopping your mother's head off." Mary lifted her nose hotly and said, in an even more insultingly pious tone, "She did commit adultery and treason." At this point Mary stopped trying to be pleasant and said under her breath, but quite loud enough for me to hear, "Besides, Anne Boleyn was a sorceress. If her treachery toward my mother was not reason enough for death, sorcery certainly was."

She ran her hand in the sign of the cross from her forehead down her chest, and then from shoulder to shoulder. Softly she kissed her thumb, closed her eyes, and muttered silently to herself. She was probably reciting a prayer for having said the words "whore" and "sorceress" in the same speech.

I watched her lips stop and her eyes open, but I could not stop glaring at her and was thankful when she turned her tightly knotted black head of hair away from me, so I wasn't caught. She was waiting for me to pounce on her as I had the last time we met, and though anger did fill me, I kept my mouth shut and let my eyes say the words she would never hear, for I was resolved to be on my absolute best behavior.

This very day I would see my father for the first time in two years. I shivered as I thought of how at the age of six I had not understood what had happened to my mother and made a horribly foolish comment to my father about his right to kill innocent mothers as he saw fit. I had been paying for those hasty, naive words ever since, so I would let nothing spoil the joy I felt at this gesture of rehabilitation. I secretly hoped that if I pleased him, my expulsion would end completely.

Moreover, I could not take offence at what Mary, or anyone else for that matter, said about my mother. I had not known her. I was three when father had her killed. I would not cling to the remembrance of a woman who I felt almost nothing for, a woman I could never understand. These thoughts brought a tightness to my stomach, but I ignored it. I would not chain myself, as Mary had done, to the memory of

and I knew that I was always able to tell more about a person or situation than what was said with words, but I wanted him to see more than that. I wanted him to see me. And I wanted him to see himself in me, for I looked more like him than anyone else, and I felt wild and adventurous like him.

But I think more than all of this, I wanted him to love me.

As I realized this, my hands began to tremble. From what I had read and what I knew of people, the fact that I needed his love put my heart at my father's mercy, and I knew that father had not treated many hearts he'd owned with kindness.

Still, every part of my body and soul wanted it.

I t was a dinner fit for the king who attended. Father had spent much of the previous day hunting and had luckily taken down a glorious seventeen-point buck, which had been seasoned and prepared and now roasted on the spit in the hall where we sat. Mary sat in her black high-necked gown with covered head, and I in lace over blue silk. The King wore a magnificent royal red doublet of crushed velvet with thick gold chains, deep blue leggings, and codpiece.

Though father had come with a party of ten other men, none of them joined us for dinner. Father, Mary, and I were the only attendees. Father started the conversation as soon as the first course was set. "Ladies, tell your father how your journey was."

Mary instantly spoke up. "The roads were tolerable, so it went quickly enough, but we had not planned on sitting about for two days waiting for a summons, Father." Her voice was even but her face scrunched just the tiniest bit when she said this. I only noticed it because I had lived with Mary for five years and knew the danger it indicated. Instantly her tone changed, as I knew it would, and she skillfully made light of the spurn. "You are a mean, evil man, forcing us to wait to see you for so long. I have missed you terribly, Father." Her lip protruded slightly, and she reached out a round hand toward him and patted his rather red, puffy-looking hand. She was very skilled at this courtly exchange. She had said and done everything perfect as far as I could see, and Father was not able to stop himself from being affected.

There had been a slight bit of annoyance in Father's eyes, but that was gone now. "I was not feeling myself after the journey here, and then the men insisted that I hunt with them. Of course, I was happy to go, despite some discomfort in my leg, and I was excessively happy when I took down that buck. I would tell you all the details, but I fear I would bore you refined ladies."

I, of course, would not be bored by any story of his, and so I decided that I would join in the conversation. "I would love to hear your story, Majesty. Pray, continue." So, he did with vigor, the exciting details of the hunt fueling his animated gestures. Unfortunately, after his story was concluded, I did not get to participate in the rest of the conversation. Though I had many thoughts and much to say to my father, Mary always beat me to it, and I had to defer to her for she was much older than I. Mary's playful banter with Father continued for a while, then she turned haughty in manner and I could tell that she was maneuvering. There was nothing I could do, so I ate and watched her.

EPISODE 2

September 1542
Royal Hunting Lodge, Pyrgo Park

As we walked from dinner down the clean yet sparsely decorated hall, Mary murmured on and on about how impossible Father was. Father, in my opinion, had behaved as a saint would. If I were queen, I never could have endured Mary's nosy comments, degrading tone, and superior manner without screaming at her in anger.

When Mary asked Father about Queen Catherine, we both watched his face go almost scarlet and then sad. Yet he did not chastise her or discipline her for disrespect.

I did not know all the details of Father's latest marriage, and I had avoided knowing because intuition told me Catherine had suffered the same fate as my mother. I had known Catherine and cared for her and I did not want to know a thing that would hurt me. She was dead and that was enough detail for me.

However, Mary soon moved on to a much different topic: Father going to war with France. She scoffed and said with her most concerned voice, "Father, I would hate to have you die in war when you are still at odds with Rome."

As if Father were going to fasten a cannon to his horse and light the charge as he galloped into enemy territory. For shame! To remind Father of his excommunication and comment on Rome's unyielding grudge toward all things English was a thrust that cut to Father's heart. The pain was evident on his face. I could not help feeling a small spurn in my direction. After all, whose mother had instigated the break from Rome? Mary could not have picked two less appropriate and awkward topics. That Father did not order her from his presence was a display of astonishing self-control.

By the end of the evening I had concluded that Mary was not trying for rehabilitation at all. She was beyond caring. She had done everything to please Father, and though he had a relationship with her now he had not put her back into the line of succession. Perhaps at this meeting she was trying a new tactic, but the way she went about it was infuriating and at moments simply treasonous. It made me so angry that, as soon as the hallways permitted me, I left Mary's side without a word and walked out to the stables.

Kat, of course, was not far behind. She was relentless in her duty. In a way, it was comforting that she was always there. Furthermore, since Kat was a marvelous equestrian, I never had to worry about her keeping pace with me on these little journeys.

It was a beautiful night and my gaze was pulled heaven-ward toward the moon, whose beams were broken up by the many trees that surrounded the house. Father had recently decided to reinvent Pyrgo Park, and there was much clearing required to transform this corner of Romford. I looked up at the sky and realized there was no way I would get a clear view of the moon amid all the vegetation, and though I loved the beauty of a well-pruned oak or beech, at that moment I could not have agreed more with his plans to clear them all out.

In the stable, with Kat's help, I stripped off my blue silk, hung it on a peg, and then donned the plain cotton dress I used for riding at night. After mounting Beaux, I instantly had the desire to race to the top of the west hill, which was a treeless plateau. I hungered for the open sky and the great celestial illumination therein.

While Beaux picked our way to the appropriate trail, I again thought of tonight's dinner and wished with all my heart that Father could see me as I rode. I wanted him to know and remember me as I was in the saddle, riding bare-back in the dark of night.

After hearing Father's story of hunting, I believed now more than ever that his heart and mine were very much the same. The pert, quiet Elizabeth who had all the intelligent, spot-on answers to Kat's questions was impressive and frankly everything a person of my standing should be. But she was not all that I was.

As Beaux and I walked toward the hilltop, we startled several birds out of the trees, but I did not look to name them. I simply pressed my heel gently into Beaux's side. As he sped up, the cool September wind brushed my cheeks, giving my face a sudden chill, but my body felt warm against Beaux's back. I could feel every strain of his hardened back muscles as he lifted us through the wood and up the hill. I listened to the sound of his shoes clicking against the small stones and roots they touched and smiled to myself, wondering if anyone else thought that the most beautiful sound in the world.

His breath remained even for a while, but soon I could smell his mouth and coat as he began to pant and sweat. I reveled in the damp air that tasted like burning wood and chestnuts, and the feel of the leather reins in my ungloved hands. My skirts rose, and I lifted my knees a little, squeezing Beaux with my thighs and heels to let him know I wanted more speed. He met my demands with surprisingly little effort, and within moments we broke through the tree line and raced along the crest of the hill.

The moment I was not shaded by the trees I knew why I wanted to come up here. The moon seemed to be right above me, and I instantly felt her shimmering glow pierce through my soul and fill me with life. For some reason I had always felt tied to the moon, always able to feel it day or night or know exactly the piece of sky it would light. Now as I raised my head up, I closed my eyes and basked in the penetrating power that seemed to surround me…to call to me.

Sensing my reaction, Beaux evened out his gate and we flowed through the night as one. Only the wind that whipped my hair and riding dress moved at a different pace than our bodies. All the frustrations of the night went through my mind. The heat of my anger burned the hottest as I thought how I had probably missed my chance to show myself to my father, but as soon as the heat overwhelmed me, I realized that the fire was gone, dissolved into the calm waves of the sea that my insides now were. Moments passed and soon, I felt completely filled and relieved of all my anger. That was the magic of my rides. Once this feeling came, I knew that it was time to rejoin Kat for she was no doubt waiting just out of view for me to turn and seek her out.

~

After putting the horses away and redressing, Kat and I walked silently back toward the lodge. Her arm rested softly over my shoulders. As we rounded a large oak we heard a deep, strained voice. "Elizabeth." We stopped and looked around. Again, "Elizabeth, come here."

I could not see where the voice was coming from, but I knew to whom it belonged, "I am here, my Lord, but I cannot see where you are. Reveal yourself and I will come to you."

Kat grabbed my arm in alarm. Of course she would not know the voice. When had she ever heard him? A tapping sound came from my left, and the voice again. "I am sitting and do not wish to get up. I am to your left. Come child, I have things to say to you."

I gave Kat a reassuring look and murmured, "It is Father." Immediately she let go of my arm and pushed me in the direction of the voice. I smiled at her and stepped around the oak, crushing a few acorn tops with my soft shoes. I'd had one wish for this occasion and I felt deeply in my gut that it was about to come true.

Looking around in the dark, it took me a moment to see him. Nevertheless, there he was, sitting in a chair under one of the most magnificent beech trees on the grounds. He wore a loose-fitting robe and held a stick in his hand. When our eyes met he smiled at me and turned his head to look forward.

Interested by what he was looking at, I glanced the same way and was surprised to see the hilltop I had just come from. It was bathed in light, almost as if the trees were leaning out of the way so that he had a direct view.

"You are very good on your horse, my Bessy." He was now trying to flatter me. I knew that few boys my age were as good on a horse as myself, but I would not blush or simper. I was a princess in training—though the one man that could make me that princess in fact sat staring at me with mirth in his eyes.

"You flatter me, Majesty, but I will not be affected. I have had excellent training, and when one loves a certain thing it is not difficult to excel when all opportunity is granted. In a way, you flatter your own self by complimenting me, for without you, I would be nothing, and thus completely unable to explore my tastes and talents."

Father raised his eyebrows at me. "I hear what you are saying, child, and no one could doubt your intelligence, young as you are." He smiled then and looked down at himself. A longing filled his eyes. "Elizabeth you are a product of your training and your position, and I understand that it is important for me to see you that way, but what I saw up on the hill just now was not a groomed lady."

I quickly began to interrupt him, to apologize. I knew that I was always brazenly immodest and unladylike when taking my secret rides, but he held up his hand and silenced me before I could properly formulate an argument.

"I am not chastising. I am trying to pay you a compliment. I myself have needed time to be free of…our duty."

It thrilled me to hear him include me in the duties of princedom and I reveled in his words as he paused to consider. While he did so, he caressed the arm of the perfectly ornate chair he sat in. With him in it, it was a throne, a throne in the middle of the forest.

"Did you know that I was not supposed to be king?" He laughed and looked up into my face. I tried to look like I did not know the story, but he knew that I was educated in family history. "Of course, you know, you bright child. I suppose that your riding has inspired me to say something. Things do not always end the way they start, Bessy. I have always been carefree and active. A fine horseman, hunter, sportsman—but look at me now." He again looked to the hilltop. "I started my kingdom by fulfilling my duties and soon realized that only doing one's duty brings but a small amount of joy." His eyes came back to mine and there was an intensity there that captured my full attention. "It is only in choosing one's own destiny that happiness may become a part of life."

He brushed a large ringed hand over his care-wrinkled brow. I saw sadness and heartache in his face and heard those when he spoke. "I have made many mistakes, Elizabeth. I need you to know that." He cleared his throat and closed his eyes briefly, continuing quietly. "There is not a single soul on this earth that I can admit that fact to, but seeing you up there on that hill, face toward the sky, I was reminded of someone whom I once loved very much. She was a lot like you, and she was also like me in many aspects. She was a fascinating, infuriating, adventurous soul, and I miss her." He sighed as he went on. "Now that all is said and done, I am sure I will never love anyone the way I loved her." His eyes drifted back to the hilltop and I waited while he thought. After a few moments he said, "You are a young, vibrant version of her." He turned to me and reached out to gently stroke one of my golden curls. "With just a bit of me mixed in."

He chuckled a bit to himself and I smiled at him, though I had no idea what he found humorous. I was struck by the mood he was in and the words that he was sharing. This was not how I thought he would be. This was so much more human.

"Mary was in rare form tonight," he said, changing the subject with a smile.

I laughed. "Yes, she was. I believe you showed a great deal of self-control toward her." Needing to open myself to him as he had done to me, I continued. "I am so thankful that

I was able to meet you out here tonight—that you called to me, and that Mary had made me so angry that I needed to ride. I feared that I would not be able to let you see me or know me. I feared that dinner today would be my only chance." I was looking directly into his face and I saw that he was affected by my words. For a brief instant I thought I saw his eyes soften, his head tilt, and I felt he might be feeling something for me.

At that moment he reached out and patted my arm softly. "We should not judge Mary too harshly. I have known her much longer than you have, and life has not been what it ought to have been for someone in her position. I am afraid the fault for that lies nowhere but on these two shoulders," he said as he touched his chest.

My hopes fell. He was not even thinking of me.

The mood suddenly changed, and he stood. It took him a few minutes, for it was difficult for him to do, and I waited silently, looking up at the hill, not wishing to shame him. "So, you are very good on a horse. Have you ever participated in a hunt?" he asked in a strained voice, and only then did I turn to look at him. There was a hint of excitement in his wide eyes. "I have a desire to gather a force to track down a wild boar. Now that yesterday's hunt broke my streak of recent misfortunes with the bow, I am eager to have some fun."

Though I was concerned that the strenuous activity of boar hunting might not be a good idea for Father, I still smiled and said as we walked, "I do love a wild boar! Very exciting thing, a hunt! Just last year Lord Compton's heart failed him right in the middle of the chase. Oh, and Kat got so involved last time we went that she fell off her horse. I am sure you saw that she is also excellent at handling the animal, yet there she was on the ground and almost trampled by the boar. It truly scared me to death. But Majesty, are you not due to be in Cheshunt by tomorrow? I think that it would not be well with the ladies there if you were missed even by one day. I know the Earl and Lady Frances de Vere, and they would not do without you for even a moment if they could manage it." I looked at him from the corner of my eye and was relieved to see a smile as he watched the ground for any unevenness. I knew that he knew I was concerned. I only hoped he did not think I was maneuvering, as Mary always did.

He did not say anything else as we walked to the house.

EPISODE 3

September 1542
Royal Hunting Lodge, Pyrgo Park

The hunt did not happen. Father was scheduled to leave the next day and he decided to honor his engagements. Regrettably, that day happened to be my birthday. When I arose, I found that Kat had a box and a note from Father. The note was in Father's own beautiful hand.

Happy Birthday Bessy. I was fortunate enough to talk with a gardener who just happened to be working on this as we conversed. I know that this may be one of the most humble gifts I have given you, but after seeing you last night I felt it to be the perfect gift for today. I even finished a few details myself. Know that I will always see you this way.

Love, Henry R

Inside the small, ornate box was a roughly carved girl atop an unsaddled horse. Her hair was flowing behind her and her face lifted as if she were looking at the sky. It was crudely made but beautiful, nonetheless. I pressed it to my chest and blinked away the tears I knew were forming in my eyes, wondering at the providence that had fulfilled my one desire. I had hoped with all my heart as I was up there on that hill that Father could see me for who I was, and I now believed that he had. Amazement and gratitude filled my spirit and words of thankfulness came to my heart. They were said silently there, for just then Mary and her maid, Susan, walked into the room. She had a pleasant smile on her face, so I knew she was not mad at me for leaving her so abruptly the night before.

She could be pleasant. Nevertheless, I sighed.

"I see mine will not be the first gift given today." She said as she walked across the room to wrap her arms tightly around my shoulders. She then said with real warmth, "Happy birthday, my one and only sister. My dear, sweet Elizabeth."

When she pulled away, Susan handed her a small wrapped gift, and she, in turn, handed it to me. I put the carving in my pocket and pulled the gauzy cloth away from what was obviously a book. I admired the cover for a few moments, for it was intricately stitched. The beauty was not merely in the tightness and evenness of the stitches, but also the boldness of the color scheme. My name and the date were attractively sewn between deep purple iris and dark green vines. Its style said *Elizabeth*, not *Mary*.

That is, until I opened the cover.

Mary leaned over me and read the cover page aloud. "A book of hours translated from Latin to English by Mary Tudor for her sister Elizabeth Tudor."

I knew such a gift must have taken Mary months. Still it instantly rankled. I knew almost every prayer by memory. I had learned many of them from her, for we said them every day the same as anyone else. Many times, I even felt her rote prayers in my heart. So, I did not understand why she would insist on giving them to me in this manner as if I were some heathen who needed to know my God better.

Of course, she saw herself as the magnificent Saint Mary who would grant me, the Protestant bastard, a book of hours so I might study and learn of my wickedness.

Or perhaps she thought that the day of my birth was the perfect time to remind me that my mother was the cause for England's break with Catholicism.

Or worse, she might think that I was so uneducated and naive that a copy of the prayers translated from Latin to English would fascinate me, as if I did not already know Latin, or any other foreign tongue. I dare say I spoke French better than even she! She could at least have presented me with a challenge by translating them into Spanish, which I had only begun learning. That, at least, would be interesting. Not to mention it would be a gift befitting a giver so obsessed with her Spanish mother's memory that she could think of nothing else.

I tried very hard to not let any of this anger become apparent on my face, and instead of saying all that was in my mind, I took a slight breath in. "Thank you, Mary. How very thoughtful."

Kat must have been able to tell my feelings and spoke up at this point. "Should I ring for breakfast, my Lady?"

I instantly replied, "I was thinking of eating in the hall today. I am hoping to glimpse Father before he leaves." With that, I left the room, leaving the book with Kat.

Several of Father's party were there in the hall, lounging in groups as they chatted.

I sat near the head table. To my left, and down a few places, sat Sir John Dudley and his son, John Jr. As Prudence filled a bowl of pottage for me, I overheard their conversation.

"If we dispatch the French over the channel, storming Boulogne-sur-Mer could be quick, and the one bit of leverage we need to succeed. Besides, I feel like this is the time to make my move. The king knows that I am loyal and useful now. He will be pleased with our success."

John Dudley was a good enough man, but very ambitious, which seemed necessary, for he and his wife were always having children, and after most of his lands fell to the hands of his cousin, he had to vie for position. The details of that loss were privileged information and he had done a fantastic job of keeping them private—not a talent to be scoffed at.

As I listened, the conversation got passionate, and tedious, so as soon as there was a lull, I quickly spoke up. "Sir, forgive me for the interference, but do you think my father the king a simpleton? He would never enter a war when the only justification is amusement." I kept my face serious and instantly saw the man's face pale.

I was, of course, playing with him. Every monarch considered war an enjoyable pastime, albeit an expensive one. After making him and his son stumble over their words for several minutes, I smiled, gave up the act, and saw their sudden relief.

"I am sorry to play with you," I said to the elder. "I only felt the conversation a touch tense for the morning meal. I thought grownups left the serious conversation for when the children were not present." I smiled merrily at him and he and his son laughed heartily at my joke.

When they were finished the son said to the father, "Her humor and manner of delivery reminds me of someone. Can you guess who?"

"No, I do not think I know," the father said, looking at his son with surprise and a little hesitancy. I was sure he did not want his son to give offense to the daughter of the king.

"Come now, Father. He is always saying things to shock us all."

"Oh yes!" He laughed again. "You mean Robert, of course." He then looked to me and said, "I assure you, my Lady, my son pays you a compliment. He is saying that your wit is in the same company as that of my younger son, Robert. He is but a few years older than yourself, I believe. He was ten this June."

I nodded my head slightly, trying not to show my indecision of feeling, and took a small bite of my pottage. This man was comparing me to his son? How very odd. I must not have hidden my slight offence too well, for the father went on in a hurried manner.

"What my son is saying is that Robert is always keeping us on our toes with his humor. He is a joy to have around. Pardon us, my Lady. I hope no offence was taken. If you could yourself meet Robert, you would understand what we are trying to convey." I wanted to relieve the panic that was forming on his face, but my mouth had food in it and I was not sure what to say yet. After a few moments of fumbling, his face lit up and he said in a hurried tone. "I have an idea. You, my Lady, are living at Hatfield, correct?" I nodded again. "Let me bring Robert to meet you there. I will go and fetch him and be back to Hatfield before a fortnight has passed. You will be home by then and will have plenty of time to prepare to receive us."

I considered this for a moment. I was curious to meet this boy I had been compared to, so I said, "I am having a birthday celebration on the twenty-second. If you and your son would do me the honor of joining me for that occasion, I would be pleased."

His eyes lit up. "My Lady, you do us a great honor indeed."

This man was no fool. What member of court in his right mind would want to come to the birthday celebration of a nine-year-old bastardized daughter of the king?

Still. he did not want to burn bridges. Very good of him. I was sure that many people would suddenly be overly obliging to me now that my relationship with Father was on the mend, just in case something came of it.

"Very well, I will see you there and am looking forward to it." I knew that my pottage was almost cold, so I ate the remainder of it as quickly as possible and left to tell Kat and Blanche all that I had schemed.

September 1542
Hatfield House, Hertfordshire

The day that Robert and his father arrived, Kat received the strangest message. We were sitting in my favorite part of the garden, discussing the properties and medicinal uses of honey and the differences between a wasp and a bee, when Alice, a gardener's wife, almost passed us by while about some task. She stopped abruptly and turned shyly back around to face us. I was watching her and not really listening, which always irritated Kat, so she stopped talking to look at Alice also. Because she was annoyed, she snapped a little at the poor woman, "What is it, Alice?"

"Lady Katherine, I was just wondering if you, by chance, got the message that a man from Hertford Castle come here to see you while you and her majesty were at Pyrgo."

Kat's shoulders relaxed, and her eyebrows wrinkled up as she replied, "No, Alice, I did not receive this message. Who, pray tell, was this man?"

"Mr. William Dunsy, milady. He said that he is a cobbler at Hertford Castle, and the story he did tell…well it was mighty strange, milady. He said that several years back, a lady all veiled in black came to him in the dark of night asking a service. She gave him a box and a letter and said he was to deliver it to Lady Katherine Champernon on the seventh of September, but in the year fifteen hundred and forty-two." Kat and I looked at one another in wonderment as Alice went on. "He was very excited to learn that you lived here but upset that you were not at home. I figured him upset because of the travel and he did not even get to deliver the box personally. But no, he said he could not leave it. He said that he would come back soon to try again." She bit her bottom lip thoughtfully. "Oh yes, and he said that the woman paid him twenty gold pieces to complete the task for her and he has never seen her again, not that he would recognize her since her face was veiled and all, but you get my meaning."

Kat looked over to me. "Well, I must say that is very odd."

"Yes, very odd indeed," I said thoughtfully. "And why would it be so important for it to be delivered on that day? That happens to be my birthday, as you well know. What an interesting coincidence."

Kat raised her eyebrows at me. "Of course, I saw that right away."

"When was this task asked of Mister Dunsy, Alice?" I asked incredulously.

"He did not exactly say, milady. I have told you all I know. Now if it please you, I will get back to my work."

"Yes, yes, of course, and thank you, Alice," I said graciously, because Kat was too involved in her pondering to pay attention to such a politeness.

The plump woman walked away, and after a few moments Kat finally started to talk.

"I feel as if I remember the cobbler at Hertford. I believe he is the very man who made my square-heeled riding boots."

I knew the pair, but did not know where Kat had had them made. "I know that I am observant, Kat, but to remember a pair of your boots? Honestly!"

Kat took one look at my face and knew I was playing with her. "You remember everything, my Lady. I know you would not let a pair of shoes escape your all-seeing eye." She smiled at me as she teased me back, but then her eyes became unfocused as she pondered. She said aloud to herself, "If you do not recall the situation then you must not have been there. Well, that narrows it down a bit. When have I been to Hertford without you?" She continued to think, and her face lit up again, "I have not been without you since I took this charge. I do not think I can recall a single day completely out of your presence."

I had been thinking also and had to agree with her. Since my late nursemaid, Lady Bryan, left to take care of my brother, Edward, Kat had spent almost every moment with me.

"It had to have been over five years ago. I cannot think of a single reason that man, if he is the same one, would have any cause for contacting me—and in such a cryptic way." She squinted her eyes in deep thought for a moment and then shook her head with annoyance. "What a story. Some woman came to him with a gift. Pah! What is he playing at?"

"It could be he is telling the truth." She regarded me with uncertainty and I instantly understood her defensiveness, so I went about reassuring her. "Kat, I do not believe that you asked some poor cobbler to meet you here for a lovers' foray. It would be too elaborate a plan, and what a faithful man to wait five years to come to you." I paused and assessed her face before making light of the situation. "A man such as that does not exist in England, but if you have found one and if he is handsome and not so very poor, I will have to give you my leave to marry him, for I doubt God made two such men."

Kat laughed at me and blushed as she always did when the subject of marriage was introduced. I did not understand why men would not see to it that this sweet lady be married. Kat was nearing forty and had never been asked. There must be some man to do the job. I could find few faults with her, and she possessed, from what I had heard, the greatest asset a man could desire: chastity.

Just then, we heard people talking rather loudly. Turning, we saw John Dudley and his son, presumably, coming up the lawn from the house. I'd had Blanche tell them it was my study time and thus they would have to wait until I was finished to be presented. Obviously, that was not satisfactory, for here they were, traipsing across the grounds to see me.

As they got closer, the first thing I noticed was that Robert had a very playful walk, sort of like he was trying too hard to look like an expert swordsman with slinky gait and sinewy movements. He almost pulled it off.

"He must practice that often," I said quietly to myself.

Kat looked over to me, smiled mischievously, and whispered, "His walk?"

I nodded my head ever so slightly and we both held back smiles.

From this distance, I could not quite see the details of his face. His hat was low and large and distracted my eye. I saw dark brown hair and a smile. He wore fashionable clothes and I thought he might be slightly shorter than me.

A butterfly landed on my shoulder and took my focus away from the approaching men. I carefully watched it flutter its wings about and extend its proboscis, testing my vivid blue dress. As I was about to try and transfer the insect to my finger, a hand gently maneuvered it off my shoulder. Annoyed, I looked up at the intruder.

It was Robert Dudley.

Hat gone, his brown waves of hair framed a symmetrically oval face. A perfectly straight nose blended into a pair of full lips which, as he looked from my face to the butterfly on his finger, parted into a gloriously uncrowded smile. His cheeks were still smooth and boyish, and they matched his expression.

When our eyes met, I did not remember how to speak. His eyes…they were glorious. Bright and wise and merry. My breath came faster, and I could not stop myself from blinking foolishly.

As soon as I realized what was happening, blood rushed to my cheeks and I quickly turned toward his father, who was watching me closely. Trying for a bit of composure, I said, "Would you be so kind as to introduce me to your son, Sir John?" It came out quite breathy.

"Yes, of course, my Lady." He cleared his throat formally. "Lady Elizabeth, this is my son, Robert Dudley. Robert, this is Lady Elizabeth." I have no idea how I did it, but I stayed erect as Robert bent and lightly kissed my outstretched hand. I could not say a thing to this boy, for, in this moment, I would sound like a complete idiot.

Thankfully, I did not have to say anything, for he started to talk. "My Lady, you do the roses in this garden an injustice! How are they supposed to carry on with their job of beautifying God's earth when the crown of his creation walks by them daily?" Inspired by my blush and breath, no doubt, he impertinently leaned over and kissed my hand yet again. "Who would look at a rose when Elizabeth is near?"

John laughed. "You see, my Lady? He is a regular riot."

I did not laugh.

I only breathed and wished he would kiss my hand again.

EPISODE 4

September 1542
Hatfield House, Hertfordshire

K at was obsessed. The identity of the man with the message was making her mad. It was all she could talk about or think of. Excepting a few quiet comments about Robert's handsomeness, and what a fool I'd made of myself in response to his ridiculous compliments, she kept up a constant dialogue about the strange message she had received from Alice.

"I wonder if the veiled woman was someone whom I have wronged and she is sending me some sort of curse."

I had stopped commenting on her absurd ideas and took to pretending to listen to her, while I thought of other things.

Robert.

I had never really noticed a boy before—well, not in the same way that I had noticed Robert, but I supposed that I had never met someone that appealed to me as much as he did. He had everything I considered beautiful in one face. Still, the only thing I knew about attraction was that it came before love, and all I knew of love was that it could come and go as easily as a head could be taken off.

Kat was in the middle of another theory when I cleared my throat and said, "Kat, I have an idea. Why not go to Hertford today and hunt the man down? It is but eight miles. We ride that distance easily when we take the horses out. Go, take Larken and Henry, the gardener's son. He will serve as an escort. I will have Blanche to look after me, so you can be away for two or three days and no one will miss you—least of all me." I smiled slyly at her. I would not miss her if this was all she talked of.

Kat looked absolutely uncertain.

"I will have Master Parry give you pocket money so that you can eat well, and a letter so that you can stay in the castle. Come now, Kat, you know that I will not hear the end of it until you find out."

Finally, she acquiesced. "I will discuss it with Master Parry, if you are certain."

It was decided she would leave before the midday meal and be home before that same meal day after next. When she finished dressing me, and we had our breakfast, it was study time. I preferred to do this outside on nice days. However, when Kat and I came out of my rooms, Robert was leaning against the rather ornate tapestry of a hunting expedition that faced my doors. He wore casual white linen and held a fishing pole in the crook of his arm.

"Would the ladies like to go fishing this morning?" he asked cheerfully.

I looked at Kat, assessing her mood while I spoke. "I have studies to attend to, Robert." I knew it was rude to not look at him as I spoke, but I did not want to chance making a fool of myself again. When I peeked quickly at him, he looked disappointed, so I sighed and stared down the hall. "Come on, then," I said to both as I swept past them. My mind continued working up a scheme as we walked. "Robert, you could join us for studies this morning. We will only work until ten o'clock, and then Kat must get ready for a little trip she is taking." At this, I turned to look at her. She was glancing sideways at Robert with a look of uncertainty on her face. I continued in a hurry. "Blanche is busy with plans for my birthday dinner, but she will be in the kitchen most of the morning. The lake is visible from there, so yes, Robert, after studies I will go down to the lake with you for a little fishing expedition."

I smiled, as he laughed and said, "Fantastic!"

I considered the morning as I sat brushing my hair.

Studies went particularly well, I felt. Robert and I both felt the need to show off, so as not to be outdone by the other. The problem was I was far more educated and, hard as it was for me to accept, he was more intelligent. He figured the problems out faster than me, but I always had the right answers to the questions. School had never been so much fun. I told him that a little competition had improved my lessons dramatically and insisted that he visit every day he could. He agreed with eagerness, but I could tell that Kat was worn out by the time we were finished.

I pulled the brush through my hair one last time and smoothed my plain linen skirt. I wanted to throw on my prettiest dress and have my hair tied back. "Not for fishing!" I told myself again.

As I exited my room, Robert's hand came out of nowhere and began dragging me down the hall. We ran as fast as we could, skidding around corners and almost sliding into furniture. Not wanting to seem too slow or not up to the task, I sped up, so he did not have to pull me.

It had been a while since I had run—really run—and as soon as we reached the outdoors, I embraced the freedom of it and pushed myself to the limit. The day was beautiful, and the grass felt marvelous beneath my bare feet. This was what my soul needed, for it was almost as liberating as riding. Kat never let me run. She thought it beneath me, but I sometimes wanted to tell her that I was only nine and running was a normal part of youth.

When we reached the lake, Robert plopped down on the bank and tossed his line into the water. I did not have a pole, so I sat down next to him and he handed his to me.

"Do you really think we will catch anything?" I asked, keeping the pole steady while I held my breath.

"Probably not. But that's not the point, is it?"

I looked at him curiously. "What do you mean? We have a pole and a hook. What other reason could we have for sitting on the lakeside?"

"We are here to talk and enjoy the quiet."

Just then a large duck quacked loudly in our direction, and Robert turned to me with a laugh. He said to the duck with mock severity, "Silence duck! We are here to enjoy the quiet." I laughed again and thought how different he was from yesterday or this morning. There were no pretty courtier words or flirtatious smiles, only funny jokes and playful laughs. I liked this side of him.

Before long, I found a wonderful muddy spot on the lakeside, and Robert and I constructed all sorts of villages in our homemade modeling clay. At first it was hard for me to get all dirty, but after Robert had thrown a few handfuls of mud at me, I gave up my attempt at staying clean.

We had a marvelous time, but the most important thing

we did, as far as I was concerned, was talk. We talked about everything and nothing. I told Robert about how my mud hut would look if I could build it the way I wanted, and he constructed a battlefield of mud men, or rather lumps, to protect my village from the water serpents. Afterward, we cleaned ourselves off in the pond and, naturally, had a water fight.

We made boats out of leaves and pushed them about the lake with sticks. I told him about my life with Kat, Blanche, Mary, and Master Parry, and he told me about his family and his life at court.

"I do not particularly like court. It is all parties, and late nights, and children are never allowed. If I did not have my horse and my brother, Guildford, I would have been bored out of my skull. Guildford and I played tricks on the maids and roamed the castle like it was our home."

"It was your home," I said with a smile. "I have not been to court for a very long time. Father banished me," I added frankly.

He chuckled. "Oh yes, I remember this story. Didn't you tell him he was a bad man for killing people?"

I did not laugh as I said, "Close." Pausing, I considered if I should tell him the truth, and as I looked into his merry blue eyes I chose to trust him. "I asked him how it was that he could chop off the head of anyone he chose. Then I told him that Queen Anne was my mother, and his wife, and it was naughty of him to kill her."

Robert stopped laughing and said, "I am sorry. That really is not funny."

"I dare say it was not. I can still remember the anger in his face, and I was just a wee child." I sighed. "Do you think he will ever let me back into his favor and back to court?"

"I am certain he will." He smiled and patted my shoulder. "It looks like your boat has been sent to the fathoms below."

I looked over and he was right. My oak leaf had sunk. "I suppose that means you win?"

"It does, indeed. Now, pay up!" he said, and held out his hand.

I reached in my pocket, fished out a smooth black rock I had found, and laid it in his palm. "You are just awful for taking my pretty rock."

"Well, perhaps one day I shall let you win it back from me." He smiled and slipped the rock into his breeches pocket.

I would one day be expected to host every holiday in the kingdom, so my education as hostess began with my ninth birthday. "I do not feel like wearing something so constricting, Blanche," I remarked as the woman cinched my waist tighter.

"Arriving early and overstaying one's welcome is the material practice of nobility, my Lady. Since your event is but four days away, I predict you will be busy receiving family and friends this afternoon and you must look the part." Blanche, who acted as my personal waiting maid, stated this information without any disdain. It was fact and not to be judged.

"Come now, Blanche. I have plans."

Blanche pursed her lips. "We shall see."

Naturally, I spent the afternoon greeting guests. Before my boots were laced, I was called down to the sitting room. My cousins had arrived.

I took Blanche with me to greet them. Bless her heart, she did not give me a single snide look, but she did talk merrily with everyone. I found I was not in the mood for talking. I was thinking—thinking about how I did not want to act like a grown up right now. I wanted with all my heart to leave all these people behind and find Robert, or have him come to me. In my mind I saw him walking through the doors, smiling at me, and kissing my hand. I sighed and could not help myself from wanting it to be so.

A few minutes after this desire settled in my heart, and I had almost decided to excuse myself, Robert and his father entered the drawing room. He quickly came over to my side. I could not help but brighten as I saw him, and I checked my dress and touched my hair to make sure all was in order. He bowed low and said casually, "Lady Elizabeth, how are you this evening?"

"Greetings Robert, Sir John. I am wonderful…now," I added quietly, and intensified my smile.

"Wonderful. I only ask, for just a moment ago, I had a strange, overwhelming feeling." Robert's cheeks flushed, and he cleared his throat unconsciously. "Never mind." There was a crinkle to his brow and I sensed a nervousness in him. "It's silly. I guess I just had the feeling that you needed to be rescued."

"Nice as it would be to call you to my side whenever I should need rescuing, sir, I do not have that power. Do you think it indigestion?" I said with a laugh on my lips.

"No, I do not." His face would not laugh. He was serious.

"Come, it is cooling down outside. Let us go out on to the terrace and talk." Robert walked next to me as we left the room. "Do you think we will be missed?"

"I am sure you will be. You're the hostess. But it is not as if we are hiding," he replied.

"I do not feel like a hostess. I feel like this is a punishment for all the fun I had with you today." I took out my fan and began sweeping it back and forth in front of my face.

With the heat, and the gown, and the expectations waiting inside, my mind tumbled and finally settled. I'd never been unhappy with my life, with its plethora of rules and intense training. I knew that some royalty balked at the control exuded upon them, but I'd never felt that way. I was a sponge, longing to know and to do and to be everything.

Until Robert came.

Ever since he arrived, a growing knot of uneasiness had been settling in my belly. Now that I had a taste of freedom, I did not want to give it up.

A touch of a breeze brushed my face and I instantly felt refreshed.

"I have thought of nothing else but all we did this afternoon." I turned to him, "Thank you for forcing me to have fun. And our conversation…I feel it is the first of its kind for me with anyone but Kat." I thought about that for a moment and realized that perhaps the conversation I had with my father at Pyrgo was in this same category. "Alright, perhaps the second real conversation I have ever had." And before I knew what I was doing, I recounted all the particulars of my visit to Pyrgo. I told him how wonderful and strange it all was.

He must have misunderstood my meaning, for his response was, "I do not assume to instruct you on your relations with your father, but everyone has been talking of nothing but Queen Catherine's beheading, and the toll it is taking on the king, so I would humor him."

Catherine beheaded? I sputtered, and my heart instantly burned with anger and hatred toward the man whom I loved so dearly moments before. Father had beheaded another one of his wives? How could he do that when he knew that I was still alive to hear about it? I thought over his words to me, for they were fresh in my thoughts, having just recounted them, and I wondered if part of his apology to me included, at least in his mind, the offense of this situation.

I wished all manner of ill on him at that moment because I was not thinking of him as a king. I was thinking of him as a man who killed a young woman I very much liked and admired. A woman whom I had known better than I knew him, my own father.

For some reason, at that very moment, Mary's face came into my mind and I knew that I now understood her anger toward our father. I needed to know everything if I was going to forgive him for this, and I wanted to forgive him. I reached into the pocket of my dress and felt the birthday gift he had helped make for me.

Steadying myself, I looked up at Robert and asked, "What was her crime?"

Absolute shock covered his face. "You do not—do not know?"

"I did not want to know. I figured he did it in some gruesome manner, but I have asked everyone to keep it from me. But now I must have the details, or I will just continue to be angry with him," I said, my hand shaking inside my pocket.

"Infidelity," he said shortly. "She was caught in the act. There was no question, unlike…" He trailed off uncertainly.

"Unlike with my mother," I finished for him. Then angry words exited my mouth. "I saw them. Catherine loved my father and he adored her." My fan beat back and forth more erratically. "Well, Robert, if that is how love ends when you are a prince, I am glad that I have been cut off. If I am ever in that high office, I shall never marry." This was said as seriously as I could say it, and when I looked at Robert's face, I knew that he knew I meant it.

He seemed very taken aback.

I did not want to discuss my now definite resolve, so I began mumbling about how I was feeling.

"I know it is feminine and insensible, but I am angry with him for cutting off her head. That is a personally offensive executionary method for me and yet"—I put my fan down— "and yet, I never truly knew my mother. So, I find myself angry, but still loving my father. Not ignoring him, despite his deplorable actions, but wanting his approval, even in the wake of them. I do not understand myself. Do you understand me, Robert?"

"Not a bit...or I think maybe a little," he said with a mischievous smile.

"Come, Robert, let us not talk like we were born north of the Northumberland."

He laughed so hard that I had to shush him. I did not want Blanche to descend upon us when I was finally having a good conversation. But, with his laugh came the light heart that I had felt before.

I would not think about this news of my father right now. I would just listen to Robert and have my mind be here, with him.

EPISODE 5

September 1542
Hatfield House, Hertfordshire

Robert and I took full advantage of Kat's absence and Blanche's unwatchful eye. I was free for the first time in my life, with no schoolwork, no forced responsibilities. Truth be told, I should have spent this time with my guests, but I did not. I spent every waking moment with Robert. I decided that my dress that had been worn to the lake that first day was now my play dress, and once I stopped fearing the dirt and embraced it, I had so much fun. Robert and I chased frogs and hunted snakes. There was an old swing hidden in a large oak on the grounds, and we spent hours taking turns swinging. Robert would always push me when it was my turn.

Once we had breached the wood, we climbed all the trees we could, and we ran and ran and ran. We chased one another and laughed. We talked of the animals we saw, and we even caught a glimpse of a doe one morning. I do not think I had ever had better conversation, for it was not contrived. It was the true and natural talk of youth.

On the evening before my birthday party, we found a small meadow overgrown with wildflowers. Robert made me a crown of beautiful tiny flowers and called me "Queen Elizabeth" when he put it on my head. Later, I found a stick and decided to knight him.

"I shall call you 'Sir Robin', but only when we are together like this, I think." He looked at me quizzically and I explained, "Not because you remind me of a yeoman or because you steal from the rich to give to the poor. Heavens, nothing that serious." I paused to be dramatic and raised my sword to touch the other shoulder; "You are Sir Robin, for you are a man in disguise. I feel privileged to be the one to whom you show your true self."

His face became very serious, and he slowly stood so that our faces were only inches apart. Even in the dim twilight, his glorious blue eyes gazed into mine with such intensity that my heart began instantly to hammer. I did not understand what he was doing as he touched my arm gently, but the touch made me shiver.

He was suddenly smiling roguishly. His hand had reached mine and it just happened to be the one with my sword in it. In one quick movement, he slipped the sword out of my hand, sprung back a few feet, and yelled, "Guard ye, filthy swine!"

Naturally, a fantastic sword fight ensued, followed by a superb defeat. He slaughtered me, and I was as humble as a mouse in my surrender.

~

K at returned the next morning, an entire day late. I teased her that she had not wanted to return, for her face was alight with something, though I could not tell what.

"What have you been doing?" she said with a *tsk*, when she tied up my petticoat and saw that my face and arms were brown from the sun. "I have not spoken with Blanche as of yet, so you will have to tell me."

I had determined to continue playtime with Robert, no matter what Kat had to say.

"I have been playing, Kat. Robert and I have spent every moment of every day together, running and jumping and playing in the mud!" My voice was haughty, and my eyes dared her to say anything about it to me.

Her face hardened. "Well, if you think that my absence has changed our relationship to the point that you can speak to me in this manner, you are mistaken, my Lady. I am almost forty years old and I will not be spoken to so disrespectfully, even by the daughter of the king." She did not raise her voice, but she did command respect.

I felt ashamed, but not so much as to give in, so I tried a different approach.

"Kat, I am sorry for being disrespectful. You know I love you as well as a mother, but you never let me play. I need it. I like it. It makes me feel free. Daughter of the king or not, I am only nine years old!"

"Yes, you are nine, and that is too old to be rolling around in the mud. I will not hear of it, Elizabeth." Her voice was final and unemotional, and I knew that was the end of it, but I protested more anyway.

"Perhaps we can reach a bargain." I looked at her hopefully. She regarded me with a straight face but nodded me on.

"I will not do anything that will get whatever clothes I am wearing dirty or damaged. That means that I can run and swing and sword fight with Robert. I can still play but not in a messy, childish way. Also, it will not conflict with my study time."

I smiled sweetly at her and her face moved a little, so I thought that there may be a chance of agreement. The terms sounded perfectly reasonable to me.

After a moment of looking at me, the corners of her mouth lifted slightly, and she said, "I shall talk to Blanche and Sir John."

I screamed with pleasure, "Thank you, Kat!" and hugged her tightly around the waist.

"That is not a yes, my Lady," she said and slipped my dress over my head.

After I was dressed, Emma, the morning maid, brought in our breakfast. Her pregnant belly was getting quite large and I asked her how she felt.

"As well as can be, my Lady," she answered and left without another word.

We sat down to eat, and I began Kat's interrogation. "So, tell me what happened on your trip. Did you find Master Dunsy?"

Kat cleared her throat and nodded. "Yes, I did, and he was a very nice man. But, he would not give me the box and letter until I had someone testify that I was who I said. That is what took me so long. Finally, I was able to get your second cousin, John Ashley, who was staying at the castle, to speak on my behalf."

She blushed so deeply when she said this, that I had to

ask, "John is moderately handsome, if I recall correctly, is he not?"

I smiled as I saw the red stain on her cheeks darken. "He is handsome and very amiable. It was exceptionally good of him to assist me, for Master Dunsy would not yield." She took a bite of her pottage and chewed slowly. "I do not think this rabbit pottage will be good tomorrow. Let us not forget to tell Agnes."

"I shall remember to remind you. Continue your story, please," I said, and took a bite. She was right as always, and I did not know if I could finish the pottage in front of me, let alone stomach more tomorrow.

"Well, Sir John must have convinced him that I was who I said I was, for he handed me the box and letter the next day."

"And was it from some evil sorceress attempting to curse you?"

Kat choked on her food and it was a while before she could speak. "I am not...I cannot...it is written in beautiful French and so I am going to let you translate it for your studies today. That way you can read it for yourself and form your own opinion."

I was intrigued, not only because I realized how much I longed to get back to my studies, translation being a favorite subject of mine, but also because I had a mystery to uncover. Kat was not telling me anything, and so it felt like a fun game she was playing, though I knew she did not play games.

EPISODE 6

September 1542
Hatfield House, Hertfordshire

Kat insisted on staying in my rooms for lessons. She did not want any interruptions today, and her anxiety over the matter perplexed me. The moment I sat down, she drew a yellowed piece of parchment from her corset and set it on the table in front of me.

The first thing I noticed was how incredibly beautiful the handwriting was, the letters narrow and slightly flourished, but straight up and down with thick-inked lines. There were no blots or mistakes, and as I began to read, I noticed the writer's French was impeccable.

I looked up at Kat with wonder in my eyes and she said, "Well, what are you waiting for? Get to work, my Lady." She smiled at me excitedly.

I spoke French better than most English women and I read it fairly well, but translating a letter could be difficult unless you knew the intent and background of the writer. However, as I got to work, I noticed that there was nothing remarkable about its contents. It was interesting because it mentioned me and my grandmother, but even more interesting was the time and effort taken to make this singularly beautiful, yet perfectly ordinary note. And there was the mystery of its mode of delivery and specified date. All these factors utterly confused me, and when I had completed translating the body of the letter, I looked up to Kat with all of this bewilderment apparent on my face.

"The postscript, Elizabeth. Finish, please," Kat said with a touch of annoyance.

As I started on the postscript, my excitement grew with each word. Immediately I asked, "Where is the box?"

"I have put it in a safe spot. Do not be anxious about it. It is made of very hard metal and is securely locked. I dare say it weighs as much as you do. In fact, I had to buy a special riding bag to carry it. Now that you are finished, I would like you to read the entire thing aloud for me, please."

Thinking that this was just a part of the lesson she had planned for me, I asked, "In French or in English?"

"English, please. Come now, Elizabeth. You are a bright girl."

I did not know what she meant by this, but I started to read anyway.

Dear Ms. Katherine Champernon,

I hope all is going well. The weather has been very pleasant here. I am currently involved in so many projects that I have no idea how I will accomplish all I wish. I guess it will all be done in the Lord's own time. I hope that your placement in the princess's house is going well. Her grandmother just told me the other day how she does not see the girl as often as she would like. I think Lady Elizabeth Boleyn the very definition of wisdom and grace, and I am sure any young girl would benefit from a bit of her council.

We will be wintering in London. Christmas always brings me such joy. I am hoping to bring joy to all in our circle this Christmas with the birth of our first son. Let us pray that he is healthy and vibrant just like his Father.

I hope this letter finds you in good time.

My best wishes for your health and happiness, and that of your charge.

A.

P.S. Lady Elizabeth Boleyn sends me with this gift for her granddaughter, hoping to entice a visit since it cannot be opened without a key.

I looked at Kat as I finished and said, "I cannot believe I have a gift from my grandmother."

"There is a problem, Elizabeth. Your grandmother is dead. How are we to get a key from a dead woman?"

"Very gently put, Kat," I remarked, a little perturbed at her crass comment. "I do see the problem, of course." I thought for a moment. "Perhaps she would have left it for me...maybe with a trusted relative."

"I thought of that, but the only close relative would be Mary, your mother's sister, and no one in court would admit to knowing where she is."

"Father would know her whereabouts, or do you think he would not keep up with one of his sons? He has only three."

"Yes, and are you going to ask him where his bastard son from your mother's sister is at present?"

It had not occurred to me that I would be the one asking. "No, that does not sound like a good scheme when my status with him is so…volatile."

"So, it is evident by this letter that I must, in the author's opinion, take you to your grandmother. It is hinted at once and stated twice." She paused to let this sink in, but when I had no response she continued. "My Lady, look at the date on the outside of the paper."

I did so. 24 October 1535. "You see it there as plain as the nose on your face."

"Yes, I see it. Kat, what is your point?" I said in a slightly whiny voice. I was growing impatient as I flipped the paper back over and saw the words "Dear Ms. Katherine Champernon," printed on the letter's top. This did make me pause for a moment, but I did not have time to think of why, for Kat had already begun to tell me.

"My Lady," she said slowly, "your brother Edward was not yet—"

"—born in 1535," I finished for her. "Which means, at this time in history, Lady Bryan was still my nurse, and you had not so much as entered my doorframe." I looked more closely at this letter. "There is no mistaking that this letter is for you, and there is no mistaking that this letter is about me. How in the world did this 'A' person know you were to be my governess? How could she possibly know?"

"That, my dear, is the question of the day." She looked at me seriously as if assessing me in some way. "I have more to say about this, but I do not want to upset you."

"Kat, how could anything about this upset me?"

After a moment more of examining me, she continued in a great rush and did not breathe again until she finished. "Do you know of a person who was close to your grandmother, spent time in court, and not only had enough gold to pay a man to deliver a letter five years in the future, but who, for some reason, would come to this man with veiled face? Also, this person was in a position where the birth of a son would be an important event in her circle. And furthermore, if there was any doubt, a person whose name starts with an 'A'?"

I looked down at the 'A' on the paper and I instantly knew what Kat was saying. I had in my possession a sketch of Hatfield which my mother had done when I was born. She had signed it, "Anne Boleyn," at the bottom and hung it in my nursery. I knew that "A." I had seen it my whole life on my wall. Shock caused my words to stutter. "This—this looks —like my mother's—mother's 'A'." I looked at Kat, mysti-fied. "Could this 'A' stand for 'Anne'?"

"I believe that is exactly what it stands for. Reread the letter. I believe she left clues to her identity there for anyone to find, if they did not just disregard the letter as drivel. She certainly made sure that neither of us would think it such."

I reread it and all the clues matched perfectly, except that she did not refer to me with any kind of affection, excepting the last line of the body, where she wished me health and happiness.

"She certainly has our attention, but what would make her go to such lengths to tell us to go see Grandmother, and why does she pretend to not know me?"

"My dear girl, she obviously did not want anyone to know who she was or that she had any connection with you, so if it fell into the wrong hands…I am sure your grand-mother had the key to that package, which very well could be from your mother and not your grandmother."

I was overwhelmed. I had no idea what to do with this information, so I went on to something else. "Well, nothing explains how she could have known about you and your charge as my governess."

"Nothing, unless she arranged this somehow. She set all this up for us, so how do we know she did not leave instructions with someone stating her wishes regarding your care?" Kat did know how to make sense when she needed to, but she continued uncertainly, "There is, of course, a very different explanation."

I saw the apprehension on her face and knew to what she was referring. "Kat, do not be ridiculous. You do not believe in that sort of sorcery, and neither do I." I considered all she said, and as soon as my mind grasped the fact that my mother might have left something for me, all I wanted to do was to get that key and open that box. "Kat, will you bring me the box, please?"

"Of course, my Lady."

While Kat was out of the room, there was a knock at the door, and since there was no one else around I went to answer it. It was Robert. He had a grand smile for me. "I have brought Emma and some tea," he said as he ushered Emma into my room and followed after her. I wondered how it could already be teatime. "I have missed you, my Lady." He bowed and kissed my hand, and for a moment, as I looked into his beautiful face, all thoughts of mysterious letters were forgotten. "What have you been doing all morning long whilst I have been pining your absence?"

He was in his role again, and I smiled widely at him to let him know how happy I was to see him. To show him I would play along, I said flippantly, "That is none of your concern, good man. I am a free woman and can do all that I want without regard to your pining or lack thereof."

He laughed heartily at me, squeezing tightly the hand he still held, and for a fraction of a moment I saw in his eyes that he really had missed me. I hoped he saw that I had missed him.

As we stood there, hand in hand, looking at one another, Kat came back into the room. She was carrying a long, flat, gorgeously ornate metal box. She stopped when she saw Robert and me. I wanted to let go of his hand, but he held mine tightly as if he were completely unashamed to be doing so. Probably because he was completely unashamed. He was obviously just touching me as he would a sister. But I was ashamed because I realized that, for me, touching him meant something.

Without letting go, he led me to Kat and said politely, "Lady Katherine, how glad I am to see you again. I have been desiring to have another lesson from you. I feel as though my mind is turning to mush without your instruction to harden it."

Kat was momentarily affected by Robert's charm, but soon enough she was looking at him with annoyance. "Lady Elizabeth and I are in the middle of a lesson right now, Robert," she snapped.

"Yes," I broke in, "but it is teatime and Emma has brought it in for us." After setting the tea down Emma curtsied and exited the room. Kat walked to a table by a window and set the box down as she searched the sky for the sun. "I cannot believe it is near noon already."

"That is precisely what I said. Now, let's sit. I want to tell Robert all that has happened today."

Kat's head swung sharply in my direction and she gave me a warning look. I knew what she was thinking. If my mother had done so much to keep this a secret, then we should as well. But she did not understand. I did not have secrets from Robert. As soon as we sat, I began telling him everything, starting with Alice's message on the day he had arrived. He of course asked questions and was completely involved in the story and mystery of it all.

"So, that box Kat just brought in is at least from your grandmother or, perhaps, even from your mother?"

"Yes!" I said excitedly.

"Well, you must rush to your grandmother's house and see if she also has left you a clue."

"Kat, do you know where we should begin? Mother grew up at Hever Castle in Kent, but I know that, after Grandfather died, the castle went back to Father's ownership, and he, then, gave it to Anna of Cleves. However, I think Grand-mother and Grandfather lived the last bit of their lives at Baynard's."

"I would think your grandmother would leave something for you in a place that would be associated with her family. I am sure that, of the two castles, Hever is the best place to start—the only problem being that it is upwards of fifty miles away, while Baynard's is but twenty miles."

I was frustrated. "So that makes neither of the castles a possibility for visiting. I cannot make a trip of that distance in the near future. I have no excuse for it, excepting this secret one."

"I guess you will just have to find some excuse for going," Robert said, as he smiled and touched my hand that rested on the table. "Do not be overanxious about it, my Lady. It will work itself out."

"Perhaps a visit to Anna. She is always inviting you," Kat said offhandedly.

"Yes, that would be a wonderful idea, except I have never showed much interest in her, and I fear to ask, now that I have refused so often." However, no other plan came to mind and then it was time for tea to be over.

"My Lady, we need to get you ready for your party. It starts shortly," Kat said stiffly as she looked over at Robert. She had been impolite to him the entire half an hour.

"Yes. Well, Robert, out with you. The ladies must make themselves beauteous," I said.

He laughed. "The men too!" Then he headed for the door, but stopped and turned before exiting. "Oh, my Lady."

"Yes," I said instantly, for I was watching him walk out.

"I know there will be dancing, and I would consider it an honor if I might share a dance or two with you."

"Robert, I would be offended if you hadn't asked. I probably would have just demanded you do the deed whether you wanted to or not," I said as haughtily as I could.

He looked at me adoringly and sighed. "You know not how you quicken my heart with your words." I giggled and watched him slide his hand just under his doublet, right over his heart, and pat it rapidly. "You see, my Lady, I shall die, it beats so quickly."

"Get out, you silly boy!" I said, and tossed a nearby pillow at him. With that, he rushed from the room. When I turned to face Kat, I knew that I was in for a lecture and it came immediately.

"The two of you act like courtiers, not like children. I thought you were playing in the mud, not making love to one another."

I felt the shock of her words flush my cheeks. "Robert and I do not—do not make love to one another." I calmed myself and thought how I did not want to explain this to Kat. But if I did not I would never see Robert again. Kat would see to it. "In public, we practice on one another because that is what is expected. However, when we are alone we play as children do, because that is what we are in our hearts."

"I am not sure where his heart lies, but Elizabeth, it is absolutely incontestable that you are smitten with him. You cannot deny it for I will not believe you."

I hated this. I did not want to have this conversation. I just wanted things to be easy with Sir Robin and me. I wanted to have a normal friendship without it leading to marriage conversations. I also hated the fact that she saw what I knew: that I was his sister, but he was in my heart. I felt spurned, rejected, a little humiliated, and foolish. However, I knew I had to tell her something.

Explaining my now-dejected attitude was important to my pride. "Kat, it does not matter the way I feel. Robert is beautiful—even you cannot contradict me there—so of course I am going to be smitten with him. Is it not time for me to have my first attraction? For heaven sake, Father has already promised my hand to four different men. Should I not discover what I like?" I realized how this sounded and quickly went on. "Never mind any of that. Truthfully, it is not important. What is pertinent is Robert. He is more than a first attraction to me. He is my playmate, my confidant, someone I trust and want to be with. He is the first friend I have ever had —that is not an adult." I looked at her and willed her to see what I meant but could not explain very well. "Do you understand me?"

Kat did not say anything for a full minute, but as her sharp eyes finished assessing whatever she was assessing, she slowly said, "I see." Then her look turned half-amused, half-conflicted, and she sighed. "Let's get you dressed. You do not want to make your guests wait too long."

EPISODE 7

September 1542
Hatfield House, Hertfordshire

The afternoon was all I had hoped. There was a large canopy with tables and chairs set up in the south end of the garden. I wondered if God had listened to all my prayers concerning the weather, because it could not have been more uncharacteristic or more beautiful. The sun was warm, and I knew that this was certainly one of the last warm days of summer, before the land would succumb to autumn. The trees were still green, the flowers were still in blossom, and the bees still buzzed.

Blanche had outdone herself. Everything was perfect. I wore my most elegant gown: gold with white silk lace borders and brown and green silk flowers embroidered onto the corset. An elegant three-tiered cake sat in front of me.

I stood to deliver my birthday speech, which I'd been practicing, for it was my main duty tonight. I did not have much to say, but I was full of gratitude. Clearing my throat, I lifted my glass. "To my close friends and family. Thank you for celebrating this special day with me. Thank you for traveling so far to see me, the humble daughter of an important man."

Many laughed, and I laughed too. "I hope this is the first of many celebrations that I host. Though I am nine today, I flatter myself that I am old enough to make a proper hostess speech, and that, my dear friends, is what this party is about: my education as a hostess." I added in a jesting manner, "Which tells you that Kat just doesn't know what else to teach me. She says I already know everything and there is considerable angst in her tone when she admits this." I giggled and so did my audience. "Really, I have invited you here because I think it important to celebrate change, personal growth, and the gaining of skills and knowledge. That is what life is about, correct?" There were murmurs of agreement. "I feel that this year I have changed. I have overcome many things, by the grace of God, and there are many things I look forward to accomplishing." I raised my glass. "So, to another wonderful year and many thanks to Blanche and all those who helped me put this together. I hope I have learned all I ought."

My friends and family saluted me, and as we commenced the feast, I congratulated myself on gaining yet another skill required of a princess. I hoped Father would be proud.

We cleared out all the tables from under the canopy to make room for the dancing, which went on until the sun was almost down. As the air cooled off we moved to dancing in the grass. The players were local men and excellent at their craft. Robert looked so handsome in his silk stockings and velvet doublet. I was proud to be bouncing around with him. There were several other girls my age attending, but I was not interested in them or their haughty, ladylike manners. I remained polite, but I did not seek them out. I wanted to have fun. It was my birthday party.

He was a very good dancer and I had not seen his face so alive before tonight. He was enjoying himself immensely and so was I. It was much different to dance in the arms of the most handsome boy I had ever met.

"This is wonderful," I said a little dreamily as I watched Robert leap and kick as the dance called.

"And terrific exercise! Do you think we should incorporate dancing into the time we spend together?" he asked.

"I think that an excellent idea, mate," I said in a Yorkshire accent. He smiled widely as he hopped gracefully past me. After attempting to dance the difficult galliard, the sun was down and so we sat. "I have not told you this, but my father and the king have arranged that I go to Ashridge in January and stay with your brother, Prince Edward, to be his playfellow and receive lessons from his new tutor, Dr. Coxe. I will be living with Edward for at least three or four months. You wouldn't happen to visit your brother often, would you?" Holding his hand out for me, I rose, and we began dancing once again.

"Unhappily, not. I miss dear Edward and wish that I could see him more. Perhaps Kat and I will have to take that up with my father." I smiled at him and he smiled back, then he began humming the melody of the familiar tune being played.

I knew the tune as well and hummed with him.

However, as I did he stopped and said with shock, "My Lady, I did not know that you had such a superb voice. How have you not sung for me before?"

I loved his praise, but it surprised me, and I looked at

him to see if he was ridiculing. "You flatter me, sir," I said with a blush. "I do not spend a lot of time singing, though I play the lute and the virginals. One really should sing if she is going to make the effort of learning to play, don't you agree?"

He nodded.

"However, I have just not pursued singing."

"You should sing whenever you can, for you will only get better as you age." He smiled at me and said, completely unabashed, "Elizabeth, I have to confess something to you." I waited, and he pulled me to a table where we sat once more. "I think you are the loveliest friend a boy could have." And with that he took my hand from the table and gently kissed it. "Happy birthday, and I hope this is the first of many we shall spend together."

I smiled, knowing he was only being charming.

Just then a lively song began. "Shall we dance again?"

He grinned as if I had read his mind and, holding the hand he had just kissed, pulled me to the grass.

Though the day of my birth had come and gone weeks before, this celebration finally made me feel that I was older. I felt nine, though I did not exactly know what a nine-year-old was supposed to feel like. It was strange, as if I had an inner clock dinging, "You're nine, you're nine."

I noticed that the night was not as dark as it should be as I walked to the barn to get Larkin, but my mind was busy, so I did not look to the sky to see why. Between a letter and gift from my mother, news of the late Queen Catherine and her dastardly deeds, knowing my Father's retaliation against her,

Robert, and my birthday, I felt as though I were swimming in a mire.

Kat was close behind me, though tonight she refused to ride with me on account of the long journey she had just returned from. She said she would watch me ride back and forth on the green. I did not think that would be a problem for I only needed the night air and the moonlight to clear my hectic head.

I walked into Larkin's stall, loving the smell of the stable. My mare, used to my nighttime rides, greeted me with a stomping foot and soft whinny. I slowly placed the bit in her mouth and then the bridle on her head. I stroked her as I did so, reveling in the chores of preparing her for our ride. I stood on a stool, pulled myself onto her bare back, then gently we walked out into the cold night air. She knew what I wanted before I asked her, and when we were out of the stable yard she instantly picked up her pace. Soon we were running through the grass. I felt everything around me, smelled every hint of fragrance in the breeze. As I lifted my face to the sky, I noticed how huge the moon was. My serenity was halted as I stared at the heavenly object. It was the most glorious sight, large and luminous in the dark speckled sky. I could not take my eyes away.

I pulled up on Larkin's reins a little, and when she slowed I noticed something strange. The moon was pulsating, or rather the light around the moon was pulsating. We stopped now. Blinking rapidly but keeping my eyes heavenward, I saw the light throb and it quickened before my eyes. Then, unbelievably, it increased in circumference to the point that the orb looked twice its normal size. I watched in amazement but completely without fear.

Suddenly a ray of light broke off from the ball in the sky and fell like a star directly toward me. Instinctively I raised my arms, wanting and willing the light to come to me, and come it did. I closed my eyes and the next second, I was hit with warmth, luminosity, and a sensation of wisdom. When I opened my eyes and looked down at myself, I was light. It radiated out of every facet of my skin. I was so bright I was like a small moon shining from the earth. I felt energy and beams of brightness, not only on my outside, but also thudding through my insides, like life's blood, and I knew that I was powerful.

I did not know what the power did or what it was for, but it felt amazing to be endowed with it. I stood for several minutes, basking in my new body. But before long I began to wonder. A million things I wondered. What was happening to me? What was this light? Why did it feel familiar? Why was I not frightened? And the scariest question of all: what would Kat think? My friend surely could see me shining like a beacon in the night.

For a moment I feared she would think I was a sorceress. I suddenly wished the brightness to go out. The moment the thought was firm in my head, the light vanished, instantly and without any warning. The void felt like devastation to my soul. I wanted it back again and willed it to be so with a desire so deep. I flung my hands again in the air toward the moon. The moment I moved toward the light I was again enveloped, and right then I decided that I did not care what people thought of my glowing form. I would never again be without this radiant power flowing through my body.

A fter taking Larkin back to her stall, I walked out to meet Kat and prepared myself for her to have a fit. She was sitting on her bench waiting for me, and as soon as I approached she said, "I do not know if it is the moonlight playing tricks with my eyes, but you look—I don't know."

She squinted at me and I thought, *I am glowing brighter than all the candles at Christmas Mass, if that is the difference you are speaking of*, but I said nothing.

"Perhaps I should have gone out with you. Your rides always do you so much good, but it did not appear to me that you spent as much time running as you normally do. Why did you stay and stare at the moon so long?" Then she looked embarrassed. "Were you praying, my Lady? Oh, I am sorry for asking. No wonder you look so divine. You have received peace to your soul. I am glad."

She rose, placed her arm around my luminous shoulders, and walked me up to the house.

She did not see it. How could she be this close to me and not feel the power that was inside of me? I was amazed to know she could not, and relieved as well for it meant that no one else should be able to see me this way, and thus, I could obey my desires and stay within the light always.

EPISODE 8

September 1542
Hatfield House, Hertfordshire

After going over and over the questions that filled my mind concerning this light that surrounded me, I finally found myself asleep, yet I had a strange awareness even in my newly vivid dreams. I kept on seeing myself arrive at Hever Castle to find my mother living there and carrying a baby version of me around on her hip. In the dream, she kept singing a song, over and over. *One day you shall catch a ray of moonlight, in the middle of a bright and starry night. Look to the women now beyond your sight, for they have bequeathed a brilliant birthright.*

The tune was beautifully haunting, and it stayed with me until the sun rose. Before full coherence found me, the faces of women I had never met, but nevertheless knew, came to me as in a vision that clouded my concentration. My mind could not stop reliving the previous night and all that I had dreamt.

As I sat at my dressing table, I gazed at my glowing body

with a bit of disorientation. I did not feel like myself at all, yet I somehow felt more like myself than ever before. Kat was running a brush through my shining strands of hair as I considered how these two opposing thoughts resided within me.

Part of my mind heard her as she spoke.

"What is that tune you are humming? I have never heard it before and it is lovely, like a lullaby."

"Hum?" I said. "What?"

"That tune you were just humming. What is it?"

I had not realized I was humming at all. "I do not know. I dreamt it up in my sleep last night."

"Well, it is beautiful. You may just have a musical talent that we have not fully explored. Sometimes I wonder if I have neglected you in that area because I have no talent there myself."

That made me think of Robert. "You know, Robert mentioned that he thought I had a pleasing voice. I think I should like to have some instruction. It seems you have taught me all you can on the lute. Perhaps I have not been as good a pupil as I should, but I am now determined to repent and do better."

"What an influence that boy has over you, my Lady," she said, and gave a very pointed look at my reflection in the mirror. Then she sighed. "I believe that you have reached the hithermost parts of my capacity in many areas, which is why I have written to Master Cromwell and asked that you be given a new tutor. A real tutor." I turned to her, half excited, half concerned. "He will talk to your father about it, and within a fair amount of time, I am sure that you will be learning more than even you can digest."

Suddenly I could not stop the bile from rising in my throat. "You will not be leaving me, Kat. You promised that you would not leave me. You will stay and continue to be my governess. Promise me that you will."

She caressed my cheek. "Of course, child. I will not leave you. I gave you my word, and like Ruth, where you go, I will go."

I turned to hug her, and she hugged me back. Then I asked, "Whom do you think Father will send to tutor me?"

"I put in a word about John Cheke. He went to Cambridge with my brother-in-law, Anthony Denny. But we will see what happens. Cheke is exceptional—that is, according to Denny he is exceptional. Have you met the fellow?"

"I do not think so, but perhaps. It has been so long since I have been to Hampton, I am sure I will not know one face the next time I go, excepting Father's, of course." I thought how my stepmother, Catherine, would not be there and it made me sad again. The very small association we did have had made an impression on me. She was the only woman I could call a real stepmother. Anna, who lived at Hever Castle now, was my father's fourth wife. She was sweet and good, but Father had only been married to her for four months and he was so miserable that, according to him, it should not even count as one of his marriages.

Kat looked down to my face with eyebrow raised. "Perhaps, while we are waiting to hear word of your tutor, we can think of some excuse to go on a long sightseeing excursion to, say, Kent. I hear there are many wonderful things to see there. Hever Castle, for example." She winked conspiratorially at me.

I looked at my glowing form in the mirror and instantly knew that God was leading me. "I have decided to go, excuse or not. We will be leaving at the end of this week, or once my guests have said their goodbyes."

Kat stopped brushing my hair and looked at me with

surprise. "My Lady, why would you decide this so abruptly without discussing it with your household first?"

"I am telling you now, Kat, and this is the earliest chance I have had since I only now decided to go. I have never seen my mother's home, and I have recently discovered a desire to know her a bit better. Do you think we could be ready to go in a week's time?"

"Yes, my Lady, but I think we will need to look over the books and discuss this extensively with Master Parry before saying we are absolutely going. You have traveled a lot this year, and with your birthday celebration, I am afraid that funds are running tighter than normal. Let us make sure it is doable before we get our hopes too high."

I had not thought of that, "Well Kat, this is important to me. If I must make some sacrifices in order to go, then that is what I will do."

Kat looked very perplexed by my sudden pronouncement, and she should have been. I did not make rash, careless, unthinking decisions. Nor had I before acted like I was the one in charge of my life. The adults could, of course, veto any pronouncement I made. I wasn't Queen, though they did let me play at it a bit. However, before I knew what I was doing, my mind had put the recent events together, and I suddenly knew in my heart that everything was connected to my mother somehow. Perhaps the only way to solve the mysteries that now surrounded me was to open that box, and to do that, I needed to go to Hever Castle.

~

I wanted to have studies outside so that I would be easily accessible to Robert, but the weather was ghastly with wind and sideways rain; so, I hoped he would come and see me, and by late morning, he did. However, he did not seem himself at all.

"What is wrong?" I asked him as we sat for tea. Kat was in her room with the door ajar, riffling around for something.

"I could ask you the same thing," he said glumly.

"Whatever are you talking about?" I asked a bit uneasily. How would it be if Robert was the only person who could see the thing that made me freakish?

"You look so radiant and happy you would think you were getting married or about to become queen," he said with wide eyes and pursed, pouting lips.

"I assure you, I am none of those things!" Thank heavens he did not see my glowing skin. Now out of danger, I focused on him. He truly looked ill. "Come Robert, you have yet to tell me what is wrong with you," I said with more concern.

"I thought you would have heard. Has no one spread it about?" he asked, eyeing me suspiciously.

"No, I have heard nothing," I said honestly.

"It's my mother. She is pregnant again and is having some complications. She sent a note last night to Father asking him to come home immediately."

I lowered my head sadly and in a low voice answered, "So, you will be leaving me then."

"Yes. At this very moment, Father is getting the horses prepared. I have only come to say goodbye."

"But, when will I see you again?"

"I do not know. Hopefully, you will be able to visit your brother while I am there. Ashridge is such a short distance from here." That was the first ray of happiness I had seen from him since he'd arrived. It made me wonder how attached he was to me. Would our friendship last if we did not get to see each other often? I hoped with all my heart that I would be able to see him in Ashridge...and, of course, I would go to see Edward, too.

"Oh Robert, I do not want you to go," I said, and tears came rushing to my eyes. Now it was time for him to act the part he always played: the gentleman.

"It is fine, my Lady," he said, and pulled a handkerchief out of his doublet. He dabbed my tears off my cheeks. "Will you write to me? Frequently?"

"Of course I will, but will you write back?" The tears were really coming now. I had not realized I had grown so attached, that the thought of being without him would have me blubbering.

Kat returned then and saw Robert and his handkerchief and me bawling into it. "What have you done?" She looked at Robert with such menace, I knew that her cold attitude had been a kind exterior, one meant to keep me happy. She did not like Robert at all. This aggravated me because she did not know him. Wanting to right an injustice toward my friend, I looked at Kat and willed her to obey me as I spoke to her. "Do not dislike Robert! He is good, and he is my friend." As I said this, a bit of the light that surrounded me, that life-filling light, left me in the shape of a small orb and flitted over to Kat's face, where it disappeared.

I instantly broke out in a cold sweat. What in the name of all the saints had just happened? My brain rushed, battling with confusion and doubt, as I watched Kat's reaction. Her countenance changed dramatically, the timbre of her voice softened, and her eyes widened in surprise.

"I know, my Lady. I just thought that he had hurt you in

some way, on accident of course." She turned to Robert and smiled, every shred of menace gone.

I looked over at Robert. He, of course, had not seen any of the light leave me, but he had watched Kat's sudden change and it shocked him. I was speechless. I could not believe it. Worse, I did not understand it at all. Had I just willed away a piece of my light and used it to force Kat to do something?

Both Robert and Kat were looking at me, waiting for some sort of explanation, but I had nothing to say. Robert said it for me. "I was just telling Lady Elizabeth that I have to depart for my home today."

"Oh no. She will be so lonely for you once you are gone, Robert." Her words were completely sincere, but her eyes held relief. She came to me and placed a hand on my shoulder. "I am sorry, my Lady, but we will make do." Then Kat walked to the window and said, "What a horrible day it is today. Not very good for traveling, I am afraid. Too bad you cannot stay until it lets up." Then she walked back to her room.

Robert leaned in toward me and said, "Is she always this strange, flipping from one sentiment to the opposite in a moment? I do not think that is healthy."

I still could not speak. My mind was divided. I wanted to think about what had just happened to Kat, but her passing words kept distracting me. I wondered if I could do a similar thing again, or if, perhaps, it was some strange coincidence.

However, if I had done it…if I had somehow, in some improbable conjecture of circumstances, happened to so quickly change Kat's mind about Robert, then perhaps I could make Sir John decide to stay with us until the weather let up.

Right then I knew that I was a selfish girl. Sir John's wife needed him.

But wasn't it dangerous to travel in such weather as this? I reasoned with myself. *One more day would not do anyone harm.*

Closing my eyes into Robert's handkerchief, I concentrated hard and willed the light to go make Sir John want to sit out the weather. I peeked out from behind the handkerchief to see if any light was moving around, but none was. I wanted to try again, but Robert was looking questioningly at me, so I decided it would be best to talk with him instead of obsess about some silly nonsense, for we only had a few moments left together.

Besides, I was certain I'd imagined the whole thing and Kat was just getting senile in her old age.

I cleared my throat and set it all aside. "Do you have enough time for a game of chess before you go?" I asked and sniffed loudly.

"Well, that depends on whether you let me win or not," he said with a smile, and touched a tear off my cheek.

EPISODE 9

September 1542
Hatfield House, Hertfordshire

I watched Robert's carriage from the sitting room window and cried long after he was gone. Kat, however, got to work straight away. She informed the house staff that I would be leaving and, thus, everything was in an uproar. When I finally cried myself out, I sat and watched the servants bustle around.

This sadness was also a brilliant distraction. I did not want to give proper thought to what had happened between Kat and the light. But, now that I was a bit more under control, I forced myself to lay out the facts in my mind: my desire for Kat to like Robert had forced an emotional reaction in me, I got upset and practically yelled at her, then a bit of my light left me and Kat changed her mind and was nice to Robert.

A chill prickled the base of my spine and my breath came a bit faster. What was this all about? I could not begin to understand. I knew nothing of what this light was and, for the first time since last night, I willed it to go away, doubting the goodness I felt with it around me.

The moment the wish was solidified in my mind, the light fled. I could no longer see it, but I knew it was within my reach, should I want it back. A hole in my being was revealed at its departure, a hole I'd never been cognizant of. I felt almost naked without the light.

Fortunately, at this moment, I also felt fear, and that abated the need to cover myself once more in illumination.

Somewhat.

Still, I desperately needed to find out what this power was, and soon, so my heart lightened a bit as I pondered my journey to Hever. My heart told me I would get answers there, though I did not understand the premonition.

∼

October 1542
Hever Castle, Kent

The first item of business Kat had seen to was securing an invitation to stay at Hever. My Father's fourth wife, Anna von Jülich-Kleve-Berg, lived in the castle but was currently staying at her main residence, Richmond Palace. Anna assured Kat that she would be more than happy to meet us at Hever, but that she could not arrive until a week after our desired date. Fortunately, she said it would be fine for us to come a few days early.

The trip took an entire week. It was long and wet, and the roads were not superb. My thoughts were torn between Robert and my mother. Back and forth I went between tears of sadness for missing Robert and excited nervousness over what I would find out from my mother's box. I hoped so much that inside this beautifully mysterious box I would find the answers to my questions.

At the same time, the god-fearing part of my soul knew that if the contents of the box told me of unexplained powers that my mother and I shared—well that would mean all the people who had ever called my mother a sorceress were right. This thought burned my stomach, for that would mean I was a sorceress too, and I had never believed in that sort of nonsense.

Finally, the castle came into sight. It was old but mighty and seemed unmodified, though the grounds were beautifully landscaped and the moat well hedged.

As I entered the courtyard, I was surrounded with the light. I'd kept it at bay for the week and was shocked to have it appear so abruptly. It was as if it was pulled from me and around me. Instantly, I knew it to be a good sign. My gut told me I was in the right place, and I settled contentedly into the comfort of the brilliant girl of light that I was.

The moment I walked through the doors, I was surprised by a life-size mural covering the opposite wall, portraying me as a tiny babe, and my mother, happy and richly dressed and jeweled. The colors were bright and beautiful, and the detail exquisite. One of my mother's arms held me and the other rested on a book. Her eyes were alight with joy, and she seemed to look toward the door I had just come through. Her realistic expression impressed me. It felt as if she were smiling at me.

I stepped closer and noticed how the mural was painted right onto the stones of the castle wall. This seemed a poor palette to me, but judging the elements of the artistry, one would never guess. This made me interested in the artist. As I stepped closer yet again, Kat came in after me, frightening me with a shrieking gasp.

"Who would do something like that? It makes this place look like a tomb!"

"Who would do something like what, Kat?" I looked at her, not understanding what she meant, and a little offended that this portrait could be construed as tomblike.

She pointed at the wall and looked at me as if I were blind. "You can see for yourself, can you not?"

"I see nothing that is offensive. It's beautiful and hardly tomblike." I was about to go on, but Kat cut me off, looking at me in an odd way.

"Well it is not offensive, per se. There are those who would like it, I surmise, but you will have to admit it is extremely strange. An entry hall shroud in thick black tar paint is not typical décor. I challenge you to disagree with me," she said, and shook the rain out of her cloak.

I looked back at the wall and was speechless. I could not see black paint anywhere. All I saw was the beautiful mural. I opened my mouth to say so, but thought better of it when Kat lifted her head and muttered, "I do not understand it. Very strange indeed." She entered the room to her left and I remained in front of the mural.

I did not understand either. How was it possible for me to see something completely different from Kat? However disturbing the revelation might be, it spurred along that other hope: the one where my mother, my long-dead mother, had left me with a great secret, and I was in the right place to ferret it out.

∽

W e spent the better part of the evening snooping around the castle. I did not tell Kat I knew exactly where I had to begin my search, and I wasn't going to go staring at the mural while she was awake. I waited until nightfall.

I lay in bed a long while before I dared tiptoe across our room and out into the hall. I grabbed the torch that was just outside my door and wandered through the castle until I was back at the entrance. Finally, I saw what Kat saw: a wall covered in a thick tar-like paint where the beautiful painting of my mother and I had been. My heart thudded crazily as I wondered if I had lost my chance. How could I find anything if I could no longer see the clue mother had left?

Then I recalled that I had the power around me when I came in the door, and so I called it to me now. Abruptly, I was able to see. The mural looked so beautiful by firelight, and I admired it for a long time before I started looking for any clue. At first, everything seemed to be absolutely ordinary, and I wondered about the seeming magic that made it. Was I the only one who could see this masterpiece? I examined every inch of the wall, but did not see anything hidden.

So, I stepped back a few feet and started looking at the painting as a whole. Instantly, I saw how out of place and uncomfortable my mother's position looked with one arm around me and the other awkwardly placed behind her, with her hand on a book. I then noticed that one of my tiny fingers was pointing in the direction of the book.

Thinking of the old, dusty, rarely used library, I saw instantly that there was no better place in the world to hide something for years and feel a modicum of assuredness that it would remain undisturbed.

I saw that the binding of the book had golden corner

pieces and a small crescent moon cut into the leather. I drew closer to the wall and stood on my tiptoes to see what the name of the book was, but my mother's hand covered it up. It did not matter. There could not be that many books that had a crescent moon carved into the binding.

"I daresay there is but one," I said quietly to myself, and touched a finger to my mother's happy face before turning and heading back up to my room.

As I walked, I wondered about the reason for the clue. If I were the only one who could see the mural, then why did she not just tell me where it was in letters of magic instead of painting a picture? I tried to think of a good reason for it, and all I came up with was that my mother was afraid that someone else would get involved...or perhaps she meant to test me in some way.

Shaking my sleepy head, I decided it didn't matter. If there was a test, I had passed. And as for anyone else being involved, I guess I would find out when I searched for the book if someone had gotten there before me.

EPISODE 10

October 1542
Hever Castle, Kent

Though Kat did not know exactly why, she helped me spend the next five days scouring the library for the strange little book. Unfortunately, the library at Hever was the biggest I had ever seen, and I felt like it was a test of my fortitude to continue searching for something that seemed not to exist. Worse, I felt anxious, as if time were running out. The hours I spent searching became longer and later, and finally, one night near midnight, Kat had had it.

"I have spent so much time looking for this ridiculous book that I cannot see straight." She took the book that was on the shelf right in front of her and said, "I am going to retire. I will see you in the morning, my Lady."

As she slipped the book into the crook of her arm, a thought came to me. "Kat." She turned to look at me but placed a hand over her mouth to stifle a yawn. "Do you know where my mother's room was? Here in the castle, I mean. Her room as a child, perhaps?"

"I haven't a clue," Kat said and turned again to leave. But she called over her shoulder, "However, I am sure one of the older servants would know."

"Yes," I said slowly. I was sure one of the servants would know. "Goodnight Kat, and thank you."

She turned before closing the door, "Wake me if you need help undressing. Goodnight, my Lady."

I knew I was acting rudely, but I did not care. I hunted down the servants' quarters despite the time. They were quite empty, since Anna was not here to need them, but finally, I did happen upon an old woman who was up to use the privy. She was not happy about my request, but she led me to my mother's old rooms, muttering the whole way as if I were a common visitor.

"And this be Sir Thomas Boleyn and Lady Elizabeth Boleyn's suite." The mistress explained as she put a key to the door. "Lady Anna has left the room alone at Lady Elizabeth's request, which is a very odd thing. There is a nice little glass table in there that has a few family portaits, a gold-leafed crest, and a few family documents. Lady Elizabeth left it as a sort of tribute to her family. She was a proud lady and wanted all to remember that her daughter had been the queen, I think. You know that King Henry himself spent many nights here, and, in fact, we still have his lock on the door to his quarters."

"Excuse me, but in this tribute, there wouldn't happen to be a book, would there? Perhaps one that has a small crescent moon cut into the binding?" I asked hopefully.

"A book, a book…" The woman thought and smacked her gums loudly. "I'm sorry, my Lady, but I don't recall any book at all." She turned a corner. "This way. Hurry along." After several more corners, the woman stopped in front of a door and said, "Here we are. And if you don't mind, I will be going back to bed now. You think you can find your way back?"

"Yes, thank you," I said gratefully as I reached for the door and went in. This room had obviously been redone as a guest room, and a quick look around proved that there were no books, or anything, left of my mother's.

Being inside a room I was certain had been my mother's did have a feel to it. She had spent much of her childhood here. I glanced at the stone floors and knew that her feet had touched them. In that moment, a spark of something started. For the first time I could remember, I felt connected to her.

Of course, there was always gratitude to her for my life, but there was also anger. Why could she not keep Father happy? Why could she not just do what he wanted and stay alive? I was angry. I wanted her. I wanted to know her. I wanted to see her. I needed to ask her a million things about what was happening to me, and she was not here. All I had of her was this silly hunt she had me on. I clutched my dress and pulled at it as I silently screamed out in anger, and then I was crying. Tears and snot were running down my face as I flung myself on the bed. I pounded my fists into the pillows and wallowed in my grief.

A long time later, I sat up and rubbed my soggy cheeks and tender eyes. This was the first time in my memory that I had cried over my mother. Everyone around me had protected me from the remembrance of her so that I would not hurt. Even I had hardened my own heart. However, now that I knew that I loved her, I missed her terribly. I did have snatches of her face in my memory but none of her words—none of her, really. I wanted her, because right now I was alone. Bitterly and utterly alone.

Perhaps if I could see some of my mother's things, or better, find something that I could keep and carry with me, I would feel the bond I now longed for. But, there was nothing in this room that was hers. Then, I remembered the servant's words and thought, perhaps, the very reason Grandmother left a Boleyn family shrine here was so that I would have something to fill the growing void I now saw in my soul. Houses were passed around so frequently that if one did stay some place long, they very well might leave a shrine behind.

I made up my mind to go and find my grandmother's rooms.

The castle was cold, and I was glad that I had remembered to bring the torch for a small amount of warmth and light. Once I was in the hallway, the darkness was almost absolute. I did remember my way and soon stood at the door the servant had indicated was my grandmother's.

Pushing the creaky door aside, I entered the room to discover an astonishing layer of dust. Thankfully, all the furniture was covered with sheets of white cotton for protection, but there was no helping the drapes, which hung heavy and lifeless at the windows. I could see the moon through the grimy windows and instantly wanted the warmth and power that came from her magnificent beams, so I called the light to me. As my body began to glow, the darkness fled from my heart as well as from my surroundings. The power also seemed to heighten my senses. I looked at my glowing arms and could not be afraid. Finally, I understood the feelings I had the first time the light came to me. I was whole. This being, filled to the brim with power of whatever nature the power was, this was me. I was not complete without it.

Quickly I looked around the room, which felt completely different now. There was something here that resonated with me now that I was shrouded in the light. No other place had ever held this feeling before. Comfort. Peace.

These objects were my mother's and grandmother's.

In a flurry of excitement, I grabbed hold of every cotton sheet I could get my hands on, and one by one, ripped the dust of time back. When the air settled, and I stopped sneezing, I saw the beautifully set room and imagined how it looked when my mother lived here, with everything clean, all in order, and the family here together. As I examined each piece in the room, I noticed a display desk with its hollowed-out center and glass top.

I ran across the room to it and wiped off the remaining dust. Words were carved around the border of wood that held the glass up, and I read them aloud. "'One day you shall catch a ray of moonlight—'"

I hesitated, because I knew these words. I had dreamt about them not many nights before. I finished reading. "'In the middle of a bright, starry night. Look to the women now beyond your sight, for they have bequeathed a brilliant birthright.'"

I looked beyond the glass and saw several small miniatures of women. I could tell they were lined up in order of age, for the back images were painted on porcelain and some sketched on worn and yellowed paper. Each face was serene and beautiful. Each face was one I had seen in my dreams.

Also, inside I saw a black leather-bound book with gold-plated corners and a small crescent moon carved into its binding. Excitedly, I felt around the edge of the desk to find the latch, but all I found was a lock.

I wanted to curse. How would I ever find the key to this lock? I bent down to have a look at the keyhole and noticed a small, carved crescent moon only a few inches underneath. It was very small indeed and I never would have noticed it if I had not had plenty of light and a reason to look down. I touched the small moon and it moved backward. Startled, I pulled my finger away and looked more closely. There, on the exact spot where the moon was, the wood was cut into a perfect square and it moved out of my way when I pushed on it. The hole was just big enough for me to get my little finger through, and as I slid it in, I ran into a thick wire of some sort. Wrapping my finger around it, I pulled. Instantly, a small clicking noise sounded and, with my free hand, I pushed on the top of the table. It came up. It was a fake lock!

Eagerly, I reached in and grabbed the book, and then I carefully let down the lid. I trembled as I carried the book over to the window and sat down in an armchair there. The letters on the front of the book were in a language that I did not know. "Fillos da Mente e da Lúa." Some of the words were a little familiar. In French, "daughter" was "fille," and in Latin, it was "filia," so I assumed that the first word was "daughter," since both seemed very close. The last word was "moon," I was sure, for in French, "lune" was "moon," and in Latin, "luna" was "moon," and, since I seemed to have an affiliation with the moon, it made perfect sense it would be written here.

"So…daughter and moon," I whispered, and it came to me acutely that the words inside this book would change me forever.

I gently cracked open the book. Inside, there were dozens of pages written in a steady, graceful hand in the same language as the title. However, as I flipped through a few pages, I soon saw a different hand had started to write, and then a different language was being written. Before long, I was looking at my mother's handwriting on the page. I recognized it from the letter to Kat. Hers were the last words written in the book. It seemed to be a journal of sorts.

I suddenly heard the scuttle of several rats right under my feet and I jumped up in my chair, searching the darkness for the creatures. In my haste, I held onto only one half of the book and let the other half dangle. Immediately, I heard something thud to the floor. There in the darkness, with only my power as the light, I saw the intricately worked silver key. I hoped it was the very one for which I had been searching.

Clutching the book and the key, I ran to our apartment. I did not want to wake Kat, so I closed the door quietly and went to my sleeping chambers. The box was very heavy, but I carried it over to the table next to my chair and, fumbling just a little, I slid the key into place. It clicked several times. When I pulled on the lid, it rose heavily.

The first thing I saw was a white sheet of parchment against a finished piece of black velvet. I took the parchment and was surprised to find two separate letters. I flipped the first over. It had my name on it. I jumped a bit in my seat as I realized that this was actually happening. I had a letter from my dead mother. I carefully opened the letter and read.

My dearest darling Elizabeth,

I sit here, knowing that my doom is come. I know that I will never again look upon your lovely face or be able to share in all of the amazing events in your life. I write this knowing that I have given you a gift which will perplex and perhaps even frighten you until you understand it, and I will not be there to help you or guide you. I am sorry for this, more than anything, but I cannot change what has happened. I can do only what I am able, and that is to set in motion

events in which you will come to those who can
help you.

I do not know what your father will do to my family
when I am gone, nor if you will even be allowed to see
my mother, but I pray with all the fervor of my soul
that those who should will keep their word, and that
you will find your way to your grandmother to get this
last letter from me. My mother will tell you what you
need to know about your birthright, so I will only tell
you about my last gift to you. Though it is not the most
important, it is still a magnificent and significant
inheritance. It rests within this box. I had it reset to fit
my taste, but the pearls date back to the first woman
who wrote in the journal your grandmother will
give you.

Her name was Sephira, and she is your ten-times-
removed great grandmother. She is the first Fillos we
have record of. You may change out the letter B, but
care for the pearls as if they were the most precious
treasure, because they are. Keep them locked in this
box when you are not wearing them. However, when
you are wearing them, my daughter, wear them with
the pride of a Fillos da mente e da Lúa.

Elizabeth, I need you to know that I love you and I am
so proud of the little lady you are becoming. I knew
that you would be a girl from the moment I knew that
you were in me. Your father had no part in that fact;
the power of the moon made it happen. You see, the
first time your father and I made love it was on the
deck of a ship under the moonlight. That is how Fillos

*are conceived—only under the moonlight. Though I
pretended a boy was all I wanted, how could I not
want the one thing more important than Henry and all
his godly kingship: a daughter of the moon, with the
mind and power of her mothers, and the wisdom of
her past as her birthright? I wanted you more than
anything, and I was so fortunate to know you and see
you grow. You are the light of my life. Know that, my
daughter, and be extraordinary.*

*With all my heart and love—
Your mother Anne*

I had not realized that I was crying until I was finished
reading. It was as if she knew what my heart needed to hear,
and she said it. I sat for several more minutes, reading and
rereading her words, and then I pulled the velvet off the necklace she had left me, excited that I would have this precious
heirloom to always remind me of her. It was more beautiful
than I would have thought. The pearls glistened in the moonlight, and the golden "B" stood out against the white of the
pearls and the black of the velvet. Carefully, I picked the
heavy gemstones up and wrapped them around my neck.
Instantly, I felt connected to not only my mother, but all the
women who came before me and had worn these same pearls.

EPISODE 11

October 1542
Hever Castle, Kent

T hinking of my ancestors brought me back to the other letter, which I was sure my grandmother had left for me. I opened it up and read.

Lovely little Elizabeth,

I am so sorry that I am not going to be around to help you through this transition. But first, I wish to offer you words of comfort. I imagine you are experiencing some fairly dramatic changes because of the gift, or, I should say, the gifts that you have. Please feel comforted. You are meant to have all the power you do. We, the last five generations of Fillos da mente e da Lúa, (or Daughters of the Moon and Mind) have done a thing which shall ensure you are the most powerful Fillos of all. But I will tell you of this later. I should start at the most important part, the reason for this little hunt your mother and I constructed. (I am sorry by-the-by for any confusion or trouble you had finding this letter. It was necessary in order to keep your mother's enemies from discovering the truth.)

My gift is foretelling. After I saw with certainty that your mother would be murdered, she gave me the charge to train you up in your gifts. However, once the horrid occurrence transpired, I foresaw my own untimely death.

So, my dear, this letter and the Fillos journal are all you will have to train yourself up in the ways of your gifts. This may be hard to understand or believe, but you must trust me, and all instruction contained in the journal. It is a record of your female line, all of whom had gifts just as you do. We call ourselves "Fillos".

Elizabeth, the women in your family have protected this great secret for as many generations as the earth has had sons of Adam and daughters of Eve upon it. We are counting on you to do the same.

I was blessed to see your endowment of power. I saw you on a horse on a green, bathed in light. A piece of the moon fell from the sky and touched you. You were still very young. This event is spoken of in the lullaby your mother sang to you as a babe and it is carved on the desk that contains the history of our power.

Now to the power. Each Fillos has a different ability through our mother-moon, and I believe each ability is specific to our circumstances. I, as I have already mentioned, see things before they happen, (and a few other trifles, like hiding the painting of your mother in the foyer, and knowing when a woman is with child) but that is the extent of my ability. Foretelling has been very helpful in raising my daughters and sons to the high positions they have achieved.

Unfortunately, they did not always listen to my advice, and you can see how each path has ended. Truth be told, Anne is the only downfall I do not pity, for she was the only one who knew my advantage and still she refused to use caution. Do not misunderstand me; I am very sorry for her fate. I wish I could have forced her to avoid it. Sadly, no one could force Anne to do anything, but I digress.

Your mother was more powerful than I, and could manipulate the thoughts, actions, and desires of those around her. My mother had a comforting or healing touch. My grandmother could call to the water and make it move with her will. I do not wish to frighten you, but you will have all of these gifts and more. I and your mother have made incredible sacrifices to secure your talents, for you alone will be in a unique position to use them.

In regard to what we do with this great, unearthly power, we have all felt different responsibilities, as you will read in the journal. We all are able to go quietly about doing good or evil as we see fit. I saw future things and was able to influence people and events because of my knowledge. I wonder, now that I am dying and am able to look back upon what I have done, if, at times, I did what I should have. Did I choose evil more than good? I guess I will know when I stand at the judgment bar of God.

Your mother was always ambitious, and I think that she was interested in making the world a better place, but according to her own ideals. You do not know the influence she had over the Privy Council and the king. She is the reason England broke with the Catholic Church. History, of course, will remember it differently, but I will tell you this right now: any brave thing your father did in regard to divorce or royal supremacy was a result of Anne's influence.

However, Henry soon began to wriggle out of Anne's control. I am not sure how or why, but we think it had something to do with his fixation on having an heir. Anne expressed how difficult it was to keep those with strong emotions under control, and Henry had very strong emotions toward the church. He did not care about anyone or anything more than those two things, and since she couldn't provide him an heir and she took away the church, I guess eventually, his obsession won.

This leads me to you. You alone will decide how to use this power. I hope that you will choose well and be happy. I hope that you will not care about what others think, and make decisions that will lead you to a moral path of love, family, and comfort, for those gifts are from God and are where true contentment lies.

Experiment, test yourself, push your limits, and see

what possibilities you can create. You have a marvelous advantage and you can make what you want of it.

You are a smart and good girl. I know that you will do very well. Know that the spirits of all your mothers are with you when you are shrouded in moonlight.

All other details pertaining to this power can be learned from the journal. Make an entry in it yourself, and most importantly, pass this power, in the proper time, to your own Fillos. Live well, my Fillos da mente e da Lúa. I will see you when we all face our maker.

With love, Elizabeth Boleyn

"Fillos da Mente e da Lúa," I said awkwardly and caressed the imperfect surface of one of the pearls hanging heavily around my neck. Carefully, I put both letters and the journal in the box, closed and locked it, and held the key tightly in my hand.

I could not wrap my mind around any of this. I needed sleep. So, I curled up in my chair and watched the moon until my eyes grew heavy and closed.

I was standing on a precipice in the black of night. My hands were raised high above my head, and I saw upon my arms golden gauntlets. Rain pummeled my face. I was light, and my hands weaved power into a web of beautiful magnitude.

Finishing my masterpiece, I directed the web downward toward the storm-ravaged sea. I watched the power as it flew just above the water's surface to its destination. When it met its target, the darkness exploded into light. The sight and sound of this terrible and mighty ripping of elements filled the silence around me. Lightning struck the face of the water, and the image of white-sailed ships covering the ocean surface became clear. There were so many of them…so many ships…but my power had just blown a hole in them, in this Armada. Smiling, I looked back to the sky and began gathering my power once more.

I yelled as I released it, "For my God, and my kingdom!"

I startled awake with a scream, and a moment later Kat came flying into the room. Morning sunshine filled the chamber, so I clearly saw how fear whitened her face. Rushing to my side in an instant, she touched me, assessing and asking questions.

"Are you alright? What has happened? You are covered in sweat. Are you ill? Are you hurt? My Lady, please tell me why you screamed!"

"Kat, I am perfectly alright. I had a bad dream, that is all. Please," I said, and touched her nervous hand. "I am sorry to have frightened you so."

She stood and assessed me with her critical expression, her eyes lingering on my neck. "Where did you get—"

"I found the key. It was in a book. I found it late last night and this was inside the box." I touched the necklace that was still wrapped around my neck.

Kat's eyes grew very wide, and her mouth gaped as she said, "Your mother's necklace."

"Yes, isn't it wonderful? I cannot believe it. I am so happy to have it. I of course will change out the B for a T or perhaps an E, but I am beside myself."

Kat's face grew serious and she gently lifted the golden B off my neck to examine it. "May I offer you some advice?"

I nodded, wondering at her austere attitude.

"I would never wear this in front of your father."

Shocked I asked, "Why ever not? If I have it changed why would he care?"

"You do not know this of course, but that necklace is absolutely the most signature item your mother ever wore, even as queen. In every portrait she is donning that piece of jewelry. I was told by a very reliable source that when she was crowned she wore it under her state robes. I think it would upset the king a great deal for you to flaunt this."

Kat was correct. I had not known, but after learning from my grandmother's letter the history behind the necklace, I understood why my mother acted thus. The thrill I felt at this small intrigue, this secret that I alone understood, overwhelmed me for a moment. I felt amazingly un-alone. I had a mother who loved me so much she lived a very dangerous life to bring me to the place I now breathed. If I were less happy, I might have cried. I never understood how huge the void in my heart and soul was. But now that that void was filled, I wanted to sing. I wanted to jump up and dance. I wanted to ride.

I bounded out of my chair and said in a hurried voice, "I am going to take one of the horses out. Would you care to come along?"

Kat sighed heavily. "I have a terrible headache today, and this little episode has only made it worse. Besides, if you have found what you were looking for, won't you want to leave?"

I smiled widely. "I have found what I was looking for. Anna will be here today sometime and after I have seen her we can leave whenever you would like. As for now, I am going for a ride," I said matter-of-factly.

Kat arched an eyebrow at me and said slowly, "Respect, Elizabeth," and she put her fingertips to her temples and began to rub. She sighed again and looked at me closely. "Stay within the grounds, please, and I will let you go alone."

"Yes, we will stay here. Thank you," I said, and walked to the door.

"My Lady."

I stopped.

"Would you care to change, or at least leave your necklace so that it will not get lost?"

"No, Kat. I do not want to be without it for now, and I do not care that I am still in yesterday's clothes. I will change later." Then, I opened the door and ran happily to the stables.

EPISODE 12

November 1542
Hever Castle, Kent

Our visit with Anna was pleasant. My father's fourth wife was small, fair of hair, eyes, and skin. Some might call her homely, for she did not have the round face that was fashionable, but I paid no mind to those things, for she was very kind. Though she did have a bit too much of a taste for the needle and thread. She enjoyed sitting with her stitching by the fire and would do so for hours on end. At first, she would speak to me as we sat, but very little, for her speech was heavily accented.

It took me no time at all to suggest that she help me perfect my German by conducting all our remarks in that language. Thus, we spent many happy hours conversing and debating. I will say I did improve remarkably. My love of stitching was small, but in those hours, I did complete several Christmas gifts for my family and household members.

One night, not too long before we were to be on our way back to Hatfield for Christmas, Anna asked, "Do you play any instruments? I feel I have heard you have a love of music."

Enthusiastic, I responded, "Yes! I do have a great love of it."

"Oh, how wonderful. It is so quiet here, I would love you to sing for us."

"Of course." A lute was summoned, and I played and sang all the old German songs I knew.

Anna stopped her stitching. She closed her heavily-hooded eyes and tilted her pointed chin upward, as if in the bounds of pure joy. It filled my heart with love for the music that much more.

Every day, as I sat, I thought of my mother. I couldn't help it. Anna liked the quiet, and though she was open enough to conversation, she did tend to sit hours on end with not a breath of a comment leaving her lips.

In this, I pondered all I'd learned about myself and my family. I wondered at how my maternal line had planned out so much of my future. How they had such great expectations for me and how in all the world could I see them completed.

I wanted to try out my power of persuasion on Anna as I had on Kat, but the only thing we disagreed on was how long one should sit poking one's fingers with a needle before one moved on. (Truth be told, I had also improved in my embroidery. A fact I suspected was the entire reason Kat had not packed us up and moved us back to Hatfield sooner. The woman would make a real lady out of me at any cost.)

Still, one morning, as the sun filtered warmly through the window and the fire cracked merrily, I knew I needed to be out of doors on such a glorious day, and I decided to give my powers a try. I had no idea how to start besides pulling the light to me, which I did.

Then, turning to Anna, I said, "Look at the beautiful morning it is. I would very much like to go for a ride."

Anna looked out the window as if for the first time since taking her station in the chair. I waited for the ball of light, but nothing happened, and Anna answered. "Yes, it is lovely. Not many more like this before the ice and snow stops all riding."

I tried again. "Let's go out. We could walk the grounds or something else…?" I left it invitingly. And I still did not get a reaction from my power.

"Oh no, dear. I don't go out until the afternoon on days such as these. It will still be cold now."

I sniffed and thought that cold was exactly what I wanted. I wanted my breath to freeze as it left my mouth and nose. I wanted the wind to whip my hair into a cold tangled bundle. The idea of spending another morning and afternoon in this room angered me. "Anna, you will come on a ride with me. Now." I said it with force and with will, and a ball of light the size of an apple pulled itself away from me and rushed across the space and air between us, hitting her fully in the face.

She was putting her needlework down within half a moment. "I do feel a ride would be fun. Let's go."

I blinked, startled, and a slow smile gathered round my lips. I could most certainly use this power for good.

December 1542
Hatfield House, Hertfordshire

W e only stayed a fortnight at Hever, and I knew my time there would be forever etched into my heart. I had come to the knowledge of who I was. I had gained a dear friend, nay, a beloved aunt (for father called her his beloved sister) in Anna, and I had come to know more of my mother and maternal line. All and all, I was very happy, and I felt a sense that I had uncovered a great mystery and been on a fairly grand adventure for a girl of nine. So, coming home to Hatfield at Christmas only broadened my joy.

I had rather hoped that Father would invite us to court, but no such invitation came. The letter that we did receive from Father held wonderful news about my tutelage, however. Father decreed that I would be sharing lessons with Edward until a proper tutor for residence at Hatfield could be procured.

I was to join him at Ashridge in January.

The joy that filled my heart bubbled out of me in the form of an excited giggle. "Thank you a million times for writing Father, Kat, for I cannot believe my good fortune. I will be studying with the prince and he is bound to have marvelously sophisticated tutors—not that you aren't sophisticated, Kat. Of course, you are. Also, my favorite of all people will be there."

I understood now that the ball of light that caused such a ruckus with Kat when last I was with Robert was the gift my mother spoke of, namely influence. I had to wonder if I, with all my hoping, had used this same gift to in some way bring about this change in tutelage. I admitted to myself I was a little hesitant to experiment with my gift, for I had no one but

Kat to use it on. I would not use her again in such a way. It frightened me.

Kat looked at me with confusion, "Your favorite of people? Will your father the King be there, my Lady?"

I had not been speaking of Father, but of Robert. Ashamed, I realized I'd forgotten to tell Kat about Robert going to Ashridge.

Feeling the need for honesty, I said quietly, "I wish Father were going to be there. Alas it was not him I spoke of, but Robert."

"Oh, I see. Robert. Well that is a lucky turn of events. How is it that Robert is going to be there?"

"He told me before he left that Father had asked him to study with Edward and be his playfellow. I can remember when I had playmates. It was a long time ago when I was still under his favor. I wish he would have asked girls here to be my playmates recently."

Kat looked a bit abashed. "I think the reason no one has come to play with you and share your tutoring is because it was I that was giving it. I have thought why your Father would neglect you in this way." Kat paused, considering, and I couldn't help but think that perhaps my mother's gifts had indeed reached into my future and influenced us all. I heard Kat sniffle. "All I can think," she continued, "is that no one wanted to come, for then they would have me as a teacher, when there are so many more prestigious teachers out there."

"Or, perhaps they did not want to live with the bastard child of the King and Anne Boleyn, a girl exiled from the king's presence for the last two years. Besides, I think word has gone about that I am of a bad disposition."

I winked at her.

She laughed and wiped at her eyes. "Yes, you are horribly disrespectful and an overall git at your studies," she answered playfully. But she sobered quickly. "I still fear our biggest problem is my lack of credentials. In this age of information, higher thinking, and educated intellects, I am not much in demand. I do not know what I would do with myself if you did not insist that I stay in your household."

There was a bit of desperation in her voice and face.

The tears had returned as she spoke, and I pitied her.

"Kat, as long as I am here to torment you, I will do it with pleasure. And I expect you to endure it the best you can, for I will never be without you."

A smile lit up her face, "You blessed girl. I would not leave you even if I should marry one day. I feel as though you are the child of my heart, and how could I leave my only child?" She wrapped me in her arms and hugged me tightly.

A few weeks ago, this statement would have brought such happiness to my soul, but now I wasn't certain how it made me feel.

I had a mother. An amazing, powerful mother, who had done all she could to help me. I had her to think about now. I had my future to think about. A future my mother had seen and planned out so carefully for me.

She had set me on a path and it was my job and responsibility to learn all I could. To experiment and grow, not only in scholarly ways, but in this new way. As a Fillos. It was my birthright.

I smiled at Kat, but also to myself, as I thought of going to school with Robert and Edward and the others; what better place to have such a power than in a schoolroom filled with boys? Boys of noble birth, no less? Boys that would think me the least of them.

I might just learn how to use my powers for evil after all.

OF MOON AND MIND

EPISODE 1

December 1542
Hatfield House, Hertfordshire

So much occupied my mind since returning from Hever. The idea of my mother, Anne Boleyn, a sorceress, the journey her power had taken her on, and her plans for me. My own power. My father finally softening toward me. Robert and Edward as schoolmates and playfellows. With it all, I admit, I was a bit flighty as Hatfield prepared for the hard winter months—the weather was so cold and rainy that we could not wander at all out of doors—thus my situation did not help my state of mind.

Christmas could not come fast enough and the distraction of preparing for the holiday was welcome. Master Parry, Emma, Blanche, Kat, and I decorated a beautifully proportioned pine that young Henry, the gardener's son, so stalwartly braved the out of doors to cut for us. We adorned it elegantly—I spent days crafting paper and string bobbles—and we ornamented the hall at Hatfield to look like a festive church. Roasted savory meats on the spit in the middle of the room and laying out pies, breads, and sweets to fill the tables, was my joy. All the fragrances blended together, making the perfect Christmas aroma.

Once the day of the birth of the Savior arrived, some of the younger children put on a small nativity play, and I played the lute, while we all sang holy carols and exchanged gifts. It was a marvelous evening.

The next morning one of the kitchen maids, Jane, went into labor. The whole house seemed to stop running when a baby was born, but I usually did not pay too much attention to the process. We would discuss when the pains started and when they ended, and after the child was washed and dressed I went with a gift.

However, Jane's screaming started around midmorning and did not cease until nightfall the next day. They needed Kat's help with the baby, so I was mostly left to myself.

On the second day, I decided I needed to go looking for Kat.

Finding Jane's small room, I quietly opened the door and instantly smelt and saw copious amounts of blood. I also saw a white-faced woman who was naked except for a threadbare nightdress, which was gathered around her breasts.

Her legs were spread open and a man was digging in her private area. He pulled and pushed at her misshapen belly and tugged on something that looked disturbingly close to a miniature arm protruding gruesomely from between her legs.

Jane's eyes were still as the man did his work, and she did not respond to the women bustling around her, wiping at her forehead, patting her hand, and saying comforting words.

I became sick. Luckily there was a chamber pot outside the door next to a mound of bloodied clothes, for I vomited right then. When I noticed the pot was also full of blood, tears and vomit came simultaneously and in abundance.

A few minutes later, after I had taken a few steps away from the door, I heard someone come out of Jane's room. It was Blanche, but she did not notice me, for the moment she was out of the door she had pulled her partially bloody apron to her face and began weeping into it.

I ran back to my room, thinking all the way of the mortality of man—for though I had not seen death before I knew it in Jane's face—but far more than that I felt an overwhelming fear of the situation itself and committed my mind then and there that I would never put myself into that fatal condition.

K at came back to our rooms a few hours later and she was haggard-looking and white. I thought I heard her say under her breath, "Never seen so much blood."

Her lips were tight, and she probed me with her eyes when I asked, "What happened?" One part of me really did not want to know the details because I knew I would see the pictures in my head, but another part of me needed to know so that I could make sense of the carnage I saw.

"Both Jane and her baby have died in the birth."

"What happened? How did they die?" I asked with real sadness in my voice.

"Doctor Flyn says the baby was turned sideways and he could not get it turned back around. Even… after…he could not get the baby out. It must have been too big or perhaps it was caught." She looked at me and stroked my hair, "Sometimes these things happen, my Lady. Do not be alarmed. It is all in the hands of God."

I had not been great friends with Jane, for she had only

become a part of my household a year ago, but I had had many nice conversations with her and had enjoyed her stories, so this information did make me extremely sad. I did not understand how God could let a nice woman like Jane die in such a horrid and embarrassing manner. And what of the child? I shivered, and bile again rose in my throat.

"Kat, is it wicked of me to say that I never want children?" I asked her as I told myself I did not care if it was wicked or not.

"Yes, child, I think that it is, for God told us to multiply and replenish the earth, and, if you are married, you should have children."

"Well, I guess that settles it."

Kat looked down at me, interested. "Settles what?"

I took a deep breath before I admitted how wicked I really was. "I just will never be married." I did not wait for Kat to register her shock. I hurried on. "All I have seen of the institution is negative, and now I do not want to have children, for though I have seen many happy outcomes, the ones that are bad are truly horrific. I simply cannot imagine the inducement."

She narrowed her eyes as if I had just admitted to seeing the sight. I hurried on. "You tell me that in God's eyes they go hand in hand, and although I know that someday I may wish to marry, I think it will be an easy thing to remember that marriage and children come together. So, I will just as soon stay single like you, Kat." Kat huffed, and I had an idea. "Why can I not just be like Father and have lovers—lots of them. They could all simper and buy me gifts and say pretty things, but I wouldn't have to marry any of them or bear them children."

Kat instantly turned a bright shade of red. She had attempted to talk to me of the relationships between a man and a woman, but she was fastidiously shy, so I had gleaned all my knowledge from pieces of random conversations, and I felt like I understood relations between husband and wife. Truly, it all sounded annoyingly complicated to me, but I accepted the fact that every person I knew seemed engrossed by love. It was reason to follow that I would probably feel the same someday.

Kat continued to blush as she said, "It does not work that way, Elizabeth. Shame on you, girl. The very thought is reprehensible."

"How so? Father has had many mistresses. Is that reprehensible? I should think not, or someone would tell him, or at least the women would refuse, wouldn't they? And if Father can do it, then why can't I?"

"I had not realized fully until this moment how truly small your world is. How little information you have on these subjects and, by being tied to me—one who does not discuss these matters—what a disadvantage you have been at. Please forgive me and let me try my best to explain."

She sat down and looked at me, but before she even started talking, she blushed again. She opened her mouth and closed it, blushing even deeper, and sighed. "Perhaps we should have Blanche talk to you about this. I cannot believe that I have not thought to do this before now. Wait here. I will return in a moment." She got up swiftly and left the room.

Before long, Blanche, with her prematurely gray bun, simple dress, dimpled chin, and bright green eyes, walked confidently into the room, all traces of blood and tears gone.

"Well it seems as though we need to discuss the facts of this life and the reasons God has made us the way he has made us." She walked up to me and lifted my chin to stare into my eyes. "I believe it is past time. Shame on Kat, but better late than never. Now, I am hoping this has nothing to do with the boy you pranced around with this summer."

Now it was my turn to blush. I could feel the heat in my cheeks, though I wasn't exactly sure why. I had never thought of Robert as a lover—Robert kissing me or peppering me with serious flattery in the way of lovers. Though if there was someone to do the job, why not Robert? He'd do it properly. I suppose I did get all funny when I was around him—but kissing Robert? The idea never had occurred to me.

I cleared my throat. "No, Miss. This has nothing to do with Robert Dudley. I simply was wondering why I had to get married instead of having lovers like my father."

Blanche's face turned stern. "That is a dangerous subject for us to breach. Heads have flown for lesser statements, as my Lady well knows. But what I will say is that any priest will tell you God's word on the subject. Women are to be virtuous. We must keep ourselves clean before God and for our husbands. This is what Christ taught us. And in a union of virtue the man and wife are for one another and none else."

"But husbands do not have to keep themselves clean for wives? I am sorry, but this is not making me feel any better." My natural instinct was to rebel against the hypocrisy.

"It is a protection for women and children that God gives this command, my dear. If any female has relations with a male, she is the one in jeopardy of becoming with child. It is a good and natural consequence of the act. Moreover, after she has a baby, she must take care of it. What would that be like for the sad young woman with no husband to support and care for her and her child? What will she do? You see the problematic situation."

I did see, but I was different. "Well I have plenty of money. I would be able to take care of myself and a child, if I were so unfortunate as to have one."

"Yes, my dear, until your father takes it all away because you have disgraced yourself and your family by becoming pregnant out of wedlock."

That closed the subject for me, completely, utterly, and irrevocably. I would never have relations with a man, even if I someday wanted to. It could not be worth the risk. However, at the back of my mind, the words my grandmother wrote troubled me. "And most importantly, pass this power, in the proper time, to your own Fillos." Perhaps there was another way to pass the power down. If there was, I would find it.

I said aloud to let Blanche know my feelings, "Well, I will not be participating in the procreation of human life. I am firm on this point. From what I've seen, it cannot be that desirable." I thought a bit more and did not understand. "I do still feel confused. How a kiss can produce the effect. I have seen so many people kiss at court without getting with child."

Blanche laughed at me heartily in that moment and then things got graphic.

She went on for what seemed an eternity about the relationship between a man and a woman, and by the time I went to bed that night all thoughts of Jane and her death were gone, replaced with less gory, but equally horrid, images. I could not believe that people, all people, did what she described. I felt vile, and yet in a very odd way—a way that I did not even want to admit to myself—I felt interested. The conflicting feelings preoccupied me, and I found it hard to sleep.

EPISODE 2

January 1543
Ashridge House, Hertfordshire

There was a very small amount of snow on the ground as we traveled to Ashridge, and it only heightened the beauty of the ride. The rolling hills and ample woods were not enough, however, to completely occupy my mind.

I could not wait to see Edward. It had been so long since I had visited my younger brother that I tried to imagine how he'd grown. He would be six soon, so he would be out of dresses and on to breeches, which was the sign it was time to find a male tutor for him, for his real education as the future king would begin. I was going to be there to witness it and, in the process, take advantage of tutelage from a real scholar for my own education. Bless Kat for writing to Father, and bless Father for letting me come.

As we entered the gate, I straightened my fur cap and coat and pinched my cheeks with my gloved fingers so that I would look as excited as I felt. I was a bit disappointed that

Edward was not waiting for me at the door, but the moment I stepped out of the carriage, I realized that it was far colder outside the contraption than in. I hurried to a black-clad man who shivered as he waited on us.

"Greetings, Sir William. How are you?"

"Well, my Lady. You look elegant and refreshed."

"Thank you," I said with a little shiver.

He smiled and motioned me toward the door. "His Royal Highness, the prince, is impatiently awaiting you just inside. I had to keep him out of this cold on account of his health. The king is most particular about the prince, as I am sure you are aware."

I was aware. I had never been in a cleaner place or with cleaner people than when I was with Edward. Though Edward was in wonderful health, Father was very anxious about him, as he should be, for there was but one son to continue the Tudor dynasty.

"Sir William, do you know, will the king be joining us here? It seems he would want to directly oversee Edwards's first bits of tutelage."

Sir William looked a bit surprised by the question and his long face held a bit of a sneer when he answered. "No, I think your father has other plans that will be taking the majority of his time at present."

I wondered what Sir William knew, but we had entered the house and so I did not get a chance to question him.

"Elizabeth!" came the eager sound of Edward's voice. He rushed up to me exactly as he'd done when he was small. His bright eyes and golden hair looked the same, though he had grown so tall and thin.

A loud humph from a strict looking man at Edward's side stalled his haste. Edward stopped just in front of me, his tight lips trying for all they were worth to hide his smile. He

straightened his fur-lined doublet and feather-plumed cap and
bowed gracefully.

"My Lady, you look ravishing. May I escort you to the
fire?" his high pitched little voice asked.

I laughed heartily and took his hand, curtseying as low as
possible over the proffered hand. "Of course, you may, your
Royal Highness. You look very handsome yourself, if I may
be so bold."

"Yes, you may. And on that subject, I'll have you know
that I find myself quite handsome as well," he said with a
serious face except for his laughing eyes.

I smiled wide and squeezed his hand. "I feel honored to
be your guest. May I inquire about your family and your
health?"

"You may, thank you. I am in perfect health, and my
family are all very well, excepting my sister Bessy. You may
know her. She is a frightful creature, a very scary thing to
behold. But it is her wit and her tongue you must fear
the most."

I feigned shock and began tickling him in the ribs. That
was his vulnerable spot. "Why, you royal rat!" I said as he
began to laugh and squirm violently. I held him fast and
continued tickling. "I will show you, speaking of your loving
sister in such a manner! It is reproachful. What if she were
present to hear you?"

Through his laughing he said in mock surprise, "Oh heavens, it is you, Bessy! How did you disguise yourself? I did
not know you."

But the laughing and playing was cut short, for I felt a
hand on my shoulder and heard another humph. I stopped
tickling Edward, who was now on the ground, tears of joy in
his eyes. I stood straight and looked around to see the same
angular-faced man.

"It is improper for the prince to be acting thus. He has guests to introduce you to."

Edward was getting up now. "Oh yes, Elizabeth. I am sorry I forgot." He took me by the hand, all courtier again, and turned me toward the back of the room. Standing there in the dim candlelight were three other boys. One of them, the beautiful one, I knew instantly.

"Robert!" I said with so much longing and excitement that even I would have been embarrassed had I time to think about it. I rushed to him and hugged him tightly. He did not hug me back and when I pulled away, I saw fear in his eyes. It was then that I remembered I was not to show this side of our friendship to other people.

"Sorry, I forgot," I said so low I hoped no one could hear, and his countenance instantly changed so that I knew he was glad to see me.

Edward came up behind me and said, "Well, I guess you know Robert Dudley. When did you meet him, Sister? I thought that you were fairly secluded from society at Hatfield."

I gave him a withering look. "I do occasionally have visitors, Edward. Robert and his father happened to be nearby and were able to attend my birthday celebration. Robert and I had so much fun dueling with one another that we became fast friends. Did we not Robert?"

He cleared his throat, put on his best courtier manners, and spoke. "Yes, we did, my Lady." I was once again thrilled to hear the beautiful timbre of his young voice. "I think that your sister here bested me in several sword fights, my Prince. She is unusually skilled, if I do say so." Before I could clarify that he was joking, the other boys laughed loudly.

The light-haired boy, who did not have as fine of clothes as I thought one of my brother's playmates ought to have, spoke. "I am sure you are telling a great falsehood, Robert, for you are the only one who can beat all of us together. There is no way a girl could best you."

He had an Irish accent, green eyes, and freckles. The overconfident way he spoke made me sure that I either would like this boy immensely or hate him with passion. I would wait to decide which after I beat him in all our subjects.

Everyone was laughing now except Robert, who kept his eyes on me, never once looking away. I felt an urgency from him that I did not understand. Unfortunately, I would have to wait to find out what it all meant.

I looked to the Irish boy. "Edward, would you please introduce me to your playfellow here, so that I might know whom I am challenging to a duel?"

Edward wrinkled his nose at my haughty speech and smiled. "Let me do this in the proper order. This is Dr. Coxe." He pointed to the severe looking man standing next to him. "He is our tutor."

I curtsied and felt worried. I did not like the look of the man and I did not like his attitude toward Edward.

"This is Henry Brandon, the young Duke of Suffolk."

I again curtsied to a dark-haired boy that had not yet spoken. He looked the same age as Edward, while the other two boys were older.

Lastly, Edward indicated the Irish boy. "And this is Barnaby Fitzpatrick, a cousin of the Earl of Ormonde. He also happens to be my best mate. As to why, I am sure you will soon understand. Unfortunately, he is also my whipping boy."

"That is regrettable," I said with a bit of sarcasm in my voice. "I shall make special effort not to get you into any trouble then, Edward, for I would not want this boy, who is intent on degrading me the moment he meets me, to find his buttocks sore on account of our folly."

Now it was my turn to enjoy everyone's laughter and this time Robert did laugh as he continued to watch me.

"Your sister has a quick wit, my Prince," Henry Brandon said.

"And a haughty manner," Barnaby said with a huge smile, not at all scared by my open threat. "I like her."

"She is very intelligent—for a girl," Edward said, "Of course she is related to me. Superb blood, that is what I say."

"Well, at least half of it is," Henry said, thinking he had told a great joke, but the room became quiet as everyone looked to me for my reaction.

Anger welled up in me at once and I felt my mind reach out for the power that was in me. As it settled around me I felt strength and a calming wisdom. I instantly realized that I needed to get along with these boys if I was going to stay here, so with all the strength I could muster, I looked at them in turn and said aloud, "None of you will refer to my mother in this manner again. While I am here, we will all get along as equals. Do you understand?"

As I said it, four small orbs of light left my aura and descended upon Edward, Barnaby, Henry, and Dr. Coxe.

Shock widened my eyes and brought blood to my cheeks. In the last few months I had tried many times to do this very thing, but it never worked. Yet here in this public situation my power easily affected everyone in the room—everyone excepting Robert, a fact which confused me more than anything.

I stood motionless and completely stunned, so much so that I did not know what to do when all but Robert started muttering confused apologies in staggered unison. Robert's eyes left me for the first time as he looked around him.

Dismay screwed up his brown eyebrows, and when he looked back at me, I knew that I would have to explain.

The rest of the evening went smoothly except for the occasional probing eye from Robert. The conversation was light and the boys were very generous. Dr. Coxe was the perpetual fly on the wall and I noticed how he focused all his attention on Edward. I felt as if he were making a mental list of his strengths, or perhaps his flaws. The constant sour expression on his face told me that it was perhaps the latter. However, his speech and manners were impeccable—perfect in fact, if that were possible by anyone but Christ. I was very excited to start my lessons with him, but I hoped that we would have some variety in our instructors or I might forget what it was like to smile in earnest.

Supper was light but expertly done, and after I finished I sat back in my chair and admired the elegant dining room of Ashridge House. This place reminded me of an old monastery, which would make sense considering Father was systematically acquiring all monasteries and giving them away as gifts. Only the prince of England could expect a house as lushly furnished as this, though. The wooden beams and stained-glass windows were breathtaking, and all the décor was exquisite in its make.

"I can see you are admiring my home. Father has outdone himself with the apartments. Just wait until you see yours. I saved the second best for you, my dear sister," Edward said happily.

"It certainly makes Hatfield feel more like a stable, my brother," I said admiringly, and I turned to watch the rain gently trickle down the windows. "I like it here, Edward. You might not see me leave anytime soon."

"You are welcome for as long as it pleases you, Bessy. Only do not begin to feel so comfortable that you forget who is master here," he said without any hint of teasing. Then he quieted his voice. "I will not hear of the cook making all those sweet things you love so much. It is an indulgence you should give up, my sister, unless you want to be as fat as Father."

I was shocked to hear him say the words, and I wondered what his feelings toward Father were. "I do not think Father is all that fat," I said, trying to let him know that I was not about to talk badly about our father.

"Yes, he is, Elizabeth, and I will not have it in you. Girls are not supposed to be fat. It is unsightly."

I knew that my six-year-old brother could not be thinking these things on his own. "Whose words are you repeating, Edward?"

He blushed but easily admitted, "Dr. Coxe. He changed my diet so that I began eating much blander foods as soon as he arrived. He thinks that obesity is equal to gluttony and he says that the Bible teaches against it, as it is a sin. He is very pious."

I knew that he had to be Protestant or Father would not have given him the position as Edward's tutor, otherwise how would it be for Father to work so hard to promote the Church of England only to die and have his own son and successor tear all his work to shreds? Yes, Father would see to it that Edward was properly indoctrinated. Nevertheless, I was concerned. Edward seemed far too impressionable. He was already quoting a man he barely knew. That was not good, and I felt I needed to tell him so. Unfortunately, I was unsure of how to go about it.

"Tell me more about Dr. Coxe," I said finally, hoping that I could somehow just bring it up.

Edward was excited. "I am so pleased to be in the company of a man. I love Lady Bryan, and she has taught me well, but it is different with Dr. Coxe. Everyone has been telling me how I am to be king one day, and now I feel as though I am finally going to be prepared for that task. You must admit, Elizabeth, that women are deficient in so many ways. They cannot be a man, they cannot act like a man, they cannot teach one to be a man. It is a man's job to teach that art."

My mood instantly changed. "Art? Edward, I am afraid that you are mistaken. We women may not technically be as strong as a man is—or perhaps we are, for consider which one of the sexes have the children. I say this because I have recently experienced something tragic in regard to birthing and I know for a fact that if that job were left to men, the world would have ended with Adam and Eve."

Edward thought for a moment, and I was sure that he pondered the fact that his own mother had died as a result of complications following his birth. However, he soon came up with an argument. "Yes. Sister, but which one of us makes war? You would not be able to fight in a war. We men do that," he said a bit haughtily.

I laughed. "You princes think you do it, but truly the men who live under your rule do all the fighting. Moreover, who has said that women cannot fight? Given equal standing as a man has in war, meaning woman against woman, I can promise you that I would do alarmingly well. Women can fight, and women have babies. And just as the entire world sees, every time a king goes off to war, women can rule a kingdom and do marvelously well. However, I will concede on this point: a woman cannot teach a man to act like a man.

She can only teach him to be the best parts of the human disposition. I am convinced that men only act genteel because women have forced it upon them."

Edward looked at me out of the corner of his eye and smiled. "Whose words are you repeating, Bessy?"

I laughed, but my answer was interrupted by Dr. Coxe, who said in a low bass voice, "My, my, we have a little revolutionary on our hands." He was standing on my other side and I had not seen him lingering as I talked. "You have been instructed well, Lady Elizabeth. I can hardly believe the wisdom and maturity of your arguments. The very manner of your delivery and soundness of your speech entices me to write to a colleague of mine and see if he would be willing to join us for our lessons, simply to observe the phenomenon that is the Lady Elizabeth."

I could see in his face that he was truly impressed, and I was astounded to find that his features had softened as he spoke, so I answered, "If you seclude a child from other children, and that child only has lessons to occupy her, someone like me is naturally produced. I can write, read, and speak some of Latin, French, Italian, Welsh, and Spanish. However, I am most fluent in French. I have read all the great works from Homer to Machiavelli. My needlework is excellent, though I hate to do it, and my calligraphy is superb. I am a talented equestrian, as well as swordsman. I love new dresses and sweet foods, and Kat says I look at my own reflection in the mirror far too often, but I disagree. I think I gaze at myself just the right amount." I smiled mischievously and went on. "I dance, draw, sing, play two instruments, and I debate with adults to get my way about things on a regular basis. Thus, I am well practiced and, as you know, practice makes perfect." As I listed my skills, his eyebrows slowly climbed higher and higher on his tight forehead, and when I finished, I blinked my lashes up at him as sweetly as I could and concluded shrewdly from his observatory stillness of the night, "I hope that all this information will help you in deciphering how best to deal with me." I glanced at Edward, who looked impressed, and then back to Dr. Coxe, with a knowing expression on my face.

He flushed with excitement and interest. "Not only are you more accomplished than most women of my acquaintance, but you are far more perceptive than I would have believed possible, and you do it all with a touch of wit." He cleared his throat and straightened his doublet as he asked, "How old are you, my Lady?"

"I am in my tenth year, sir," I said, knowing that now I would get the best this man had to offer. He would not assume that I had received inferior training because it was given by a woman, or that I was unable to keep up with the boys. Thus, we could get straight to learning.

EPISODE 3

January 1543
Ashridge House, Hertfordshire

As Kat and I walked to my apartments, I heard footsteps following us. Apparently, so did Kat, for we both turned around at the same time.

It was Robert. I stopped and waited for him to catch up with us, and as he did he said, "I know that it is late, my Lady, and you are no doubt tired from your journey, but I was hoping to beg an audience with you."

I looked at Kat, not only for permission but also because looking at Robert's face for any prolonged amount of time made me begin to shake. I was again unaccustomed to his beauty. Thankfully, I knew my reaction to him would lessen with time and exposure.

Kat nodded and said, "But come into our sitting room so that we can get warmed up. I have our things to set out, so I will be able to watch you."

Robert smiled debonairly and said, "Thank you so much, wonderful and beautiful Lady Katherine."

I shivered with cold, excitement, and a touch of dread. I wondered if he was going to ask me about the strange things he had seen.

Edward was correct in saying Father had outdone himself with our apartment. It was magnificent. Thick rugs littered the floor, plush chairs reposed in every corner, and freshly beaten velvet drapes swooped across windows. The tile-worked fireplace was intricate with gold-carved flourishes and ebony inlays. I walked directly to the flames to warm my hands. It was so cold here. Robert joined me, and Kat went about lighting more candles before going to the bedchamber to warm herself there.

I looked over to Robert to find that he was staring at me. He looked so amazing by firelight. His dark eyes did not leave me as my eyes moved from feature to feature on his face.

"I have missed you terribly, Robin," I said, my voice a bit wobbly.

He nodded and opened his mouth to say something, but his countenance changed, and he looked into the fire for the first time. "I have missed you as well, my friend. I did not know how difficult it would be to act my part around the other boys, but I find I can do it."

"Sometimes I wonder what you are talking about, Robert. Are your parents cruel to you that you must always play a part when around those who could report on you?"

He stiffened and looked at me in alarm. "What do you mean by...oh, never mind. I can't fight with you right now. All I came to tell you was how I have missed you and missed being able to be myself with you. I also wanted to warn you about the situation here. I think that there is a delicate balance I have to maintain. Because I want to stay, I must act my part.

I need you to know that if, at any time, I say something that in any way is unkind, I do not mean it. You are my closest friend, but I think it would serve us both if no one found that out."

My eyes narrowed. "So, you want to keep the depth of our friendship a secret so that I will continue to be the outcast of the group? Or are you asking me to forgive you if you have to be unkind at times in order to maintain your clout? Which is it, Robert?" My voice rose as I spoke, and I knew that I was nearing anger.

Robert looked at me as if he had never seen me before.

"My Lady, you have always been able to read into what I was saying, but to have my own thoughts untwisted and regurgitated in this manner is quite alarming. Moreover, when you lay it all out in that way, I must say my whole speech was quite unforgivable and I am ashamed of it. What kind of thing for me to ask of a friend? How am I such a numbskull?" He looked down at the fire again and shook his head at himself.

As he always did, Robert dissipated my anger with his humble wit and charm.

I smiled slightly and turned to warm my backside. "You are not a numbskull, Robert Dudley. You are just a boy," I said with a bit of degradation in my voice.

It was then that I realized I was somehow so much wiser in the matters of human nature than I ever had been before. What had happened to me? I thought for several moments on this subject, but then looked back at Robert, whose face was downcast.

"Oh, Robert, forgive me! You are not as stupid as a boy— well, not all of the time." I elbowed him. "You see, two can play your boy's game."

It struck me just then that Robert had always treated me

as an equal girl. Here was the proof. He came to apologize in advance if he ever accidentally acted like the other boys. More proof was how he acted when they were mean to me, like about my mother. He did not laugh or joke because he would never do such a thing.

A thought occurred to me then. What if the reason my light did not touch Robert was because he was already aligned with me and my request? This made me think how important a distinction this could be for me. By intentionally manipulating the minds of all those around me, I could always know who agreed with me.

I imagined myself as queen and my whole Privy Council always agreeing with my silliest whim. That, however, could cause some difficulties. All my opposition could not suddenly be on my side without raising eyebrows. Those not manipulated would sense strangeness, just as Robert had done both times it had happened in front of him. I wondered if I could choose whom I wanted to affect, and if I could do it at varying levels.

Suddenly a surge of delighted excitement tickled my mind. I knew exactly what I would do with this time surrounded by the rougher sex. I would glean all I could from Dr. Coxe, of course, and I would have as much fun with Robert and Edward as I could. But I also now had subjects to practice my gift upon. I would hone and perfect my gift until it was as sharp as a rapier sword.

I knew that I could use this opportunity to experiment with my power as a stepping stone. I could make myself into something great. What if I could manipulate my way into a crown someday? My thoughts had betrayed me for had I not just thought of myself as such? I had, and I felt, in that moment, as if I understood exactly how it could happen for me.

And what a thing it would be. A woman, a single woman, uninterested in having children or getting married ever…queen.

A woman alone on the throne, powerful yet loved, feared yet respected. How would that be? I truly could be all that my mother wanted, for look how far she rose with this power.

I turned to my friend and took his hand. I squeezed it with as much affection as I could muster and smiled, my very skin and breath and fingers anticipating the future ahead of me. But as I looked into Robert's beautiful face, with its bright eyes and full mouth, I understood something about myself. Of all the scary, seemingly impossible things I saw ahead of me on that futuristic path, having my beloved Robert by my side felt like having a suit of armor, a buffeter against my own cowardice. And it was not the hope of being queen or the power of my magic but Robert's face before me, in my future, that sent a chill of excitement up my spine.

February 1543
Ashridge House, Hertfordshire

The bitter January weather kept us in the schoolroom for the majority of every day, and I felt distracted from my practice of manipulations by the rigor of our studies. In the mornings, we would go through language exercises, and then we would move to science and math. I was at almost the same level as the boys in these two subjects. However, since math and science were considered unimportant for me to know, Dr. Coxe asked if I wanted to be excused so that I could practice my needlework with Kat. I quickly informed him that I would much rather stay and learn the new subjects.

After the sciences, Dr. Coxe had us read history, and then we would conclude our studies with him by listening to him read out of the Bible. He would often give us a sort of impromptu sermon on the meaning of what we read.

I was thrilled by the stories of Christ, his miraculous healings and superb manner of teaching his followers. I felt the words flow from the scriptures and touch my soul with such force that I often wept. I wanted to do what Christ taught. I had heard sermons before, but not anything like what I was hearing from Dr. Coxe. He was a Catholic bishop, but everything he said suggested his inclination toward Protestantism. I loved the God that I met while listening to Dr. Coxe, and I knew in my heart that I agreed with this religion and not the one which my sister Mary was always subjecting me to.

Besides, I was proud that my mother's work as a monarch was one reason Dr. Coxe was able to hold the scriptures he read from, and proud that the religion my father was forming was one my heart loved. I had an awakening in my soul as I heard the sacred word, and I treasured Dr. Coxe's explanations.

As I learned more about the teachings of God, I wondered what he would make of me. I had a power that was otherworldly. How did I fit into his master design? Then Dr. Coxe read the beginning of the Bible. As I heard the story of Adam and Eve's creation for the hundredth time, I learned something new. No matter how strange I seemed, I was created in God's image and I was his child. Moreover, when we read of Noah and Moses, how they not only walked and talked with God but had great duties to perform in his service and with his power, I knew that I had also been given a power that could do God's will. This brought me great comfort and I was surprised by my strong desire to do good with what I was given.

Dr. Coxe noted my devotion and sometimes I felt as if he gave his lectures for my benefit alone. It was one subject in which he could openly pay me attention without seeming to neglect Edward, his primary charge. However, I soon saw that I was receiving attention from our tutor outside the schoolroom. Every morning Dr. Coxe had a different and invigorating lesson for me which I could only assume he had contrived in his off hours.

I watched him try not to praise me too highly or too often. However, the boys did notice his attention and I could see that at times even Robert got a little offended by my abilities. I did not care. I felt as though a veil had been taken off my mind and I was able to perform far better than I had come to expect of myself. But, then again, I was always shrouded in the light of my power.

One day in early February, wondering if my heightened astuteness was due solely to my power, I let the light around me go out. Dr. Coxe asked me if I was feeling well because I was not doing my figures correctly. He also commented that my countenance looked all wrong and wondered if he should not send for a doctor. Consequently, I had to spend the rest of the week confined to my rooms to make certain I was not ill.

While quarantined to my apartment, I had a lot of time to myself to think and to read. I thought of my gift and how it seemed to work. I mentally listed what had happened the two times I had used it openly. Firstly, I had gotten angry. Secondly, I had spoken the words that I wanted others to believe, and then the power left me. The other times that I had tried to work the manipulation I had not been angry, nor had I said anything aloud. This made me wonder if that was how it had to happen. After going through each circumstance repeatedly in my head, I finally realized that I would not be able to figure this out on my own, so I turned to the only place I could: my mother's journal.

I could not understand many of the languages, but for now it did not matter because my mother's words were of most interest to me. I began at her first entries and marveled at her experiments. It seemed that my mother and grand-mother had the power at the same time. Having someone to guide my mother made the learning go smoother for her than for me. This was evident in the fact that her entries were experiences while mine were all questions. Mother wrote of the first people she had manipulated, and then she shared how her skill grew with practice. When she was ten, she wrote, "I have found that I can now choose how strong I want the manipulation to be. This makes things much better, for that way I do not cause trouble for myself."

This was wonderful news for me. I too wanted this type of control and understood just what troubles she meant, for I had already foreseen the problems that could arise by not limiting the strength of the manipulation.

Mother talked of how, when she got angry, she had a reaction similar to mine and she could not control herself at all when upset. However, as I read on, she became better.

By and by she talked of Father. They met when she was very young. Out of curiosity, she tried her hand at manipulating him. At this point, I was surprised by her words.

*I was in the Lady Queen's antechamber when the king
entered. He saw my sister Mary for the first time, and
I could tell that he was interested in her look. I*

concentrated on him and mentally demanded that he make Mary his mistress; and you will never guess, but within a fortnight she was one of the Queen's ladies-in-waiting, and within a month the king had called her to his rooms.

It was a shocking story, but I focused on the fact that Mother had singled out Father. There were many other people in the room, yet she had only used her power on one. This was wonderful news and I was anxious to try my hand at it. I would need to get the boys one-on-one and then see if I could get them to do something small, using so little of my power that it might seem like their own idea. I thought of practicing on Kat, but Kat and Robert were both out of bounds. I loved them and did not want to manipulate them. Besides, they were usually on my side anyway.

When I returned from my confinement, the boys showed their happiness to see me again. Barnaby was the most enthusiastic. "I fear we're all quite bored without you here to make cheeky comments," he said in a whisper while Dr. Coxe was busy helping Edward with something.

I replied, "Yes, well, I missed you too, Barnaby." When he smiled overenthusiastically at me and his face flushed, I decided that he would be the perfect test subject. Having no idea what my limitations were, I determined that I would wait to force an action and just practice changing his mind, as I had already done, but hopefully in a more controlled fashion. I waited for an ideal situation to present itself.

However, when an opportunity arose, it was not with Barnaby.

Edward and I sat together at dinner. We ate baked fish and winter vegetables—again. The menu Dr. Coxe had us abiding by was not at all varied, and I longed for a tart or some hearty venison soup. When Edward pushed his plate away from him, food half-eaten, I decided it was time to take matters into my own hands.

"Excuse me, Edward," I said politely as I got up from our table to walk over to Dr Coxe's. With all the energy of mind I could muster, I looked the man in the eye, and in a voice so quiet no one else could hear, I said, "You have decided we are all in excellent health and that the variety of our food should not be restricted anymore."

I waited for the light of my power to go to him, but it did not.

"Excuse me child, I did not hear you. There is a terrible clattering of dishes and you were speaking so softly. Kindly repeat yourself." he said and wiped his mouth and beard with a napkin.

I panicked. What could I say? The blood rushed to my cheeks and before I knew what I was doing I seized the power and with every part of my mind willed my words to be heeded.

This time when I said them they were rushed.

"You have decided we are all in excellent health and that the variety of our food should not be restricted anymore. Tell the cooks now!" As I spoke, a strangely large orb of light left me and went to Dr. Coxe. I saw his mood shift at once.

"I am sorry, child. I know that you have something to converse with me about, but I need to talk to the cooks. It is a matter of urgency...I think." He added the last with a confused look on his face and raced off toward the kitchen.

I smiled to myself as gratification fumbled through my tense nerves. I had done it. Though it was rather awkward to have all the boys gawking at me for yelling at our tutor, their expressions frightened as they turned confused faces toward the tutor for not censuring me, but obeying me instead.

After, I made my first entry in the diary.

A Lady should not yell an individual manipulation at the top of her lungs; those should be quietly spoken so one does not get found out and burnt to the stake for a witch.

EPISODE 4

February 1543
Ashridge House, Hertfordshire

I had to practice my skill, so practice I did, on everyone. I endeavored to keep my manipulations small, singling out some one person. I figured since I started with food, I should see that through, and talked Nan, the cook, into baking a plethora of tarts, meat pies, and crumpets. Everyone seemed pleased about the change except Dr. Coxe, who still looked a bit perplexed.

Once, when we played hide and seek, I told Edward not to find me just as he was about to do so, and at once he went off in a different direction.

I had our dance instructor, Marvelo Baroush, convinced that I needed to dance with Robert more than with the other boys. As a result, we became quite accomplished together.

Dr. Coxe suddenly felt the need to instruct me most intensely in the subjects I liked best. This brought my knowledge of languages along so quickly that even I was astounded.

Sir William wrote to Father telling him that for some reason my dresses were getting a little ragged and I needed new ones. I was still waiting for that one to pan out. I hoped Father did not wonder why the news had not come from Kat.

Moreover, this one made me wonder if there was a distance factor, could I influence someone far, far away from me? How much energy lived within the little balls of power? This would be an experiment for later and the idea of unraveling that mystery intrigued me.

Entrenched as I was, I left that question and focused on enticing Henry and Barnaby to play a terrible prank on a grouchy maid, and that resulted in Barnaby getting a whipping of his own. I decided that, funny as a wet maid could be, it was not worth watching Barnaby protect his tender bottom for the next few days.

The skill I gained from these small manipulations was priceless. I could now manipulate one person in a room full of people to whatever degree I wanted; I had but to whisper my desire. It had to do with how much power I seized. When I was angry, my tendency was to grab far too much, which resulted in the person I manipulated acting rashly or feeling a sense of emergency and leaving him confused about what he had done. Once I could do it without anger or excessive fear, I figured out how to control the amount of power I took. The resulting orbs of light that broke off from me were very small indeed.

It was not until the first of March that I controlled a direct action, and I did it by hope alone.

After dinner, rain or shine, we would take a walk out of doors. Dr. Coxe believed that cold, fresh air was invigorating to body and soul, and I agreed with him. Then we would all go in to be instructed in dancing, swordplay, and often we would have chess tournaments. I never won. Robert always did.

However, on this day, I somehow bested Robert in the first game and, amazingly, so did Edward. Therefore, Robert was out. As we played on, Barnaby, who was always good, beat out Edward, as did I, and we both beat out Henry. Finally, it was Barnaby and I, to win.

I quickly set up a trap for Barnaby and, as I sat hoping he would fall for it, a smug look crossed his face. Quickly I began to chant in my mind, Move your queen to f4. Move your queen to f4. Light left me without my seizing it. Barnaby had already picked up his knight and was about to place it when he suddenly returned it and grabbed his queen instead. He proceeded to move her to the exact place I wanted. I could have sworn that his hand did not move with his permission. When it was over, and I had won, I did not feel the pride I might have. Barnaby seemed upset, especially when the other boys jeered at him for falling into my easily recognizable trap.

And here I had a war with myself. As much as I loved winning, as much as I wanted to squash these boys and teach them I was their equal; forcing them with my power to lose a hard-fought game seemed beneath me somehow. Manipulating someone into making you sweets was one thing; it was harmless, and the myriad of other small things I'd done fell into that category also. But this...it was not fair, and it weighed on my conscience.

After a week of struggling with it, I knew then that I did not want to act thus ever again. I also learned I needed to keep my hopes in check for, with me, hopes turned to magic.

Spring came in April, and with it sunshine and afternoon rains. We took full advantage of the sunlight. Because Edward was still a child not quite six, it was appropriate for us to all play together. However, his nurses were always at the ready in case he got hurt or we became too rowdy. We danced, ran, and played as much as Dr. Coxe would allow us time to do it in.

We all got accustomed to being together, and, though all the boys had their peculiarities, I got along famously with them all. I did take issue with one thing in our living arrangement. It was hard for me to watch how all the adults smothered Edward. He was such a good boy. I watched him carefully and noticed that his animation and happiness seemed to be ebbing. He became more serious and guarded. It worried me. The bond between us had grown, and sometimes, when his guard was down, he would hug me tight and say, "I love you the best, Bessy."

Though I did not want to think of this, Kat reminded me that soon Edward would be king and that it was important to stay within his favor. I hated this. I loved Edward and did not want my actions to be influenced by the fear of death if I someday displeased him. But her warning was true though. Everyone knew it, and before long I saw that Kat had been correct to remind me.

Many afternoons I spent much of my free time admiring the early vegetation with Kat, Robert, Henry, Edward, and Barnaby. Kat would drill us on the names and properties of the plants we saw and teach us about the ones we did not know. She had a great interest in plants, an interest I did not fully understand.

After one such outing, when Kat left us and Sir William called in Edward, I decided to explore the wilderness that was outside of Ashridge's grounds. I had wanted to do this on several occasions but could not because Edward was not allowed to leave the grounds. So today I went, and the other boys joined me.

It was lovely in the woods. We remained within sight of one another as we each explored different things. While Robert looked for frogs and spiders, I looked at the birds. My desire to fly across the ground overwhelmed me, for I had not ridden Larkin in months. Just as I was about to open my mouth to say so, Robert spoke up.

"I long for my Bessy," he said, without the slightest care who was listening. The other two boys stopped what they were doing to look at him and then at me. I stared at him in shock, but he did not look over at me. He just continued to lift rocks and poke interesting objects with his stick.

I decided I needed to say something, "When did you start calling me Bessy, and how could you long for me when I am here?"

Robert looked up, confused, and saw everyone staring at him. He blushed deeply and spoke in a rush. "My mare—my mare is named Bessy."

I arched an eyebrow at him. "So now you are naming your horses after me?" I looked at the other two boys, who were now laughing quietly to themselves.

"No, no, no, my Lady! Heaven forbid! I named Bessy thus when I was but six, long before I knew you. In fact, I was rather shocked when your brother called you Bessy. I thought then I had better never mention to you that that was my horse's name, but now look what I have done."

Henry and Barnaby burst out with laughter, unable to hold it in any longer. I sniffed haughtily and turned my back on them.

"My Lady, do not be offended. All I was saying was that I long to take my horse out. I feel it has been an eternity."

I turned around swiftly and glared into his face. Now that I was part of the world of impossibilities, I was aware that there could be other powers out there, perhaps powers that could read minds.

He blinked and wrinkled his brow at my expression.

"What is it?" he asked slowly, walking toward me.

I took him in, uncertainty in my gaze, but as he neared I knew that it was just that we were so connected that he felt the same as I in that moment. "I was just going to say the same thing as you, that is all. Riding is my passion and I was confused that you stole the words from my mouth."

He smiled and came to me then more quickly, climbing up the boulder I was atop and saying so only I could hear, "It is just that our souls were cut from the same fabric. I was sure you had already concluded this, being the insightful genius that you are."

"Well when you put it that way, I either have to admit I am a fool or that I am a genius." I looked at him smugly then sighed. "Yes, you are right. We should be brother and sister, for our minds are in agreeance on everything."

I saw his smile fall a bit, but I did not know if it was because he did not like the statement or the comparison.

Henry spoke up at that moment. "Do you think we should get back? I feel as though it is getting late, though it is hard to tell when one cannot see the sky."

I looked around and the forest was significantly darker. "Yes, we should be going."

I hopped down and Robert jumped after me. After he caught up to me, he leaned over to whisper in my ear, "Now that the ground is not so soft, would you care to join me for a ride late tonight?"

I turned to look in his eyes. "A nighttime ride happens to be one of my favorite pastimes. When shall I meet you in the stables?"

～

When we entered the house, it was to yelling and screaming. Edward marched his small frame up to me and said, "Elizabeth, if you take my playfellows and keep them all to yourself through our entire playtime again, as you did this evening, I shall be forced to have your head cut off! I am the prince here, these are my friends—not yours—and I can cut off whoever's head I wish!"

I could not believe what I was hearing. I was so hurt and astonished that I had no reply for him. It was Barnaby who suddenly stood forth to reply, "My Prince, we are truly sorry that we left you out. We all had a desire to go into the woods and we knew that you were not allowed. Therefore, we mutually agreed that, so as to not cause you any pain, we would go while you had other obligations. Please do not be upset with Lady Elizabeth, for it was all our decisions."

Edward was not affected. "Then you all shall be punished! Sir William, I want them all to receive a good whipping."

Sir William looked as if he did not know what to do. It really was not in Edwards' authority to have anyone but Barnaby whipped. But then he was the prince and how could you disobey a direct order from a prince, no matter his age or the stupidity of his request?

It was my turn to be mad. With the power of moonlight radiating around me I stepped forward, looked Edward boldly in the face, and whispered with rage, "You will not have any of us whipped, and you will apologize at once for your child-ish, impudent, selfish behavior."

As an orb of light flew to Edward, I knew that I emanated the power of the man whose daughter I was, for everyone in the room stared in shock at me. Though angry beyond belief, I had used only enough power to make the manipulation strong, but not so much that Edward would be confused by his actions.

I had also done it in front of everyone. Unfortunately, there was no way to explain away his reaction to my words.

Edward flung himself toward me and started to cry. "I am sorry, Bessy. I am childish and selfish. I would never cut your head off or have you whipped."

At that moment, Dr. Coxe entered the room. His long beard was flowing and his face sour-looking. Instantly he began scolding. "Edward, why in the world are you crying like a child? Stand back up at once and dry your eyes. You are a prince of England! You do not cry into little girls' dresses!"

In that moment, I knew that Dr. Coxe would soon enough rip all of the child out of Edward, who wiped his tears away as his tutor led him from the room, rebuking him all the while. Now that the situation was resolved, the other two boys sighed audibly in relief and thanked me with a pat on the arm before walking to their apartments. Only Robert looked at me as if he wanted to know what in the world had just happened.

That night I met Robert in the stables. Kat accompanied me and said, as the three of us walked into our respective stalls, "After all these years I must be taking after you, Eliza-beth, for I have found myself desiring a nighttime ride for weeks now."

I had left Larkin at home and so I pulled myself atop a

bay gelding with long legs and a long mane. He seemed a little thin compared to Larkin, but pranced about as if he was just as excitable, and I wondered if I should not put a saddle on him.

When we took the horses out, I was sure that a saddle was needed, for he did not give me time to feel his stride before taking off. He sped across the park at a race-winning speed. I held on to the reins and mane as if my life depended on it. After pulling the horse this way and that so he would not think that he was the boss, I let him go where he wanted.

I was very surprised when I looked to my left and found Robert next to me, chest against his stallion's neck, smiling at me as if he were seeing me for the first time. The fact that he was just as graceful as I, atop his white-spotted stallion, made me laugh aloud. But that was all the noise I made, for in the moonlit flora, astride the greatest animal God ever made, there was no need for talking, and Robert understood that.

We galloped over hill and valley, through forested acres and farmland. I had no idea how far our galloping took us and I did not care. The horses seemed able to go forever and I had Robert smiling at my side. Frankly, I never wanted the ride to end.

The next day, Kat received a letter from Father stating that he had found a tutor for me and that I was expected to return home to meet him on the first day of May. Everyone was in the school room when Kat came with the letter.

"William Grindal is a renowned scholar; a student of Roger Ascham, I believe," she said excitedly.

I was very excited for myself until I looked over to Robert, who suddenly seemed very interested in his book and would not look at me.

Edward jumped up from the table and said, "This is not fair, for I just got Elizabeth away from Hatfield. I do not think she should have to go away so soon."

All of the boys were murmuring their agreement, which of course pleased me, but I was surprised the most by Dr. Coxe, who did look truly upset by the information. However, his face instantly hardened at Edward's outburst and he began lecturing him, as he always did when the prince acted his age. I spoke up quickly to avoid another lecture.

"Well you are all invited to come to Hatfield and join me there. I would love it and will insist that plans be made for such a trip."

All seemed happy at this and plans were made.

At dinnertime, there was a new person Dr. Coxe introduced to us as Dr. John Cheke, who I recalled Kat naming as her brother-in-law's associate. He was a dear friend of Dr. Coxe's and would be joining Edwards's household in October, when Edward turned six, as an assistant in Edwards' tutelage. The man was tall and dark with a kind yet serious face, and he seemed to never speak but to mention what Jesus said about this or that.

I did not have much time to get to know him, because Kat said we must leave by the next day in order to get Hatfield ready to receive Dr. Grindal. I had to say goodbye to my dear brother and friends that evening, for we would not have time for goodbyes in the morning.

Edward's was the hardest for he was the saddest to see me go. He hugged me long and hard before turning to leave the room. Robert had his courtier face on and swept my hand up for a kiss. "You shall be missed, my Lady. Hopefully our paths will cross again and soon."

I saw his eyes before he turned and walked away, and they were not as carefree as his face. However, he did not look back.

May 1543
Hatfield House, Hertfordshire

D r. Grindal was all I thought he would be: a man in his later years, yet intelligent, passionate, and funny. He complimented me so freely I often felt myself blush, and the letters Lord Cranmer sent from Father stated how pleased the King was with me and my progress. Dr. Grindal added two things to my studies that Kat considered inappropriate: archery and in-depth swordsmanship. I loved them both and was so happy to have someone to teach me.

One day I told the swords master, "I shall beat Robert and Barnaby next time we are together."

"Indeed, you shall, my Lady. Unless they work as hard as I see you do every day, they will be in a bit of a pickle the next time they cross blades with you."

I laughed heartily but knew that he was just being kind.

After a particularly hot and tiresome day, I retired early to my bed and fell instantly asleep. Kat woke me in the middle of the night, white-faced and frightened.

"Elizabeth darling, it is alright. I am here," I heard her saying to me.

I sat up, confused. "Kat." I rubbed at my eyes. "Whatever is the matter?"

After searching my face carefully by candlelight, she responded, "Why, my Lady, you were screaming. Quite fiercely, in fact."

My brow wrinkled. "Screaming? Screaming what?"

Kat sat on my bed and set the candle on the other side of the drapes. "You kept saying, 'Cicely! Cicely! No, not Cicely!'"

"Cicely. I know no Cicely, unless it was the mare? Why in heaven's name would I be screaming about her?"

"I have no idea, child. You must be overworked for the day."

"Yes, I must be."

She stroked my hair and took up the candle. "I will leave you to get back to sleep."

I complied gratefully, completely unperturbed, in spite of Kat's insistence that I was very upset only moments before. It wasn't until the next morning, when I lay in that splendid state between sleep and waking, that I recalled my dream.

Quickly I dressed myself in a simple frock and tied my hair with a ribbon. As I rushed out of the house and down to the stables, I had a sinking feeling that I was too late, that all was done, and when I arrived, I saw by the blood and the downturned faces of the stable hands that I was correct. I made my way through the mess and found what I'd feared.

The mare was stiffening already, her foal blue and bloody. The straw was littered with water buckets, clothes, tinctures, and solutions procured by the stablemen to help the poor horse, yet all to no avail. Salty tears burned my eyes and Henry the riding boy took me by the arm.

"My Lady, I wish you would not see a picture such as this. Come away with me please."

I did not need to be prodded. I left and returned to the house. When I went toward the stair I heard the adults speaking.

"Yes, it was a bloody affair. Both mother and foal perished."

"I do say that is a pity. Cicely was one of those rare mares that are both beautiful and docile."

I heard Kat's familiar voice ask, "The name of the horse was Cicely?" I started and for reasons I can't explain, I hid behind a door.

"Yes, I believe it was." The stable hand answered my governess.

Stunned, I backed away from the door and hurried up to my room. Kat would for sure ask me about this. Unfortunately, I had no answer for her. Could I see the future as my mother did? I felt that perhaps this element of magic was manifesting itself.

Once I'd run that line of wonderment into the ground I turned back to a much muttered-about topic. Childbirth. Even the beasts were not free from death in birth. This topic perplexed and frightened me. How could God expect me to take my own life into my hands so carelessly through childbirth?

I did not understand the allure, and the commitment I'd made to myself so long ago again formed itself in my mind. I would not marry. I would not give birth. I could not do it. I understood that I was wicked for thinking this, but I loved my own self too well to risk it on something with so little return.

Furthermore, I needed desperately to understand if I

could see the future. Turning to my mother's part of the Fillos journal, I read and reread her passages about how it happened for her. Then, I search for her first-acknowledged forethought. I found a passage stating her need to go to France to be taught of courtly ways. There was an edge to how she wrote of it. Even her quill seemed to press the words harder into the page, for I could feel them when I ran my finger across the paper. Then later, there was a revisit of the topic and a comment on how it was absolutely necessary, and it was this that convinced me that she knew. She was but eleven. I was in my tenth year. So, I was a bit early, but that was such a regular occurrence for me, I could not give it weight.

She never wrote the words "I have seen the future" until she was nineteen.Though there were many instances of her mentioning how she was always right about this or that.

I was convinced by all I read that she did not want to acknowledge that she could see the future. She had other gifts to attend to. But she was at odds with her mother who had the same gift. I was not, and I had no mother to guide me but in this displaced way. So, I promptly wrote the words in my part of the journal.

I can see the future.

Then I shut the book and pondered what this could mean for me. I wondered if I would be gifted with strong sight like my mother or just occasional sight like my grandmother. And I wondered how it would affect me. Would I see my own death, as my mother had? Would I see the deaths of those around me, as my grandmother? Was I cursed to see only death?

For the first time, I felt fear. I did not want this part of my power to be great. I did not want to know what lay on the path before me. I did not want to be responsible in that way.

Closing the journal, I looked at my shaking hands and, for the first time, wished I was a regular girl. I feared myself and my future. I feared what I could see.

In the middle of May, Kat received a letter from Father, one that she did not want to show me. Telling me I must wait until studies were over for the day to have the letter, she folded it up and stuck it in her corset. Of course, I fretted all day long over what she did not want me to know. When the time finally came to read it, she hesitated giving it to me.

"Kat, you can have no reason for keeping this from me. I will have my father's letter. Please hand it over."

I tried to say it with as much respect as I could muster, but when I saw the determined look on Kat's face, I reached for my power to surround me with its protection and almost sent her an orb. However, remembering my oath, I did not. It burned me to force myself to stand there as she looked me up and down with an eye of anger. After a few moments, she retrieved the letter and handed it to me.

My Lady Katherine,

The king has requested that Elizabeth be brought to Hampton as soon as is manageable. The king would like his children to meet Lady Katherine Parr, for within the month she will be our newest queen.

Lord Thomas Cranmer

Royal Secretary to the King
Henry VIII of England and the Isle

"Father is going to be married again?"

I could not believe the words that were on the page. Part of me hoped so much that Lady Katherine Parr was one whom I could call stepmother, but I did not want to have one more woman in my life who could be dead by my father's hand within a year.

Kat was watching me closely, so I looked to her with a smile filling my face and said, "I suppose this means that I shall be at court for a while, and you know what I expect if I shall be at court?"

Only one corner of my governess's face lifted wryly.

EPISODE 6

June 1543
Hampton Court Palace, London

My new dresses filled an entire trunk. The yellow satin and green embroidered one I wore as Mary and I entered the hall of Hampton made me feel like the princess I was, in all but name. Father was absolutely resplendent in his gold and white satin and velvet doublet, with black breeches and hose covered in gold embroidery and pearls. His gold chains, staff, and crown sparkled as the noonday sun glittered through the windows at the height of the long hall. Well-dressed courtiers lined the aisle as I walked slowly down with my sister, but they did not have my attention.

My eyes were upon the lady at my father's side.

She was nothing like what I expected. Katherine Parr was very handsome, yet middle-aged. She had dark hair and bright eyes, with a round nose, mouth, and body. She was dressed in crimson and gold with a white starched collar and feather-plumed diamond hood. A thick necklace of gold and rubies flattered her thin neck and gold encircled every finger of both hands. Most importantly, she had a very sweet countenance and a motherly smile. I found myself smiling back at her with exuberance as I curtsied in front of them.

After a rather formal greeting, one that silenced the hall, a courtier with a deep resonating voice spoke. "What a very great pleasure to finally meet you, Lady Elizabeth. Lady Mary, it is likewise always an honor to meet with you."

I tuned out the niceties to pay attention to an exchange between Father and Katherine. She placed a hand on Father's and looked at him with adoration and maternal love. He looked back to her with happiness in his eyes, but it was not the same look I had seen him give Catherine Howard. This woman had had two husbands previous to Father and it seemed she knew how to treat a man. Nevertheless, I saw that he was not in love with her, although he did care for her.

Father smiled, spreading his arms wide as he turned back to look at me, and the silent chamber seemed to sigh as he bellowed, "Bessy, Mary, come give your father a hug!"

In that moment I did not care who was in the room. I rushed to hug him. This was one thing known about my father: if things were well in his life then things were well for everyone around him. He doted, laughed, and ignored proper form when he pleased; however, when he was unhappy, heads flew for the slightest misstep.

As I buried my face in his neck, I smelled the medicines he had on his leg and the unwashed hair of his head. But none of that mattered as I squeezed him tightly.

He whispered in my ear, "How is my little nighttime equestrian?"

When I pulled away to look up at him, I saw a small sparkle in his eye. It warmed me as much as the letter from my mother had. He saw me. He remembered our special conversation and he let me know that he remembered. I felt loved. It was a new sensation for me and I wanted to jump up and down with happiness, but I resolved to control myself and only spoke in a lively manner.

"I am well, Father, and very pleased to see you and meet Lady Katherine. I am very excited to be at court. Very excited indeed."

Father smiled broadly and the courtiers behind me laughed at this comment. I stepped aside as Mary bent to hug my father, and who should be the first person I noticed in the crowd but John Dudley. He had an admiring smile on his face as he glanced up at me and I nodded to him. He was standing next to a very handsome man whom I had never seen before. The man smiled adoringly and winked at me, making my cheeks flush. Katherine must have noticed and wanted to relieve my embarrassment for she took my hand and pulled me in front of her as she cast a hard glance over my shoulder.

When she met my eyes, she smiled warmly. "I am Lady Katherine and I will soon be Queen and your stepmother. I hope that you will come to love me as a stepmother and that I can be a comfort and joy to you. I can see that we are going to get along wonderfully, and if what your father tells me about you is at all accurate, we shall have many amusing and stimulating conversations." Then she turned to Mary, "How lovely you look today, Mary. I am always telling Henry how beautiful his children are. You shine like a Spanish jewel today, my dear."

"I do not assume that I am beautiful, my Lady, but I think God has given me all I need," was Mary's curt reply, and she looked around the room uncomfortably.

Katherine smiled a tad smugly. "Yes, my dear, I believe he has. You are such a good girl." There was a tiny bit of condescension in her voice and I had no idea what would make Mary and Katherine behave so.

We all proceeded to the dining hall where an elaborate dinner was served. I sat close enough to Father to speak with him.

"Thank you so much, Father, for letting me study with Edward. It was so enjoyable I thought I would never want to leave. Nevertheless, I am not ungrateful for my new tutor. He is all I hoped, and I am learning so well I doubt even the princes of France could do as well as I."

"You seem to know that we are at odds with France again, my wise little one. I wonder what your tutors are teaching you."

"Oh, Dr. Coxe is always at Edward to recall political information. I could not help but learn it," I said with a smile. "I fear I always learn much more than my teachers intend."

Father laughed so that his big belly shook. "You are right, my little Bessy. All that teach you are impressed. I hear that you are becoming quite accomplished on the lute. I would love to hear you play."

"I will oblige your smallest whim, Father. Name the hour," I said, eager to share my talents with the crowd.

Father laughed again, "She is eager," he said happily to the table of guests, and all laughed with him. "I like that in you, Bessy. I like that very much I have always been a bit eager myself." I glowed with exultance at his words and he eyed me with real notice now. "Do you not think it time we find a real suitor for this young lady?" He turned to Katherine and smiled. "If we wait too long to marry her off she will be so independent and stubborn that we will not be able to find anyone to please her, for women are not in the same situation as men. They do not need to marry. Why, look at Mary. She is already twenty-seven and is so set in her ways that she will not have anyone."

Mary blushed deeply, and I could tell she wanted to excuse herself from the table, but Katherine spoke up. "I think that we all could work a bit harder at finding a proper husband for a…woman of Mary's standing. I do not think she would be opposed to the situation of marriage if a suitable man were found. Would you Mary?"

"The lady is quite right." Mary seemed to get her back up, then her face went white and I knew that I would not want to hear the rest of what she said. "I would like very much to have a suitor, if Father would be so kind as to tell me what station of man I am to expect. I am neither princess nor mere courtier. My mother was a princess and a queen, and my father is still the king, yet he is unwilling to claim me as his own in the way that would affect my rank and thus my marriage. So, what is anyone to think? I am just as confused as everyone else."

Father slammed his hand down on the table, silencing the whole room. "That is enough, Mary! Your provocations will not help your case! Better for you to be willing and happy as your sister is, for this attitude will get you no further with men or with the king!"

He had knocked his wine goblet over and a servant was bustling to clean it up as Father cleared his throat and straightened his sleeves, which now had tiny droplets of wine splattered over the white satin. Suddenly he called out to the musicians, "I want to hear Lady Elizabeth play. Bring us a lute."

Startled by this pronouncement, I quickly wiped my fingers on the table cloth and rose from my seat. As I began playing, I noticed John Dudley watching me closely. His nose twitched and his finger bounced upon his lips as if he were deep in thought. The man that sat next to him was the same handsome man that had winked at me. He had an odd look on his face, intense and hungry, like a bear being kept from his dinner.

As I came to the part of the song that I was to sing, I cleared my throat nervously and surrounded myself with the power, willing my nerves to stay calm. My voice came out clear and sweet, the sound of a young girl with great singing talent, and I myself was extremely pleased to hear it so. As the melody swelled and became more elaborate, I watched eyebrows rise with wonder and I smiled inside, knowing that my wish of silencing a room with the beauty of my music had just come true.

Robert had been right, and I knew deep within me that he would be right where I was concerned regularly, for who knew me and loved me as well as Robert?

~

July 1543
Hampton Court Palace, London

Though I was only allowed into the daily parties of the court on special occasions, it was all I dreamed it to be. There was always something entertaining going on. Father's fool, Will Somers, kept brightly colored balls up his sleeve and would juggle the most intricate patterns on demand. He would also tell jokes and sing songs. There were dancers and lute players, card tables and food, laughing and scheming. I loved it. It was all new and interesting to me. I had spent so little time in court or around so many adults that now that I was old enough to understand, in a way, what was going on, I was fascinated.

No, it went further: I was addicted.

I watched and learned the way a woman and a man acted while they were together. Married men and women conversed flirtatiously with those other than their spouses, and I saw more than one or two hands in the wrong places on the wrong person, but only because I was at the perfect height for observing. I also saw the tension between certain individuals and I imagined that they loathed each other, or perhaps secretly loved one another. I always watched those people the closest, for I was curious to see if I could figure it all out and was perpetually absorbed, yet shocked, by what I saw.

However, it did help me understand what exactly Robert had been practicing on me. There was a defiant art to these flirtations. I soaked it all up and hoped that soon I would be able to practice some of the more mild tricks on him.

The second time I was allowed in a court party, it was due to many courtiers wanting to hear me sing and play again. However, I stayed far after my singing was concluded. It was then that I noticed something. Katherine and the man that had winked at me (I learned his name was Thomas Seymour) watched one another a lot. It did not take me long to realize that, although Katherine was completely devoted to my father, she was in love with Thomas. He may have been in love with her as well, but he was far too distracted by other women for me to make that determination a certainty.

I caught him on more than one occasion groping a maid's bottom or playing at innocence when kissing a lady's hand then letting his lips go to her wrist. These things always happened in the darkest corner of the room where no one normally would see. But I saw. He did not care about the station of the woman he flirted with, only that she was young, petite, handsome, and of course willing.

This was interesting to me and I wondered if I could not

cause him a little trouble. He was, after all, making Katherine —who was the sweetest of women—miserable. I watched her watching him; she was no fool. Even more troubling to me than this was what a man so carelessly forward in front of God, king, and the whole court, might be doing to these women behind closed doors.

I set myself to surveying him at every opportunity. At first, he noticed me and gave me far too many winks to be proper, but I met his gaze with one of my own that I hoped conveyed my thoughts. *I see you for what you are, you scoundrel.*

I focused on watching his eyes and contrived to know, long before his intended prey, what he had in store for her. As soon as he would approach her, I would fill myself with the light of the moon and send a message to the woman. "Find your husband," or, "Someone is calling your name. Find them." Sometimes I would say, "You are very sleepy. Make your excuses and retire—alone."

I found that certain ladies were not as susceptible to my subtle power and I would end up using much more of the power than was necessary, and then they acted strange and confused because of my manipulation. As I studied these situations, I found that, nine times out of ten, the woman was staring down Thomas as much as he was her.

They were not receptive to my power because they wanted him to come to them.

I noticed how these specific women—mostly pretty servants—sought him out. *They* sought *him* out even though they were married!

I was shocked and dismayed by their behavior. What in the world was this man's allure? That these women knew the certain consequences of being with a man, was undeniable. Yet they still chased him? Sure, he was handsome, rich, and single, yet, he was a self-proclaimed rogue. Why would any woman put herself in the power of a man such as him? This was so shocking to me that I decided I needed to understand. I was too perplexed to let it go.

One evening an opportunity arose for me to follow him. I only wanted to catch a glimpse of what he would do to the young serving girl he brazenly pursued out of the party. The girl had bright, friendly eyes and long blonde hair that was braided neatly and tied around the top of her head. She was perhaps four years older than me, so she was still youthfully slender, yet she had a disproportionately large bust. The blending of these two features was something I had seen rarely, perhaps because it was not natural to look that way. Yet I noticed how all the men eyed her, even though her face was rather squished and homely. This bizarre notice of a plain, yet buxom girl was helpful in educating me on the subject of men.

I was sure that he was too busy to see me following him, for I kept a safe distance behind and used a manipulation to influence him to keep looking ahead. I followed the two of them to a small room that had been lined with bookshelves and served as a makeshift library for long-staying guests.

It did not take me long to reach the room and peek in the door Thomas had entered, and by the scene before me, all I could assume was that he had attacked her upon opening the door. Several comfortable chairs and a few side tables littered the room, but in the center was a larger table. It seemed upon this the young girl had crassly been thrown, for she was in some sort of aroused panic. Presently Thomas handled her large breasts in a vicious manner ripping and clawing at them. Yet the girl did not complain, she only pulled on the strings to his codpiece. After sweeping her skirts out of the way, Thomas Seymore mounted the girl in a most grotesque manner. I could only watch for a moment before I felt so ashamed I had to turn away.

Closing my eyes, I flattened myself against the cold stone wall beside the door and felt my heart pounding in my chest. I could hear moaning and the creaking and screeching of table and behind my eyelids I re-saw the event. I did not under-stand it, but something happened to me in that moment, as I saw in my mind his actions and her pleasure, something that quickened my breath and my heart.

It gave me much to think on, but it also sent me running for Kat.

After that experience, I avoided Thomas Seymour, for when in his presence, my eyes could not stop from wandering to his hands and seeing anew what those hands had done. Thankfully, several weeks later, Father sent the racy scoundrel away on a diplomatic mission to the Netherlands. I wondered if there was more to his reasoning than just the need to have someone act as a diplomat.

When I saw Katherine's face I knew my suspicions were correct. It was in the smallest downturn of her round mouth as she gazed around the room, the slight wrinkle in her fore-head when someone mentioned Sir Thomas' name.

Father did not want to have another wife beheaded for treason, so, though it did Katherine harm, I was doubly glad of it, for Thomas felt dangerous to me. I wasn't sure how to justify the strength of the feeling but in the pit of my stomach, I knew that he was to be avoided and feared.

July 1543
Hampton Court Palace, London

Finally, July and the wedding came. The chapel was simply decorated, a sharp contrast to Katherine's jewel-encrusted dress of gold and crimson. These particular colors accentuated the paleness of her skin and thus were a favorite combination of hers.

Father waited on her procession patiently, a man completely at ease with the ceremony. Archbishop Cranmer was short in his words, and once he laid their hands together, there were giggles and murmurs of congratulations while the bride and groom walked among their guests. When all the religious had been said and done, a great celebration commenced.

I was in cream gauze with pearls intricately woven throughout the flowing folds. Accents of embroidered green satin climbed my sleeves, bodice, and forepart. I had tiny white flowers woven into my hair, which hung in loose golden curls to my waist, and as I walked through the crowd of people, I felt someone's hands touching my hair. I turned to see who it was and almost jumped when I found Robert.

This was the first time I had seen him since I left him in April.

"Hold still my lady, you have a loose flower. I am attempting to situate it." I turned back around and felt Robert's other hand touch the satin at my arm as he held me still, working with the small flower. As he did so, he whispered in my ear, "I am so glad to see you, I am sorry for the way I left you at Ashridge. Will you forgive me and understand that it was just sorrow at your leaving that caused me to be so abrupt?"

I turned back to him after I felt his hand leave my hair. I understood why his goodbye had been cold and I did not hold it against him.

"Oh Robert, of course I could never stay mad with you for long." The smile that filled his face was magnificent. With the word and the smile, the tension between us faded. "Although I would be even more apt to completely forgive you if you would whisk me away to the dancing area and show me how much you have missed me."

I raised my eyebrow at him and wondered what he would do, but I did not have time to fully wonder for he took my hand and pulled me to where the music was loudest. Many of the lords and ladies were dancing and I instantly felt nervous, for as Robert deposited me in the line of women who were in the middle of the galliard, I noticed that my father and Katherine were sitting on a dais watching us all. Katherine's sharp eyes found me and pointed Robert and me out to Father.

Not wanting to look as if I were seeking attention, I

averted my eyes and smiled brightly at Robert as he moved around me. He smiled his best smile and I could tell he wanted to please me so that I would forgive him, and thus was going to be enthusiastic. Soon I forgot about Father. All I thought of was keeping my steps as beautifully executed as Robert's were. It was exhilarating, and I forgot myself several times and laughed aloud with glee, lifting my skirts to have more freedom to move.

Robert laughed too. However, halfway through our second dance, he looked in the direction of the dais and frowned. I turned to see what the problem was and saw Robert's father standing before the king, talking animatedly and pointing in our direction.

Father had a knowing grin on his face and he watched every move Robert and I made. I am not sure why, but right at that moment I blew him a kiss. I laughed and bowed slightly when he snatched it out of the air. He smiled widely at me and turned back to John Dudley. Robert stepped out of the dance as he watched the two of us, and when I was expecting his hand to twirl me, it was not there.

When I turned to him he said, "I think you might have just let your father think that you want to marry me."

I felt the blood drain from my face. "What?" I exclaimed, and I looked back at Father, who was now speaking to John.

"Don't look so scared. I told you this would happen. Father told me he would look for an opportunity to talk to the king tonight while he was in a good mood." He took my hand and stood close enough that I could feel his breath on my cheek, but I did not take my eyes off of Father. "Why do you look scared? Do you fear you are not good enough for me? Let me assure you, my Lady, your lack of rank can be overlooked."

My head swung around to face him with narrowed eyes, but his smile was so big and mischievous that I could not even pretend to be mad. To my everlasting shame, I laughed. This boy was going to think he could say anything he wanted around me, and it would not matter. My eyes went back to my father.

"In truth, Elizabeth, why do you look so?" Robert asked and turned me to face him. "It is as if I had just told you that you were to die within a fortnight. Whatever is the matter?"

I took his hand and looked into his eyes. "It is just that I was not…"

His eyes were so beautiful, so open. I saw in them hope and happiness at this prospect, and it was then that I knew he loved me more than any sister. He was so vulnerable, yet also so sure of me that I simply could not tell him I would never, never, marry—not even him, however I might like to.

He continued to wait patiently as I gathered myself, and finally I rallied my courage and put on a smile, simply saying, "It is nothing. I suppose I just was not expecting to be married off so young."

"Nor I, but neither one of us has a choice, really. We are pawns that our families may use to gain prestige at their whim." Robert sighed, walked me toward the dancing couples, and twirled me into the current set. "I will tell you this, my Queen. If I must marry, you are the only girl who would do the job properly. For I love you as a sister and admire you as my natural better and am awed by your wit regularly. You are the best companion I have ever had—and that's saying something. Do you know how many siblings I have?"

I blinked at him and smiled half-heartedly at his jest. His speech was so pretty, I felt something stir in my heart. Or was that my heart just racing with out-of-control fear?

Robert went on. "I do think we would get along famously. I only hope I can challenge you enough to keep you happy."

This speech made my heart completely stop and for a moment that felt like I had left reality and entered a world unknown, I saw myself, my life, my future with Robert. Hatfield and parties. Games of chess and books. Horseback rides at all hours, and smiles and laughter. Love and children.

Children.

The blood drained from my face. I saw Robert mount me the way Sir Seymour had mounted the maid, and the happy heart-racing twisted darkly. My insides swirled and roiled, and I felt ill. Cold and clammy and sick.

That could not happen.

I stopped dancing and looked into Robert's face, his beautiful face was now warped with an animal grimace, full of lust and male power.

I shook my head. I did not want to think of Robert that way, but I now knew that a beast resided inside of men, and Robert would soon have one, if he did not already.

He could tell something was amiss, so he said, "Do not be anxious, my Bessy. We will see what happen. These political moves can change direction quickly. Besides, we are still young. I do not think that the event will happen until you are at least sixteen and I seventeen."

This caught me up short. So not only was I to be betrothed at the age of ten, but I would be forced to wait to be married for six years, knowing all along whom I must marry but not enjoying the benefits of a married person. That was not how I wanted to have it done if it was going to have to be done. And I felt the need to have the deed done now.

I shook my head again. I felt like my mind was jolting through feelings and determinations as a flat rock skips with velocity over the water. This was all too big. I knew that if I would marry, it would be Robert, but I truly had no intention of making those sacred promises. Can a person want two opposing things? I did. But I did want one side more than the other and I knew only one way to save myself.

Right then I did something I had not ever done before. I looked at my father, surrounded myself with the power of the moon, and I brought my hand to my mouth as if stifling a yawn. Into my light-filled hand I silently spoke the words I was desperate for Father to know and inconspicuously pushed the light toward him.

It flittered and flew and quickly reached his ear. He did not change his expression, but John left only a few moments later and Katherine looked at my father as if she were truly puzzled by what he had just said. I smiled to myself.

I did not want to be forced into a betrothal—not now, and perhaps not ever—and now, while in this room with my father, might be the only time I could do anything about it. Moreover, if my manipulation at some point wore off and I were forced into it, I absolutely did not want to be forced to wait.

I saw Thomas Seymour and the maid in my mind.

No, if I were going to do that thing, waiting and imagining would be a punishment I couldn't bear.

I had used my power to induce Father to not make that choice for me and I was glad I did, for I did not see him for weeks afterward. Who knows how many chances John Dudley would have to talk privately with father and influence him.

I influenced Katherine to invite me to spend time with her so that I might keep my ear to the situation, so to speak.

One morning as we walked in the garden, I said as convincingly as possible—for I would not admit what a sinner I was— "I do not intend to marry young. I want to wait until I am older and can make the decision based on love and situation and not other inducements." I hoped that I had gotten my point across, but I could not tell because Katherine just smiled at me in a humoring way.

I had called the power around me, preparing to sink the thought in a little more convincingly, when she said, "Yes, child, yet we all do as the king commands."

This did not give me hope that I would win the battle.

She continued. "Surely you can see that he is in the best position to choose a husband for you and he knows when the proper time is. I myself followed my parents' wishes and was betrothed and married at the age of twelve. Of course, I was a widow two years later, but I passed those two years happily and with a kind and loving man who, though he was much my senior, was able to educate me in the matters of marriage. On the other hand, there is benefit in marrying someone the same age as yourself. You grow together. You have all your firsts together. It can be magical." She paused and looked as if she were reminiscing before going on. "Of course, this only is practical for those with wealth and high position, such as yourself. I believe you are extremely blessed that your father is considering a boy who is almost your same age—one with whom you are great friends."

These words all but made my heart leap out of my chest. I absolutely saw the sense of what she was saying. Still it did not quiet the frightening possibilities and circumstances (possible death by childbirth being a chief concern) that arose simply because of my sex. I simply could not take my life into my hands.

I hoped I had done enough with Father to ensure that no

agreement would be made and, if an agreement was made at some point, I could only promise copious amounts of kicking and screaming and wielding of power against any and all who tried to force me into matrimony.

EPISODE 8

July 1543
Hampton Court Palace, London

As July slowly passed by, Katherine included me in all her outings and invited me to stay long hours with her in her apartments. I was practically a lady-in-waiting. Every morning when I arrived she would have someone read the Bible to us for hours. She also spent a great deal of time at her prayer bench. I did not realize how religious she was until I sat day after day with her. It was refreshing in a way. She spoke of things that I had heard my whole life but that I was just recently beginning to understand and love.

She leaned very Protestant and I was sure that she was trying to influence me to think that way as well. However, as I listened there were things that I was not completely convinced about. I did not think that all one had to do was to claim Jesus as her Savior.

Perhaps I'd had too much Catholic education.

While I knew that nothing we did could possibly make up

for the debt we owed Christ, I still thought that he expected a certain level of good behavior, and I was positive that good behavior brought good things into every person's life. I could not help but read history that way.

Though there were those who were punished for standing up for their beliefs, I contemplated those who were not martyrs but everyday people. The majority of the populace who acted in an honest, Christlike manner, were the happier, more prosperous people.

The more I thought about it, the more certain I became, so Katherine and I had many animated and honest discussions about this facet of religion, and many others that I did not understand or agree with. She was obliging in her method of indoctrinating me and listened to me carefully, but she always came to the same conclusion: I was wrong. I was not a scholar or a priest, and I had not convinced her, nor had I made her think.

Soon, I was convinced that she was a highly stubborn soul, and somehow this made me like her even more. She did not just lie down and wallow in the dogma. She thought it all out, carefully made her choice, and stuck with it.

"It is just not so, Elizabeth. The holy word clearly states, 'This do in remembrance of me.' The bread and wine do not actually turn into the body and blood of Christ."

"I know, Majesty. However, I believe that we are to think that they do, so that we will remember the price the Savior paid for our sins. It is a symbol, as so many of the scriptures are."

"But you say the same things over and over again, and I say that you are wrong. Will you not be convinced?"

I sighed. "I will think more about it and perhaps tomorrow we can discuss it again."

Then Katherine sighed too. "I always hate it when you

say that, for I know you will come to me tomorrow with logic that will make my head spin, and passion that will knock me off my guard. I do not wish to fight with you anymore. Let us ask the priest."

I laughed. "And I hate it when you say that. He only spouts the same words you use, for you learned your answers from him."

She put her hands on her hips, anger in her face, but she held her tongue and a few moments later burst out laughing, "Your father was so right about you. I have never had so many spirited yet intellectual conversations in my life!"

I laughed with her. "I am glad that I amuse you."

"You do, my child. You most certainly do."

And we would always end with a great hug and kiss to the cheek.

It didn't take long for me to realize how much I loved Katherine. And I was changed by my time with her. I spent more time than ever at my prayer bench and I think that even Mary was glad of it. She always assumed that I was a heathen because I did not conform to all her ways. But, I did not agree with Mary's strict observance and highly judgmental attitude about everything non-religious. Then again, I did not think Katherine's way was the complete answer either.

I felt strongly about being a good person, but I also felt that life was made to be joyful for the wonders and beauties of nature and the intimacy of friendships. There was much more to life, I felt, than contemplation and prayer, though I did feel that those things were an honored duty of the Christian person.

I soon discovered that this problem of religion was what stood between Katherine and Mary. But it would not stand so with us. By the time Father decided I was due to go back to the schoolroom, I had formed a true friendship with

Katherine and was so glad to have found such a kindred soul in the Lady Queen.

~

August 1543
Hatfield House, Hertfordshire

Father changed his mind and sent Edward and me, along with Robert, Barnaby, Henry, Dr. Coxe, and John Cheke, to Hatfield, which of course delighted me. There were few places in England I enjoyed more than Hatfield. When we returned, though, things were different. My tutor, Dr. Grindal, had a bout with the plague and was thus sent away and I did not know when he would return. I had only studied under him a few short weeks and was eager to continue. Dr. Coxe, however, was an excellent tutor—for me, that is.

Edward had not come to court for the wedding, for Father was afraid that through the crowd he would catch some disease. Thus, the prince spent those many months with his tutors and without any of his friends but Barnaby, for their families had all attended the wedding.

When I saw Edward next, I was highly aggravated by his disposition. The expression on his face was grave and he did not have the smiles I expected and deserved as his favorite sister. I instantly began the task of livening him, but no matter how I tried, he would not be tempted, and by the time of his sixth birthday in October, all would call him the most sober youth they had laid eyes upon. I put the entirety of the blame on his tutors and Father's fear for his health.

When I listened to his teachers as they spoke to him, the comment I heard repeated over and over sounded like a threat. "Edward, you will be king soon and if you are not this or that, how will you ever live up to your father's reputation or the expectation of a prince?" It made me sick.

One day I'd had enough, and after one such comment I said, "How indeed? Edward will not be able to become anything with you telling him that all his actions are reproachful and that the whole world will be watching him and comparing him to our father. I myself would rather go out to the privy and clean it with the servants than sit and listen to you tell him again about how his duty is so grand and how he will never live up to it."

I had not used my manipulations on them, yet they seemed to listen to my words and take them to heart, for I did feel that things became better after that. I was just ten, but I realized at that moment that I had a mind that could reason out problems, and though I did have an advantage when it came to getting my way, I did not always need to use that advantage.

My mind was very capable.

As we ran through the beautiful fall countryside that was Hatfield, I found playtime somewhat strained between Robert and me. He seemed more than ever the courtier and less the friend I had wandered these woods with last summer. I wondered if it was because of the marriage talk we'd had as our fathers discussed the same topic, or if it was because of Barnaby, who was undergoing adolescent changes and now took to paying me ridiculous compliments and lingering by my side when it was not completely appropriate.

He might only be following Robert's lead, for I doubted

he had been to court more than a few times. However, it was obvious that it annoyed Robert to have a third party always following us into the groves and to have said party constantly vying for my attention.

Most of the time, I forgot that Robert and Barnaby were both at the age where they began to notice girls. I was ten and only after Blanche told me all about relations between a man and woman did I have some dreams that involved Robert. I convinced myself they were due to my mind struggling to comprehend the process, not because I really wanted to act out that sort of thing. It—as Blanche described—was too disgusting to think about for long.

There was a single exception to my distaste: Thomas Seymour.

I had pondered on the act he facilitated with the maid many times. I did not understand how changing the characters involved moved my mind from revulsion to fascination. Yet it was a fact, it was as if the fascination had a moat around it and only Sir Thomas Seymour could enter.

The fact was Robert did not make me feel what Thomas did, though I liked him best and thought him perfectly hand-some and genteel.

I definitely did not have any feelings for Barnaby or anyone else.

Blanche had said that courtiers lived in a sexual environ-ment, and children who were exposed to that environment naturally acted like the adults surrounding them. This made me wonder if the interest between boys and girls at my age was not forced. It was possible that I was unique in my nonin-terest, or perhaps Blanche was right when she said that the inclination developed at different times for everyone.

No matter what the reason was, I noticed as the summer months passed that anytime I brushed Robert's hand or got close to him in any way that was normal as a result of playing together, he stiffened, his cheeks flushed, and he would walk away as though he were embarrassed about something. Even his manner of walking seemed stiff.

But at other times, I was certain he stared at me all day and lingered by my side.

It was all so strange that I resolved to ignore it entirely. I spent more time with Edward and my studies, though Robert and I continued to ride horses together several times a week.

Only on his horse would I consistently see the Robin I loved.

School crept along, and as winter descended, I had another manifestation of my power. It was October, and Kat, Robert, and I sat under an apple tree that had just given the last of its fruit, when I suddenly felt an icy wind blow past me. Next, I could smell firewood and frozen straw, and I felt tiny prickles of ice on my skin. All this culminated in a single sound: the hush after a new snow.

As the frigid air blew past, I felt as if my hair should be whipping wildly around me, yet my shawl was still, and Kat's own loose hair remained in place. Neither she nor Robert seemed to share any of these sensations.

"It is going to snow," I said in a thoughtful voice, my focus far away.

Kat twisted to look at me, and when our eyes met, she smiled. "Why do you say that, my Lady? I have a very good sense of when the weather will be changing, and I feel that fall will hang on a bit longer. What do you say, Robert?"

My head was reeling with the knowledge that I had just had an experience that was beyond my understanding. Robert was looking at me strangely. Shrouded in the power of the moon, I felt I knew what he was thinking. He had been present almost every time I had used my power and he might very well know what I could do, although he surely had no explanation for it. I searched his face as he searched mine, and finally, he glanced away to peer around him.

"I would say that there were no signs of winter yet." He looked back at me. "However, I have come to realize that our Ladyship here is more than just wise beyond her years. I believe her to be something of a seeress. She seems to know things before they happen, like what people will do or say." He ran his fingers through his hair, then finished in a softer voice, "Yes, I do believe I should always listen to what she has to say and take it to be truth."

Kat looked at me, suspicion in her dark piercing eyes, and I wondered if she also knew. I had not shared with her what the letters from my mother and grandmother had said. She only knew that they held something secret. As I looked into her eyes, I saw questions there.

So, I did what I had to do. I put them off. "Robert, what in heaven's name are you talking about? I have heard Dr. Grindal talk of astrologers as seers, and Father does see one —I know that for a fact. But the future cannot be told by any but God. Are you saying that I have the same talents as the Almighty?"

Relief flooded Kat's face, and I could tell that Robert's held a touch of the same sentiment, however, in my attempt to logic my way out of this situation, I had happened upon a premise that captured the full attention of my mind. Was I like God?

By the time the sun touched the horizon, massive black clouds filled the sky, and the looks of dismay I received from Kat unnerved me. I lay awake most of the night pondering my question. It was only at night that I took my mother's journal out of its hiding place and read it by candlelight. Skimming through the pages, my eyes fell upon the word GOD, written in capital letters. I stopped on that page and read. It was an entry from my fifth great-grandmother, Edith DeGray.

I wonder at times how I fit into GOD's plan. I have his power, and from my reading in this book I have concluded that I am to be in partnership with him in a great work. This is a gift and a treasure, one I have not seen nor ever heard of anyone else having.

I watched my relations and saw how they loved and worked together thru health and sickness, thru wealth and poverty and I think that there must be a reason that I have been given something that no one else but my mother has. So, my thoughts are thus: I, my grand-mothers, and my daughters are here to do the female half of the work God has. I do not wish to sound wicked, but this is my journal. Is it not a safe place for me to write out my thoughts and feelings where no one may judge me but God? I only hope to understand myself and the power I have, and perhaps help my daughter who may have my same questions.

What I think is this: Jesus our Saviour worked his mighty miracles on the earth and he used the power of God to do it, and I believe that we as a line of women are here to continue Christ's works. We cannot be partners with Him in sacrifice, though we do sacrifice in our service. However, we can continue His works. We have the same power, only it is the opposite, or female half of it. For I have many times wondered where His works have gone. Does God not love us as much as He loved those long dead people and prophets? Or with His infinite power and knowledge has He given us all He has, all we need, and done all He can for us? Or is He just no longer powerful? Or no longer interested in us? Has some horrid heavenly battle taken place and God has lost the fight so that we are no longer under His hand? Where are His apostles today? We have men who tell us what the scriptures say and what Christ did, but where are the men that testify of Him because they know and have seen Him and have worked with His power? I believe those men are gone and all that are left are women... women with the power of God. A power given while Christ sojourned on the earth. A power passed down from generation to generation in a process that can only be attributed to God, for is not creation His domain? Yes, and is this a reminder that we are more than just animals? We are apprentices to Him and has He not given all of us the right to participate in the most miraculous, most powerful, and most godly event: procreation?

I and my posterity are here to break the tides of evil, to fight them and to set the course of mankind on the correct path. One day, one of us will be in a position of power, and then let evil try and stop us from bettering the world and bringing about the truth of God's plan.

There is power and knowledge yet, and He is mindful of us.

The moment I read the words, I knew that Edith was correct in all her thoughts. I had never had a truth so burned into my soul. It was as though I felt warm water rushing down my skin, caressing and comforting me. My mind blazed with the power this knowledge gave me. I could someday be in that position of worldly power. I, more than all the Daughters of Moon and Mind, besides my mother, might be able to change the face of the world and to bring about what was right.

But how would I know what was right? How did my mother know what to do? She had to have read this and understood what it meant for her.

Perhaps this was part of what my mother was doing—trying to change the face of history and the world. In order to divorce Mary's mother and marry mine, Father had had to break with the Catholic Church. My grandmother told me that my mother caused this break, had pursued it single-mindedly, and the Protestant Church was created, using many of the new ideals, protestant ideas. She had also helped him with Royal Supremacy, setting it up so that the king was considered the direct servant of God and was thus over his church, like a prophet.

I could see the logic in that action after reading this journal entry, but I was not sure my mother was correct in her application. Father was just a man, an unholy one at that, nothing like a prophet. Also, I felt there were equal parts good and evil in the Catholic Church (evil mostly because of the men in charge). Nevertheless, this was the task my mother focused on.

She made all the present religious turmoil come about and then, somehow, she lost control and was killed.

That was something too. How was it possible for her to lose control of someone? Even with my tiny experience I could control anyone I wanted. So how did Father get out from under her spell?

Perhaps this was not her main goal. Maybe she knew that she was not to be the one with the opportunity, but that she was to be the one who laid the groundwork for someone else —for me. Perhaps she always knew her life would be sacrificed for a greater cause.

I had always had so many questions about my mother's actions in regards to my father, but what if she was only attempting to secure my place in the royal line? It all made perfect sense. If she could have a daughter by royalty, that would ensure that such a princess would marry a prince of some land and thus be in a position to lead.

Perhaps she accomplished these important things only so I could accomplish more.

It was all very romantic to think of my mother in this light, but I had read her entries and they sounded rather selfish and vain to me. However, I did know that even the servants of God were imperfect, for they were human. All of the Saints had weaknesses and struggles, and I would not assume my mother was void of any good motives just because I knew that she was not holy.

The more I thought of this possibility the more right it seemed, and the more it resonated with my soul. I concluded that I would have to go back and read again all that she had written. I knew that in my current frame of mind I would be most likely to pick up the small hints and nuances, if there were any, so I began right then.

EPISODE 9

October 1543
Hatfield House, Hertfordshire

W hen I woke the next morning, I felt the silence of new snow on the ground. I jumped out of bed, cold prickling my skin as I raced to the window and flung it wide. I smelled firewood and frozen harvest straw that had only been cut the day before. It was my exact experience, only in the opposite order.

At that moment I knew I had seen the future, but I wondered if it was a premonition or if I was now somehow connected with the weather. Grandmother did say that the powers of the moon and of the water were connected. My great-grandmother could control the water, but Grandmother could see the future. So, I was not persuaded either way, and not knowing what had happened made me want to run back to my book to find another answer.

Unfortunately, Kat came in at that moment with a tray of breakfast and she had a look in her eye that told me she was troubled.

Apprehensively, I watched her set the tray down and look out the window I had just shut. When she met my eyes, she hesitated, and so I had pity on her and relieved her of the duty of speaking first.

"I have no idea how I knew it was going to snow, Kat. Truly I do not. It is as odd to me, as I am sure it is to you. Shall we talk of it, for I do not want you to be troubled?"

Kat's face softened, and she spoke in a quiet voice. "I just…I thought of your…I am sorry, Elizabeth, it was just so odd. And the way you have acted on occasion of late—I just wondered if maybe there are things you are not telling me, or if…well never mind. If you do not know, you do not know, and there is nothing we can do about it, is there?" She smoothed her light blue velvet dress and cleared her throat as she lifted the lid of the tray. "Nevertheless, I am happy that only Robert and I were there to hear you, for neither of us would betray you or claim that you were a—anything other than what you are."

"I do not think there is anything to betray," I said as I came to sit at the table. "You yourself said that you could tell the weather sometimes. I just happened to be right this time." I took a piece of bread with butter on it and tasted a small corner.

"Yes, my dear, but though I say I know the weather at times, I have never known it would rain on a day without clouds. The entire circumstance has a feel of something unnatural, as I fear others would recognize." She lifted a bowl of porridge off the tray and set it in front of me. It had a delicious aroma of dates and I took a bite while Kat continued. "Moreover, if you yourself did not think the situation odd, why did you assume that was what I was upset about when I arrived?"

I swallowed hard and cleared my throat. She had trapped

me, and I had not even seen it coming. I instantly surrounded myself with the power and my mounting anger melted away into the glorious gleam of the light. Without the intelligence that filled me when surrounded by power, I was just a regular ten-year-old arguing with an adult. Though my brain worked swiftly, I could not reason a way out of her comment, and I had made a promise not to manipulate her.

I said coolly, "Kat, I do not understand why this is such a marked thing for you. I would appreciate it if we could move past it and you could assume, as I do, that it was a coincidence."

Kat looked at me with uncertainty. "As you wish, my Lady." And I hoped she meant that was the end of it.

January 1544
Ashridge House, Hertfordshire

News came at the new year that my aunt's grandchildren would be joining us in our studies. I was interested to watch how the older boys reacted to the arrival of Lady Mary Grey and her sister Jane. I was not surprised though when they acted as I suspected they would.

They flirted with, cajoled, and teased both girls mercilessly—especially Barnaby—and I knew it was because they were pretty and shy that the boys were enamored with them. It was only then that I realized they had never paid that sort of attention to me, and this told me a few things about myself. Firstly, I was not pretty, or I was not as pretty as these girls were; and secondly, boys were mean when they liked you as more than a sister. These boys were always talking with me and joking with me, but they never made fun of me and I was sure that it had nothing to do with being the king's daughter. We had acted as brothers and sister from the start.

However, there was one boy in the crowd who never looked at Mary and Jane twice. Robert talked with them and we all played together, but he never acted toward them the way the other boys did. Then again, he had never acted flirtatiously toward me, aside from playing the courtier. This was telling, and in a way, I did not like it. I learned that Robert's deference, or lack thereof, was quite devastating to my ego, and this shamed me.

Soon, Dr. Grindal returned to us and we floated between Hatfield and Ashridge as we became educated. In late January, we received word that Father was planning to attack the French at Boulogne, and was about the countryside raising an army. This of course worried me for I did not want to see Father plundering the French when he was in such bad health. On the other hand, I had never seen Father at war and I had been told by a great many nobles that he was at his most splendid when there was an enemy to vanquish. So, Edward and I kept our ears open for news of how things were maturing, as we both hoped that Father would give up the notion but were nonetheless excited by the prospect of his defeating the French.

There was something else that kept my mind off Father, though; namely, Kat and her lonely state. In midwinter I dreamed of Kat and my cousin, John Ashley, together in a lovers' embrace. Uncertain if this dream resulted from my gift or if it was just random, I acted on the premonition, asking Sir John to join my household as my senior gentlemen's attendant.

This would be a great test of my understanding my gift.

Interestingly enough, from the day of Sir John Ashley's

arrival, Kat and he were enamored with one another. From then on, I did not see Kat for two minutes together. Really, I was very happy for her. She and Sir John would soon be married. I felt certain of it.

And with this small test, I knew I had my grandmother's gift of telling the future.

Still, a part of my heart felt a stab of fear that Kat could leave me, and the notion began to drive me mad. But loving Kat, I did nothing to show my fears. The only solution was to attach myself more fully to my stepmother, whom I wrote almost weekly.

My studies were becoming far more vigorous and thus were also a great distraction, for I enjoyed the challenge very much. The work I did with numbers and languages was always praised by my teachers, and I loved to hear their pride in me.

But I excelled most in gospel studies, and I spent a lot of time at my prayer bench, wanting to know if God had a work for me to do. Finally, I came to the conclusion that if he did, he would put me in a position where I could do good. I realized I had given myself to Great-Grandmother Edith's ideas. These beliefs cemented into my heart and soul and they instantly gave me a goal which made me more eager and more grateful.

God would guide me, and so I prayed that his will would be made known to me and that I would be ready to do my part, though it took my life from me. I found that my conversation with deity changed, or rather grew. When I talked to him now I spoke as I would to a loving father and divine leader in my coming service. I wanted to do what I could to help my relationship grow with him, so I became devoted to study of the scriptures.

I also felt it my responsibility to practice my manipulations as much as possible and seek within myself any other parts of my gift not hitherto manifested. Though my conscience told me that I needed to set some rules for myself when it came to who and what I manipulated, I recognized that I did not have many opportunities as it was, and thus, had to do it when I could.

I redoubled my reading in the journal to try and figure out what had happened with forecasting the snow. Since seeing Kat's future, I thought that foretelling came to me in dreams, just as it had my mother. Thus, I assumed that my prediction of snow wasn't a foretelling.

Perhaps it was water talent, yet I hadn't had any other signs of it. I learned from the book that Grandmother had her first foretelling when she was fifteen, but Great-Grandmother had not moved water until she was in her twenties. With only these clues to go on, all I could do was watch for any signs in myself that would tell me what I needed to know.

EPISODE 10

April 1544
Hatfield House, Hertfordshire

In March, Robert left for several weeks. Though I missed him, it was a bit of a relief. Since the girls arrived, Robert and I were flung together as playmates more and more, for neither of us cared to be always bossed around by Mary and Jane. Thus, things had become awkward.

The boys were so besought with Mary and Jane, that every Saturday, they took to the music room and put on plays, for that was what the girls loved. Normally, I loved it too, but one Saturday, I did not feel up to it. However, I decided to go anyway, for what else was I to do?

As I left my room to perform said duty, I found a familiar sight. Robert stood outside my door in a white linen shirt.

I would never tell anyone, but Robert's face had filled every moment of my dreams the previous night, and most nights since he left. As I looked at him now, sleep still in his eyes, hair tousled, my assessment of him shifted. He was more appealing than my dreams or my memory had portrayed. I could not take my eyes off him. The most beautiful boy of my acquaintance was back, and moreover, he looked relaxed when he saw me, instead of stiff. This gave me hope.

I beamed at him and he asked, "Would you care to go fishing?" He pulled an old fishing pole from behind his back.

I looked at his homemade stick and said what I should have the first time he asked, two years ago. "Of course! I am just hoping you do not expect me to use that hideous thing. I will never catch anything with it."

He smiled so brightly, I should have looked away at once, for a strange thing happened. My breath came faster, and my face felt on the verge of flushing.

"Of course, if her Ladyship prefers a pole designed by a master craftsman, I would not stop her from acquiring one. However, shabby as it may seem, this was made many moons ago by a world-renowned magician."

I laughed. "You are trying to tell me you made it two years ago, with a dull knife and little light, out of a castaway limb. Am I correct?" I checked his expression. Yes, of course I was right. "Tsk tsk, Robert! What an opinion you have of yourself." My voice was playful as I admired his pole. This was a lot easier when I did not have to look into his eyes.

Now it was Robert's turn to laugh. "Her Ladyship is witty as well as beautiful, and she can fish!" He sighed contentedly then said, "Heart, where hast thou gone?" He was in full courtier mode and I loved it. For it was playful instead of awkward.

Still, I smiled and blushed scarlet with pleasure. My Robin was back, and I could not wait to see how he acted when we were alone. Fortunately, I did not have to wait long to find out, for as soon as he saw that I was serious in my consent, he grabbed my hand and pulled me uncomfortably behind him. We raced down the hall and out of doors just as we had done before.

It was a glorious April afternoon and, as we ran through the west garden, I smelled everything. The sun was high and the rains had not yet started, but I could feel them on their way. It was so magnificent, I almost forgot that Robert was holding my hand.

We quickly got to the lake, but Robert did not stop running. He held my hand tightly and, before I knew what was happening, he ran us right to the water's edge, leaping with me ungracefully over the high cattails lining the bank, and we splashed into the shoulder-deep water. It was shockingly cold, but wonderful. I came out of the water laughing, and so did he.

"I cannot believe you just did that to me," I said, and I splashed him right in the face. "Did you even know if I could swim with this bulky dress on?"

Robert laughed. "I was hoping that you could not swim, if you must have the truth, so that I might have an excuse to take you in my arms and rescue you." He winked and splashed me back.

"Robert Dudley, you have spent too much time in court. You have the flirtations of that place mimicked perfectly," I answered tartly.

"Well, if I am to someday make a good impression on you in front of all the other gentlemen in court, it seems I should begin practicing now."

I wanted to cry. He did not mean what he said. He was only practicing—honing his skills on me. What else could I expect? As I tread water in my thick skirts, I thought about why I was suddenly so upset by his teasing. I never had been before, but I found that I had to turn my face away from him so that he would not see how hurt I was. Sometimes of late, it seemed I only had two temperatures, hot or cold, and right now I was ice.

"With that sort of talk, it is no wonder courtiers cannot tell if they are in love or not. I will not be a practicing arena for your games, Robert Dudley. You go practice on someone else. I am sure Mary and Jane would love to have someone new to flirt with." And with that, I started for the bank.

When I got to the bank I heard him quietly say, "Forgive me, my Lady. I find it difficult...I mistake..." He sighed and splashed at the water with his hand. "Isn't it hard to try to be an adult when we are only adolescents? I know I botch it up all the time." Then he laughed. "I am only in my thirteenth year, yet my father is already looking for a girl with good blood and fortune to be my wife. I know he is seriously considering you, Elizabeth. But we have talked of this before."

I turned around slowly. He was bringing it up again. I wondered what had happened while he was gone. When I looked at him, he smiled mirthlessly.

"Watch out or you might get the job, and I know that would be a punishment for you," he said bitterly. I started to contradict him, but he turned angrily away from me and ground his teeth as he continued. "He sent me back here to woo you. Did you know that? He has all of these plans, but what is he thinking? Scheming against you is absolutely unthinkable! Furthermore, the farthest goal in my mind is matrimony. I would rather talk about the properties of lake moss than the arrangements of a marriage."

Shocked as I was by these confessions, I laughed and said nothing. Somehow, his words had taken the anger and spurn out of my soul, and looking at him now, all wet-haired and gloomy, made me melt. My dress clung to my beginnings of a womanly shape and so I sat on the green grass next to the water, concealing myself as best I could, and patted the ground next to me. Slowly he swam toward me and when he was about to come out of the water I turned my head to give him a little bit of privacy.

When I felt him sit next to me, I turned back. He had his knees pulled into his chest and was leaning forward, resting his chin on them. His wet hair stuck to his forehead and cheekbones. I could not help but notice how incredibly smooth his skin was and how dark and thick his eyebrows were. He had a small mole near his ear and a little scar near his chin.

"Where did you get that scar?" I asked, wanting to say something.

His hand moved to his chin to touch the exact place the scar was located. "I tell everyone who asks that I got into a knife fight with a brigand last year. It is a thrilling tale—not that people believe the story, but it is fun to tell and to do so is expected of me." He paused to smile at me and pull a piece of grass out of my hair before continuing. "Do you sometimes feel as though there are two Elizabeths—one that you use in front of regular people and one that you save for special friends and family?" His focus went far across the lake now and he bit on his lip as he thought to himself.

I wondered why he had said deception was expected of him. I certainly could understand expectations, but what was the source of his feelings? His parents? His situation? All of these mysteries I suddenly wanted to know. However, this was a Robert that even I had not seen before, and so I kept my mouth shut and my ears open.

"Only when we are alone am I the Robert who can tell you that deep inside I am a child who wants to run and play— and jump into lakes with pretty girls. I want to hunt snakes and frogs and make wood boats to sail down a stream like we did when we first met." He looked at me. "I still want to play with children my age and not feel like I have to talk about politics, religion, and the weather with them. I do not want to force my body into court apparel, tights, doublet, and uncomfortable shoes! These things are not for me. I do not want to have to like killing a deer, or jousting, or simpering for ladies, or perfecting the art of a courtesan. I love school—math, mostly—and I love God. I want to spend time learning things and having fun, not focusing on family traditions or Dudley pride." He breathed in deeply but would not look at me. He focused on the blade of grass he had extracted from my hair and started twirling it around. The next moment he squeezed it between his thumbs, placed it to his lips, and blew. It made a garbled whistling sound and we both laughed. When he pulled his hands away, he touched his scar again and said, "I haven't a clue about this scar. It is the result of some folly as a child, my parents tell me, though they say they do not remember it either." He looked at me with a serious face and said, "I think that I must be mad."

"Or you could be absolutely ordinary." I said this with a note of finality. "Being here with others my age has been so wonderful, but before I came here, I felt exactly the same things and I know that I am not mad!" We both laughed.

"Are you certain? I just told you that my father was planning our wedding and that he asked me to scheme with him, and yet you still sit here next to me. Think hard, my Lady, for madness is a very tricky thing."

I just looked at him and thought to myself that there could be worse ways to spend my life than with this honest, good, and beautiful boy, but I said, "You do have a point. I shall have Kat give me the mad test straight away." We smiled and stared at one another for a few moments before the wind came up. A chill came over me and I realized we needed to get some dry clothes on before we caught cold. With a sly look in my eye, I asked, "Race me to the house?" I jumped up before he could say yes or no and took off running.

The musicians began a slow waltz and dancing lessons commenced. Robert grasped my hand in his and held me confidently in his arms. We began dancing in earnest and I thought how I would love to dance with him in front of a crowd. We were very accomplished for our age, and I was sure Father would love to see how we had improved since the wedding. As I fantasized about this, we turned and twirled.

Robert's voice took me out of my reverie. "You have particularly slender hands, did you know that? They are graceful and soft. I like them."

I had always admired my hands and was so pleased that he had taken notice that I decided to return the favor.

I lowered my voice and said right into his face, so others would not hear me, "You, Sir Robin, have eyes that will someday melt a heart so thoroughly that I pity the girl unfortunate enough to fall in love with you, for how will she ever be able to regard another set of eyes with any passion when yours are still on the earth to be seen?"

Robert's face for one instant held a look of…longing? I did not understand his expression, but it completely changed in an instant. He looked away and then laughed at me.

"Perhaps I shall die early so that I will not cause anyone harm." His magnificent eyes considered me again. "I do not know if you are practicing on me now. That was as flamboyant a compliment as ever I heard in court." Before I could become offended, he cleared his throat and a wobbly smile curled his lips. "But I must caution you to worry for yourself, for my father has decided that you will be that unfortunate girl forced to look into my eyes with regard. I received a letter today."

He watched my reaction carefully, but I gave none, for I did not know how I felt about it myself. So, I continued dancing, but in the back of my mind, I considered what my father might say to such a proposition.

EPISODE 11

June 1544
The Palace of Whitehall, London

I was excited when Edward and I were summoned to court, for I could see Father and Katherine and hear all the news of the upcoming war. However, in the week since we had been at Whitehall, I had only seen Father on a few occasions. Katherine and I had taken up our usual routine of prayers and scripture study, and I was eager and pleased to spend the days by her side.

She strived to help me improve myself and to help me understand what Christ and the Apostles meant by the different scriptures. Father would occasionally join us in her rooms and sit with us while we sewed or debated, but when he was present, the tone and veracity of our debates was quite subdued.

He would talk of the war with France. It sounded to me that he would be leading the armies himself and that it would be happening very soon. Father was highly pleased with all the men he had recruited, and the gathering of warships around the Isle of Wight seemed to be happening as planned.

He would not invite his children to join him in the courtly gatherings that happened almost nightly. There was a rumor that he planned on presenting us for a special event and was saving us for that. I had no idea what it could mean.

Finally, the day arrived. Father summoned us to join him for supper and I hoped that we would have a wonderful evening surrounded by courtiers, as I had the previous year. Mary had only arrived the day before because she had been far to the north and had to travel. As I looked at my older sister, I realized that I was almost as tall as her now, and though she was not a tall woman, I was still surprised to see it. I had new dresses, but they were all made long so I could grow into them a bit. I suppose they did fit me a little differently now. I wore my most formal one tonight—burgundy velvet with gold stitching and small jewels sewn around the neckline.

The private dining room that Edward, Mary, and I were led to was lavishly decorated. Thick purple curtains draped the window and plush chairs surrounded the thick mahogany table. A giant bear skin covered the stone tiles and the fireplace was encased with swirls of gold. Sugared fruit stood high on trays decorating the table, and the plates looked as if they were out of a Far Eastern storybook, so beautiful were they with cherry tree blossoms and delicate fans painted so skillfully.

Father sat at the head of the table and, as I stood before him, he had a pleased look on his large, red face. "Edward, my boy, you are in fine form today. I admire your cap." Edward nodded, and Father went right on. "How are you, little prince? Feeling well? Your tutors say you are keeping up with Bessy as best you can."

Father patted Edward on the head as he soberly said, "Yes, Father."

Then Father turned to me, "You have grown, Bessy. I suppose I shall have to call you Elizabeth now, hey?" I smiled and rushed to hug him. He patted me, but said, "Come now, child, go back to your place." A little saddened by his rebuke, I stepped away and his eyes went critically toward Mary. "So, you are here at last, my eldest daughter. How was your journey?"

Mary stiffened. Her black dress and tight coif made her appear sickly. I thought she looked very ill indeed and worried for her. "As well as it could be, Father. The roads were mostly good, but the spring rains have held out in some of the north county, which was why we were delayed."

Father cleared his throat and waved to Mary as if she had apologized, then he raised his voice as if speaking to a large crowd, though it was only the four of us in the room. "I am happy to have you all here, for I have something important to tell you. However, we shall eat first so that your minds can be contemplating my news. I do enjoy the air anticipation stirs." He laughed and popped a grape into his mouth.

We sat and servants began to bring out trays of food. The meal was magnificent, though light, for we had already feasted that day. A thin, flavorful bouillabaisse with stock of pheasant looked beautiful in the colorful bowls, with every kind of bread I could imagine for dipping. The first of the green and yellow vegetables were cut and organized so picturesquely that I hated to take them, though they were deliciously fresh, slightly covered in olive oil and salt to enhance the flavor. I will admit to partaking in more than my fair share of sugared fruits. I could not help myself because only in Father's house could I have such a luxury.

I was excited and nervous for Father's mysterious

announcement and wanted a bit of conversation. Father did seem in a mood, so I asked hesitantly, "Father, may I ask where the Queen is?"

Father frowned slightly. "That information is too closely linked with my announcement, so no, you cannot ask. Only hurry with your food and I will tell you all when you have finished." He smiled mischievously and glanced around to make certain everyone was following his orders. It seemed that he himself could barely keep the secret in.

I wondered what kind of secret would keep the Queen away or how it was connected to her.

Finally, when we had all finished, Father snapped his fingers and a man came in holding an easel covered with a large cloth. Father pointed to where he wanted it set down and looked at us expectantly. I met his smiling eyes with wonder and confusion, and finally he laughed aloud.

"Remove the cover."

The man did so with a flourish and the stirring of the air brought the scent of oil paint to me before I looked to see what was before me. It was a long, almost blank piece of canvas. In the exact middle was a portrait of father sitting on his throne.

Edward spoke up a little uncertainly. "Father, that is a masterful depiction, but whatever is it for? Why is it almost completely blank?"

He laughed, "Oh ho, my wise son! You bring me right to the point." He looked at each of us intently and spoke quickly. "This is to be a portrait that will hang in this very castle. It will be one of my family, but more importantly, a picture of my heirs." He said the word slowly. "Edward, you will stand here at my side." He looked at me and Mary and rushed on. "You, Mary, will be here on my right hand as the second in line to the throne, and you, Elizabeth, will go on my left as the third in line."

Mary gasped and rushed to hug Father. I could not take my eyes from the canvas as I tried to imagine what all this could mean. But Father interrupted my confusion by saying, "Edward of course will outlive you all and his heirs will be those that take the throne, but before I go away to war I want to acknowledge you all as what you are: my dearest children. No matter who your mothers were, you are mine and I love you."

Those words made tears spring to my eyes. My father did love me. He did. I ran to his arms and hugged his neck and cried into his hair. Before I let him go, I whispered in his ear, "I love you, Father, and I am so glad that you love me too."

When I pulled away from him big tears filled his eyes and he pulled me in to whisper in my ear. "I have always loved you, my little Bessy. Please forgive me for taking so long to tell you so." Tears ran down his face in earnest now.

No wonder he did not want anyone to see this gathering. He was soft, and I liked to see it, but it would not do any good for his reputation.

Later that same evening, we met for the void Father had planned, and he announced this change in the line of succession to the whole court. Again, the queen was not there and so I asked Mary if she knew why.

Her nose rose a bit and she said in a vile tone, "Father will not be including Katherine in the portrait of his family. Jane Seymour will be painted in as the true queen. I think that Katherine does not feel welcome at a void that is so clearly a snub to her relationship and status to us."

I squashed how incensed I felt at these words. I had to support my father, especially in front of Mary. "Oh, well that would make sense. Father does not seem to play anyone's pipe but his own," I said and gritted my teeth. Looking up to my tired-looking sister, I asked, "Mary, are you alright? You really do not look well."

She sniffed and glanced at me out of the corner of her eye. "The traveling was hard on me, and I have been having pains in my stomach and headaches that I cannot get rid of. Furthermore, I think my courses are about to be upon me, though I have not seen them in many months. Perhaps I have just forgotten what it feels like when they are here."

I had not started that womanly circumstance as of yet, so I did not know what she was talking of exactly, but it did not sound pleasant, and if there were any way to stop that from happening to me soon, I would do it. "I am sorry. Is there nothing to take for your relief?"

"No, one must wait it out with the patience akin to that of Job. You will understand soon enough, my dear young sister." She caressed her stomach in a tender way and looked over to me, "I hear that you are very friendly with the queen and that you study and pray with her daily." I nodded. "Well that is good to hear. I only wish that you would take mass with me while I am here with you. I do not believe that the queen is keeping the ordinance pure." She turned hotly away, and I knew that I must not say a word or there would be a fight, and that was the last thing I wanted.

After a moment she looked at me expectantly, and when I smiled at her, she wrapped an arm tightly around me and said, "I have missed you, Elizabeth. Perhaps I will come to Hatfield and stay with you awhile. I did like living at Hatfield, after I got over the shock of being treated like your servant, that is." She smiled again and said, "No matter. That changed soon enough and now I am in the succession ahead of you. Isn't life strange? Yes, I do think I will see you there. I really am fond of Hatfield."

Before my temper could get the better of me and I told Mary that she was not wanted at Hatfield House, Father rose out of his seat with the aid of a cane and cleared his throat. The room silenced instantly. "I have already made one announcement tonight, but it is getting late and I have a big day ahead of me tomorrow—when I ride for the coast and on to France." There were great shouts of approval and "Long live the king" before he continued with a smile and a jolly, red face. "So tonight, I say goodbye to you all and I hope that you will keep England's soldiers and her king in your prayers, that we may ride home alive and successful."

I was again in shock. Father was leaving tomorrow, and he was going to fight the French. This meant that Katherine would be highly busy taking care of the affairs of state in his absence.

This was going to be a very interesting stay at court. As I thought this, a familiar voice whispered in my ear, "I think this might be a very interesting stay at court," and I, of course, knew it was Robert.

I turned to my handsome friend just as he swept me a bow so low I thought his nose might touch the floor. "My Princess, I am so honored to stand next to you."

When he rose, I saw the color in his cheeks and the serious glint in his eye, but I felt a change in him. He was very much the courtier tonight, but an embarrassed one, and I wondered why. It was soon discernible when Robert talked of my new high station and how it seemed possible that his dearest friend might one day take the throne. "What would I be to you then?" he asked petulantly.

With my father recognizing me as an heir, all prospects of me marrying Robert were out of the question. My marriage would more likely than not be brokered off to some prince as an alliance piece. I blinked at the thought. I might be forced to marry some stuffy old prince from Spain. "Oh Robert, that would be just the most awful thing in the world. How would I get over it?" I answered him with no regard to his question.

"Being queen? Awful? How so?"

"No, not that! What if Father or Edward forces me to marry some old man twice my age and smelly to boot, just for the sake of an alliance or a trade deal or some such nonsense? How will I bear it?" Taking hold of Robert's arm and turning him away from the crowds, I looked desperately into his eyes. "I love you more than anyone, and if I cannot even make myself marry you, I could never face the institution with someone I loathe."

"Make yourself?" I looked into his eyes and saw the hurt there. He blinked a few times and looked away from me. Then, sniffing, he said, "I see my aunt. I should go and greet her. "You will excuse me, Princess." And he stepped around me to enter the crowd.

The entirety of the night was ruined for me then, not only with the startling premonition of a future unwanted marriage, but by the knowledge that I hurt my friend. A friend who could have saved me long ago from this startling fate by becoming my intended husband. However, fool that I was, I meddled in that prospect. And I did it out of fear. Stupid fear. But here I was, afraid again and with a much worse fate on the horizon. This all burned me up inside and the only relief from my torment was to repeat the manipulation I'd done one year ago and hope it lasted. I turned toward my father and pulled the light to me.

I n July, I sat for Hans Assouline, a Flemish man commissioned to do the family portrait. I stood in a brightly lit room in my hot, embroidered green and maroon damask. My hair was up and back, and my mother's necklace was wrapped neatly around my neck. The white starched lace at my wrists itched, but I dared not move for fear the anxious artist would yell at me—though he would be yelling at a princess now, and not Lady Elizabeth. What a difference my Father's acknowledgment made.

After what seemed like an eternity, the man finished painting my likeness and I went straight away to change out of my gown. When I entered my room, Kat was there. Tears were running down her smiling face and she dabbed at them with a white handkerchief.

I went to her side at once. "Whatever is the matter, Kat? Are you hurt?"

Kat shook her head and sniffed. "No, I am perfectly at ease." She smiled as if that would convince me.

"No Kat, you must tell me why you are sitting here crying. What has happened?"

"Sir John. He has just—just asked for my hand." She sniffed loudly. "He has already received consent from all the proper places, but I—I just am not sure how I feel about it."

"How you feel about it? Kat, are you mad? What did you tell the poor man?" I was very upset now. "Did you tell him that you were uncertain if you wanted to marry him? Oh Kat, please tell me you did not."

"No, I told him that I needed to discuss it with you," she said in a frightened tone.

"With me? As far as I am concerned the situation is perfect and I am happy for you both," I said with utter conviction. "Why on earth would you need to talk to me about it?"

"I did not know how you would feel and I knew that I could not leave you."

My pulse raced and I swallowed hard. "John has said he wishes you to live elsewhere?"

"No, not exactly. But he wants to have children, and have a life like other people, and not be servants as we are now. Not that either of us is complaining. We are so grateful to be with you, my Lady—Princess—" She sputtered to a stop.

I understood. Of course, I did. But there was no way I was going to allow Kat to be married if it meant she would leave me. "Kat, you will not have to act as my servant, or even a lady-in-waiting. I will find someone else to take over your duties. Only stay with me. And if Sir John is unhappy at his post, we can find something else for him to do also." I began to cry a little. "Just do not leave me, Kat."

She grabbed me and held me to her chest. "Of course, child, of course. I promised that I would never leave, and just because I am going to be married does not mean that I can go back on my word. Shhh, it will be alright," she said soothingly and stroked my hair.

June 1544
The Palace of Whitehall, London

Katherine managed the affairs at home beautifully, and I learned so much as I watched her. If this was my one opportunity to watch the Crown rule, I thought that things were just as they should be, with Father off fighting and Katherine handling the delicacies of home. I saw rulers and those of the Privy come to her and bend ear to all she had to say. They respected her, and, though they did not always do exactly as she wished, they did listen and take her counsel nine times out of ten.

Because I maintained the belief that someday I would be queen (in fact, I had many fantasies of how I would one day rule England), all I gathered in at this time was of utmost import to me.

I began to understand as a woman the measures necessary to keep the council in its place, and without the backing of a powerful king, such as my father, those measures would be grand indeed. It would take all my talents and skills, I knew, for though I saw that they humored Katherine and did as she bade, it was obvious that they were not beholden to her as they were my father.

I began to say such things in my head as, "I want, as queen, to enrich and prosper myself and my people," and, "As queen, I want men to come to me and do as I bid them." Thus, I felt a switch in my thinking.

Of course, in all these schemes and imaginings, I had no husband off at war to worry about. One of my dearest hopes was to never to have war in my kingdom. I saw the moral and financial toll war took on a country and its subjects, with the dead leaving orphans and widows everywhere. I privately thought badly of Father for the frivolous act, and yet, all the while, I still felt proud of how brave he was. It was an interesting mix of emotions.

I learned as I watched, and as months turned to years my relationship with Katherine grew so firm that I knew I could not, though the entire world should be searched, find a kinder or more involved guardian.

Our companionship even helped me to become closer with my father, for they were in constant communication and I was one of her most notable companions. When I'd helped with a little thing or two, and we received word back from father on what a smart idea it was, my ego was duly petted. Thus, my love and admiration of my father grew more than ever. I had the feeling that the next few years would hold my happiest memories, and they did.

Returning triumphantly from France, where he won the war, and also defending our shores when the French counterattacked, may not have seemed a big victory comparatively, but for Father it was. He handled the armies with the superb touch of a man in tune with his soldiers. He was again the lion king, fighting for what was rightfully his. As Father told me the story of the French general kneeling at his feet, I knew that God had placed this man, my father, on the throne to head His church and to rule this people.

Sadly, after Father returned he was not the same man as before, though his spirits were high, and he was ever talking of his last hurrah and how even in his old age he'd spat in the face of the French. We all agreed that the war was exactly what his spirit needed, but his body continued to vex him greatly. All sorts of ailments grieved his legs and hands and innards, making us all realize that he would not long be in this world.

Queen Katherine continued to help with matters of state but dealt more with matters of the king's health. I watched her become a nursemaid to my father, preferring to care for him herself rather than turn the duty over to servants.

This was inspiring to me. As I watched her take him for walks in his chair and feed him and clean him up, I saw Christ in the woman I loved as a great guardian. This service put her in a special place for me and taught me so much of what being a Christian really was.

Father oftentimes would go into a rage and torture all those around him, throwing things and screaming and cursing. Katherine attempted to shield Edward and me from these behaviors, as well as the rest of the court. When things became too bad she sent us all away, and I left knowing I might never again in this life see the man I loved as my king and father.

Still I felt so grateful. I had grown so much. My mind had been enriched by my time under the tutelage of Doctors Grindal and Coxe. My heart had been warmed with the love of my father and Katherine and God. I had practiced and very closely mastered my skills with my power. I had made choices for my life. I wanted the throne; I wanted it by my own right and not that of a husband. I felt hopeful and useful and wiser than I'd been before.

However, I felt a testing of self on the horizon. I did not know if it was a premonition or if I was calling bad omens my way. Whatever the cause, I felt prepared and willing to grow more if that was what my future held.

SEASON OF TEMPTATION

EPISODE 1

February 1547
Windsor Castle, London

In the winter of my fourteenth year, I became an orphan.
I had known about Father's death for a fortnight.
The day they would entomb him in St. George's chapel
at Windsor was upon me now. It seemed like it took me
weeks and weeks to finally grasp that he was truly gone.

It was too dangerous for me to attend his funeral, so I
mourned him in my rooms. I did watch from the window of
the Castle as throngs of angry people arrived to protest their
dead king's rites. It broke my heart how the country had
turned against him now that the effects of the war were being
truly felt, and it further hurt me that I could not pay my
respects without being accosted.

This all vexed me greatly. I spoke to God often about how
heavy my heart felt and he quietly reminded me of all the
lovely times Father and I had shared. The solace I found in
having been near him in his last months pulled my sorrow

out, but it was a hard relief, like of extracting a splinter. In some moments sweet, yet at other times like a festering sore.

I truly had never seen him so alive and vivacious as I did near the end, even though he was confined to a chair. It made me know him as he would have been while a young lion, and I liked seeing that side of him. He felt proud of himself. He had a legacy. He had Edward and all he'd done to better England.

He'd been God's servant too in so many ways, though he might not have known it.

Thinking of him in this light, though, always brought on a crying fit. I felt the stinging of my eyes and the ache at the back of my throat, telltale signs—which would not do, for I was waiting for Robert.

And, sure enough, as the first tear fell, I heard his light tap on my door.

As he entered my chamber, I ran to him, tears pouring down my cheeks. I held onto him tightly so that I would not collapse with sorrow as I cried into his shoulder.

Robert had been in and out of my life the last two years. School with Edward and I. Visits when he was at court, for it was but a half day's ride for Robert to get to Hatfield. And when I was at court, as I had been quite a bit of late, it was easy for us to stay close.

However, recently, our closeness had a tension to it. I did not want to think about what that tension could mean.

"My father is dead, Robert. How can anything be right again?" I said and snotted all over his beautiful buckram waistcoat. I cried even more as I tried to wipe the mess away with my handkerchief. "I am sorry I have ruined your new coat."

He patted my hair and held me tight. "He is with God now. He will be missed, but at least he is with God…and he does not have to get snotted on by you." He added the last as a quiet afterthought.

I looked at him sharply, but his face only mocked me when his perfect lips curved slightly up and his beautiful eyes twinkled.

I smacked his arm and sniffed loudly. "Can you not be serious for two minutes together, Robert Dudley? I have lost my father. I can snot on whomever I like." I began to push him away, but his strong arms would not let me go. Soon I gave up and put the handkerchief to my nose, feeling another bout of crying coming on.

He must have seen it coming too for he said, as sweetly as he could manage, "Come now, my sweet princess, I am sorry. I know you loved your father. You will miss him. You are very much without immediate relation now. I am certain that is difficult. But Bessy, you still have Edward, and Mary, and Kat, and me. We are all here to be snotted on whenever you desire. See here, I still have yet another shoulder." And pulled my head to his clean shoulder. "Have a go."

I clawed at the embellishments on his sleeves, and pushed my face into his shoulder, not able to allow myself to smile for him, even though I knew Robert wanted to see that smile, so he could feel as if he'd helped. I just felt overcome.

He snuggled me tightly against his chest. "I am sorry for this loss, my dear princess. He was a great man and will be missed. I am just so glad you grew closer to him in his last years." He smoothed my hair as I cried on him heartily.

March 1547
Windsor Castle, London

The day was extremely cold, but I did not care; I needed my horse. I was bundled in furs as much as I could be while still holding on to the saddle and reins. Fowler was a beautiful animal and his feet and legs were as sturdy as any I had ever seen and good for winter's icy months. Robert rode next to me on the stunning black mare he called Blacket.

Father had been gone another fortnight and I still felt the loss keenly. Edward, now age nine, was king, though with a regency council to help him rule. The political state of the country was full of tension as each house tried to gain the favor of the new king. I had so many feelings swirling around me that even filling myself with the power of the moon failed to comfort me as it should.

I wanted to talk to my dear brother and have his reassurance that he would take care of me. Father had of course provided for Mary and me in his will, but a new king could change all of that if it was his pleasure. I did not think that Edward would do such a thing, but Father's war had left the country near bankruptcy and Edward might be convinced by his council that England needed the money. That serious-natured boy would not stop until he made it all as it ought to be, but who was to be the judge of what was necessary?

I had not realized what a protection Father was to me until he was gone.

A tear rolled down my cheek and I wiped it away before Robert saw it. It seemed all I did of late was cry, and in the last few weeks Robert had been my only confidant. Blanche left me six months ago to retire to her family estate, and Kat was married just before Father died, so she was still busy being a new bride. Therefore, my beloved friend Robert took on the responsibility of making me smile and listening to me when I needed to cry. He was only fourteen but toward me he acted as only a dear friend who knew me inside and out could. I felt the same about him and knew I would still choose to confide in Robert if Kat or Blanche were available to me.

I wanted to weep again, for I knew that Robert and I would be going our separate ways in a few short days—I back to Enfield, until things could be settled as to where I would reside, and Robert to his family home in Sussex. Robert's father was on Edwards's council, and so Robert would be at court sometimes, but for now it seemed as if we would be on opposite sides of the world.

After clearing my throat to try and hide my emotion, I said, "I hate that we must separate." Surely my petulant tone told him how upset I was. I heard it with disgust myself. When had I become such a ninny?

"Yes, I do not like it either," he said shortly, and his glance in my direction was harder than I was sure he intended.

"When shall we see one another again?" I asked with a bit of whine in my voice.

"I am uncertain." I missed the usual way his mouth curved as he spoke, for the air froze his breath, blocking his lips partially. Those lovely lips should never be blocked.

There were so many things that I would miss.

"Do you think you might come and study with me? I am sure that Dr. Grindal would be most obliging, for he loves you as much as any of his other students." I sniffed and patted Fowler.

"I do not think so. Because I will be at court more often, Father has informed me that he will have an informal position for me to fill." He looked over at me intently. "He thinks that under Edward, our family might gain the esteem to merit a nobly born wife for myself and even for Guilford, though he is only ten."

"Yes, your father is always in a hurry to marry you all off, isn't he?" I said a bit testily.

"My Lady Princess, once you have had thirteen children, as my parents do, you will understand."

Robert did not know that I did not want children. I had told no one but Kat and Blanche, and they of course assumed that I was being ironic.

"Besides, I feel it is time to whittle down the choices, for there are many fine-looking girls my age."

He was trying to goad me, but I would not bite today as I was in too sober a mood. "Yes, well at least you have the happiness of having choices and the knowledge that your fate should be secure. I do not know what I am to do if Edward sends me to stay with someone awful, or if he takes my inheritance away or banishes me."

"Do not be dramatic, Elizabeth. Your brother loves you. How many times must I tell you that he will never do such a thing as that?" There was a touch of aggravation in Robert's warbled voice, though his eyes lit, and he smiled as he reached over to take my gloved hand. "You could always just run away with me. I would take care of you and buy you so many sweet things to eat that before you were thirty you would be fat as Emma." He laughed loudly and I laughed with him.

When the laughter died down, he said to himself in a quiet voice that I almost did not catch, "Then we could stay together forever."

He was looking far away now, and his smile brightened as he thought. I watched him closely and wondered if he was imagining the same things I was imagining. I was trying very hard to keep my thoughts under control, as Katherine had told me I should, and so instead of lingering on the thought of Robert and I together forever, I said, "I will race you to our spot." He looked over at me and I knew that he knew I would not wait for his response, so with smiles on our faces we took off at the same time.

Our spot was at the southernmost edge of the grounds. There was an ancient oak tree there and the foliage which was wild and unmanicured in the summer was a bramble of skeletal twigs now. There was also a wild blueberry bush that we had enjoyed before winter hit and a small pond with huge rainbow fish in it. At each home we stayed at or visited simultaneously, we always picked the most beautiful unusual spot on the grounds and called it "our spot," or "Queen Elizabeth and Sir Robin's spot." Besides having the fun of exploring the grounds to find such a place, we also had the pleasure of enjoying it over and over again when we returned to that particular house.

There was at least a foot of snow in some of the deeper rolls of ground and a significant amount of ice, which we avoided. The crunch our horse's hoofs made as we raced over the acres of land was beautiful to my ears. I loved to hear Fowler's slow breathing and feel his body move and strain. Robert kept in perfect speed with me until our goal was in sight and then, as he always did, he kicked his horse in the ribs and the mare took off at an alarming pace to reach the finish line before me. Robert was excellent on his horse. He always had been. I had decided it was his passion for the animal that caused him to excel, not any innate gift. If you did not care about the creature or take the time to ride it every day, then how could you excel?

It took us at least twenty minutes to reach the old oak tree.

Both of our faces were bright red and freezing cold by the time we slowed the horses. I walked Fowler up to the tall frozen branches of our tree and turned to Robert. "I love that I share this passion with you. I do not think anything helps me get myself under control better than riding."

He beamed. "I feel the same. I have never seen a girl with skill to match my own on the horse. I believe it is because you love it. Loving it makes all the difference and you know we choose what we love. I am just glad we both chose the same thing."

Robert so often took my own thoughts and repeated them back that it did not surprise me anymore. We actually had a word we used when this happened, and I said it now.

"Precisely!"

He smiled wider and nodded his head with a jerk to help him emphasize the word. "Precisely!"

This was one of our private routines.

I looked around the pretty little spot and remembered that the last time we were here we found a doe and her fawn. They had taken cover in the thick heather behind the pond. I slid off of Fowler and said, "Shall we go see if that doe is still keeping a den in the heather?" And before Robert got off his horse, I started to walk across the frozen pond.

As I got to the middle of the frozen water, I heard the eerie sound of cracking ice. I took one more step and heard Robert yell as I fell.

Freezing water surrounded me instantly and my breath was swept away by the shock of the cold. After several frightening and bitterly uncomfortable scrambling moments under the icy water, my mind cleared slightly, and I considered my own demise. It was long enough. I called my power to me, though I did not know what I could possibly do with it. Kicking my heavy legs and flailing my encumbered arms, I forced my way to the surface. As soon as my frozen eyes opened, I saw Robert's hand grabbing at me, his face grave with concern as he heaved me out with all his might. I tried to help him, but my gloved hands would not work. Finally, he got me out of the water and was ripping at my soaked layers of clothing.

Sudden clarity hit my mind, as if my body had finally processed what was happening and was now ready to fight back. I saw that the power was around me, but I also felt the icy cold water touching every portion of my light-infused skin. Holding that light to me with fervor, my frantic mind willed the water to leave me, to get away and make me cold no longer.

In that moment, the light around me surged and all the freezing water that covered me was pushed away from my body and clothing. It rose from me in a clear aura of rolling waves. As it passed over Robert's frantic hands, it left his gloves soaked through. Naturally, he jumped back in alarm.

It rose further and further away from me and I felt again as if I were snuggled in furs, dry furs, warm except for the places where my skin was exposed—those places where Robert had loosened or undone my clothing. I pulled one such place closed, and when I did, my elbow should have brushed up against the pale water surrounding me as it hung in the air, but it did not. The water bulged outward to make sufficient room for my movement as if it were repelled by me. Then it grew cloudy and suddenly stopped moving. I had thinned the water so much in my pushing that it froze in a dome around me, clouding my view of Robert and all things outside of the dome.

I instantly felt fear and began kicking at the ice, which shattered into jagged shards on first impact. I looked at my now ice-covered fur and sat up. Amazingly, I felt fine. The glow of my power still surrounded me and its light helped me feel some warmth in the freezing air. As if the sky were threatening me ominously, a loud crack of thunder sounded, and I jumped to my feet, brushing myself off. An unusually dark, low cloud had gathered above us. Rain would soon be coming.

After all that, I did not want to be rained on.

I looked over at Robert and his face held an expression I had never seen on him before. I could not tell if it was fear, amazement, or a combination of both. I cleared my throat and started for my horse.

"It is going to rain," I said in a tight voice and got onto Fowler with little difficulty. Before seeing whether Robert followed, I kicked the horse hard in the ribs and Fowler took off at a startling pace.

EPISODE 2

March 1547
Windsor Castle, London

I entered my room, knowing that Robert would not be far behind me. I was glad that Kat had a fire lit, though it did worry me that she sat in front of it with her needle and thread. She was working on a pillow and smiled at me as she opened her mouth to say something. Without even considering what I was doing, I took a piece of my power and flung it at her to cut her off.

"Go somewhere else." The words cut me internally as I spoke them but there was nothing to be done about it.

Instantly she stood and said in a quick, jerky voice, "Good evening, Princess. I think I will go somewhere else." And she grabbed all of her needlework and opened the door for herself and, as it were, for Robert, who threw himself inside my room.

I looked at him once and saw he was covered in sleet and snow. Part of my frantic mind wondered why he was all wet, but I was too angry, confused, and frightened to think on that question for long. I began taking off my furs and laying them on the chair where Kat had been sitting.

The moment the door closed behind Kat, Robert spoke.

"I see it now."

I did not look at him as I focused on my buttons.

"I see the light that surrounds you."

My head did whip about then.

"I began to see it as I followed behind you. The sleet...the snow...it did not touch you." He looked down at the carpet and I saw him shiver. "It moved out of your way." He looked back up at me and I saw how wide his beautiful eyes were, but I also saw how his jaw quivered.

It only took a moment to understand that he did not shiver because he was frightened by me, for he did not look frightened. He looked cold and wet. This realization made me furious. I was the one that fell in the pond and Robert was the one who came home wet as a dog and in danger of getting ill. In a thoughtless flood of emotion, I willed the water to leave him as it had me. A large shield of my power left me and raced across the room to him. He must have seen it too for his eyes got even wider, but he did not shrink back.

It was then that I realized how much he trusted me.

Soon the light surrounded him and pushed the water away from him in the same manner it had me, but instead of freezing, it fell to the floor in a puddle. Robert watched it splash and then turned to me with amazement.

All I could say was, "Come to the fire, Robert. Let it warm you. I would be positively heartbroken if you were to get sick after rescuing me."

He did not hesitate. We stood next to one another, looking into the flames for what seemed like forever before he spoke. "Elizabeth, we have to talk about this. I am so scared to start for I do not know how to ask what I need to know."

Fear again prickled my skin. What could I tell him? I must say something. He had seen. He could see me now for what I was. Instantly I pushed the power away from me and looked over at him. His eyes seemed to take in the change in aura but remained silent, waiting for me to speak.

I found my voice. "Then do not ask me, Robert, if you are unsure or scared. Do not make me say something that would cause problems between us." My voice seemed to almost beg. I hoped that he did not want problems more than he wanted answers.

He looked at me, his face as serious as I had ever seen it, and considered me for a long moment, staring into my eyes with such penetrating intensity that I could not look away. Soon his look changed from seriousness to loving understanding, and he exhaled. "Alright. If you have not reasoned out what to say, then I will wait. Only tell me this: if I do not press this now, will there ever be a good time for me to hear the truth?"

I looked at my hands. Must he prove to me how trustworthy he was? I thought of how he did not flinch away from me when my power went toward him. Was there a soul more trustworthy than he? How could I doubt him? I was not supposed tell anyone my secret, but I wanted to tell Robert. He was the only person I had ever wished I could tell.

However, though my heart wanted it, I could not find the words. I could not fathom explaining it all.

Feeling desperate, I tried to think of a way out. I looked at him and he stared right back, watching every mood pass over my face, listening to every huff of frustration I let out. I decided I would have to deceive him. I did not want to, but my mind would not allow words of explanation to form. Looking at the fire, I quickly said the first thing that came to me.

"I am only allowed to tell one person—my husband—and only when I can no longer hide it from him."

Why had I said that? It might make him think I intended to marry.

I touched his arm before continuing. "Do you remember that conversation we had where you told me of Catherine Howard's death for treason against my father?"

He looked at my hand on his arm and then at the fire, his forehead scrunched up. A moment later he said, "I do not recall every aspect of the conversation, but I do recall you being highly upset by the information."

I pulled on his arm so that he was facing me, and bent my head to catch his downcast eyes before I continued. "I am determined to honor what I said to you then. I have no wish to marry. I will never have a husband, I will not do it if I can help it."

"You will tell no one?" Then his face flushed. "But I thought—" His gloriously vulnerable eyes flashed, and then looked away from me. "You would not even marry me?"

I knew that he was the only person in the world who could tempt me to forsake my resolution, but I did not want to forsake it, and I could not give him hope that I would someday change my mind. Better to deal with this situation now rather than later. In two short years, Robert would be old enough to marry and his father had already singled me out as the young lady for the job. My being reinstated in the succession was only a hiccup in his plan, for all John Dudley needed to do was distinguish himself a bit more to the king. Then his son, eldest or not, would be enough of a match for a princess third in line to the throne.

Yes, better now than later. I made my voice as loving as I could, but also firm. "I will not marry even you, Robert. Not if I have my way." I quickly went on. "I love you as a brother, but if you ever did want me for a wife, you will change your mind after you hear this." I waited until he looked up at me. "I do not want to have children. I will not bear a single soul out of this body, Robert Dudley. I will not do it, even if I have to die a virgin." And I added regretfully to myself, "Though I do not think I will like celibacy very much."

My body had been changing since I began my courses, inside as well as out. I was now thirteen and felt a strong urge for physical gratification. It was a constant struggle not to give in and touch that raging river of pleasure.

Even as I thought of it and looked at Robert in all his young beauty, I longed for him. I wanted to kiss him, and touch him, and mostly to have him touch me. Imagined scenes of us together bombarded me and I cursed myself for not having more control over my thoughts.

Instantly, my heart began to race, and I felt the beast of desire deep down inside me raise its lusty head. I involuntarily took half a step toward Robert, who seemed to sense what was happening inside me for he went suddenly rigid and I saw in his eyes what he probably saw in mine. Hunger. Young, vibrant, erotic hunger. I heard him start to breathe heavily. His eyes looked uncertain, but something in my face must have consoled him for he stepped even closer and his hand touched my waist, his eyes moving slowly over my face and stopping on my lips. I suddenly did not want him to be a novice like me; I wanted him to be like Thomas Seymour, to throw me onto a table and have his way with me. I wanted it so badly, my body ached, and it took every shred of my control not to attack him.

However, I wanted what could never be. Even as he slowly leaned toward me, I found strength somewhere and turned my head, taking him in a tight hug instead. I held onto him, tightly pressing myself against every part of him, noticing how he felt different, and closing my eyes to block out the thought. I would not do this. Not to Robert. As much as I wanted it, as much as my body craved it, nothing could happen between us. I had to gain control. It was what God required of me and it was what I had chosen for myself.

I surrounded myself with the power, and wisdom instantly told me that once I started down this path there could be but two endings: marriage or heartbreak. In the sane part of my mind, I knew I wanted neither.

Then I realized I had unknowingly tricked my way out of telling Robert anything, and though I knew he could see me for what I was now, hopefully once he left this room, the words would never have to be spoken. Pressing my advantage, I turned and whispered in his ear, "Robert, will you be a gentleman and leave me before…before things become…"

I purposely left it hanging as I gently pushed myself away from his embrace.

Being true to who he was, he looked at me a moment longer, breathed deeply as he took my hands in his, brought them to his lips then turned to leave. There was a fair amount of regret on his face.

When he reached the door, he turned around and said, "You know, it would not have mattered, Elizabeth. None of it. I see you, and that is all I will ever see." There was a deep, quiet anger in his voice, an anger and a hurt that I knew was completely my fault. Then a strange softness touched the anger and his eyes grew watery. His hands tightened into fists and he concluded, "By the way, I have never seen you look more beautiful than you do right this minute, surrounded by light. You are as glorious as an angel." With those words he turned on his heel and slammed the door behind him.

～

I sat with the morning sunbeams warming me through my window. Kat sat with me, but we did not talk. I was still feeling frustrated about all that had happened the night before. Frustrated that I had to fall into the silly pond and use my power right in front of Robert. Frustrated that, yet again, I had discovered another facet of my gift that I had no idea about. Questions plagued me. Why could Robert see my light now? Is this what had happened to my mother? Perhaps Father had seen her light and then she was never able to manipulate him again.

And I was fascinated. Fascinated at how Robert could let me off the hook so easily. If I were he, there was no way possible I would have left that room without some sort of explanation. It made me wonder at the trust he had in me that he would just take my words without argument. It was amazing. It also made me wonder if Robert might know more than I thought he did, which of course sent me back from fascination to frustration again, for how was it possible that Robert could know anything about my gift? My mind went in circles about what his easy acquiescence might mean.

It was so obvious that Robert wanted me as a wife and that he would not be angry with me for letting him down easy as I did it. That was just Robert. He was a gentleman. It was all my fault if he was hurt, for we had been joking about marrying one another for years.

My thoughts were interrupted by a tap at my door. When Blanche, my new lady-in-waiting, opened it, Katherine strode in. "I am sorry, my Lady Princess, to come unannounced and so early, but I have the most wonderful news which I could not wait to tell you."

Katherine had stayed out of sight for several weeks following my father's death and funeral. I had not even known she was still here. Though we were close, I would not have gone to her with my troubles on any account. The poor woman had just buried her third husband. She did not need to hear my small problems.

"My Lady Queen, it is so wonderful to see you." I walked to her and, hugging her, said, "Now come, you need never feel uninvited. I am so happy that you are still here. What is your news?" I motioned to a pair of chairs and we sat down.

"I have just finished speaking with the council and they have consented to allow you to live with me. I shall be your guardian. Your father left me many houses, but I am planning on making Chelsea my home for now." There was a little expectant hitch on the words *for now* and I wondered what it could mean. "You are going to come and live there with me. What do you have to say?"

A small squeal of excitement escaped my lips and I leapt up.

"Kat, did you hear what my dear stepmother has come to tell me? I shall not go live with an evil lord who beats me and makes me take care of his children. I shall be living with the queen!" I grabbed Katherine's hands excitedly and jumped a bit up and down. "Oooh, I am so pleased. I was so frightened that I had done some bad thing to Edward in our youth and he was keeping it secret until he was crowned so that he might punish me by taking away my inheritance, or making me live with someone awful, or heaven forbid both! And now you see all my worry was foolishness. I am to be supremely happy. How wonderful."

Kat stepped in and said, "Most of what you do think is foolishness, girl—I mean, my Lady Princess. Sit yourself down and act like a lady. I am sure that the queen is not thinking of taking a four-year-old into her house. She is expecting a young woman with proper manners and the air of a princess. Am I mistaken, my Queen?"

Katherine laughed deeply, "I expect her to be what she is. I know Elizabeth. She gives herself to whatever she is about. Whether that be music, riding, or excited exclamations, she puts her heart and her young enthusiasm into it. I could not love her so dearly if she was not this way." She sniffed and smoothed her black mourning gown. "Her father and I talked of this gift she has on many occasions. She was a light to him in his old age. He said her enthusiasm kept him young." A small tear leaked out of her eye and I knelt before her, her hands still in mine.

"Did he really feel that way about me?"

She nodded with a smile brightening her face. Then she put fingertips to my cheek and stroked my hair, "You look so much like the man himself. I see his face in yours. I think you will be a great comfort to me in the next hard months." And she squeezed my hand.

I left for Chelsea with Katherine and the Ashleys before the week was over, because now that Edward was crowned, women were not allowed to stay at court, not even the sisters of the king.

Robert did not come to me again. Though I sent him notes begging him to see me before I left, he did not come, and the tears that I cried as our carriage departed were not for the absence of court but for the absence of my best, most dear friend. God only knew when I would see him again. But when I did, I told myself, I would not speak to him. I would stick my nose in the air and walk the other way. That was when my tears became angry and fierce, for I knew I was lying only to myself.

EPISODE 3

April 1547
Windsor Castle, London

In April, I went to Windsor so that my likeness could be painted. Mary was there for the same purpose. I had done my best to avoid her, and yet. Her depression seemed deep, her face grim and grey. I worried for her, but I did not enjoy her company. Edward, on the other hand, I wanted to see and had not.

Kat had come with me, but Katherine had not, stating that she had business to attend to at home. It was just a brief visit, so I thought nothing of her bowing out.

The artist, William Scrots, was not well known, but I trusted he would do me honor in his portrayal, for he was ambitious, and an ambitious man will make use of the opportunities that are afforded him. This was his opportunity. Doing the likeness of a princess as she entered womanhood was no small thing. Many people would see this painting for years to come.

Likewise, said princess needed to make a statement with said painting.

I chose the setting, and as I assessed myself in the glass that was positioned to help me remain in the same attitude whilst standing for him, I knew that I had chosen correctly.

I stood in a lush, coral-patterned silk that went almost off my shoulders. The tightly fitted bodice showed how nicely my bosom was blossoming and it tapered to show off my small waist. The neckline was exactly proper in its lowness as it accentuated the one necklace I proudly wore: my mother's pearls. I had switched the "B" pendant for an "E," and the pearls seemed to make the cream color of my skin look more lustrous. My red hair was pulled tightly back and shrouded in a French hood, also a tribute to my mother, for she preferred the French style. In my visible hands, I held my black leather-bound Fillos journal, and I had placed a single finger inside to signify how important the book was to me. It was a frequent read.

Behind me on a stand, I had the other book that was of greatest import: the Bible. This signified how I knew God had a work for me to do and I would not forget it or leave my Lord unrepresented in this historic portrait. Also, behind me was a bed with curtains slightly open. I wanted to allude to my womanhood.

For years, adults had told me I was wise for a girl so young and that my manners were that of an adult (they of course never saw Robert and me together). But now I felt older. I looked more like a woman and I wanted to be treated as such. It seemed that without Robert around, I was finally able to grow up.

I had another reason for wanting to seem more like a woman. In the last month, Admiral Thomas Seymour, the man himself, the man with the hands and the very wicked way about him, had begun visiting Chelsea. At first, he just stopped by chance, though I thought it was to see Katherine, since I knew that she was in love with him, but soon I was sure it was not because of Katherine. The man would go into the house and talk with Katherine for a while, then he would search me out wherever I was and spend hours talking with me. And before long, he came daily and didn't bother to see Katherine at all.

Perhaps it was I he wanted to woo. I, a girl that was twenty-five years his junior! At first, I did not know what to do about his attentions, for it did not take many such visits for my mind to start creating wild fantasies about him. I could not understand the pull the man had on me. But pull he did, ever so strongly.

As we walked in the garden, the tiniest brush of his hand left bumps on my skin. The smell of his skin as he moved past me to fetch a flower and put it in my hair made me swoon. His voice, as he told me stories of war and the sea, had me longing to be on a ship pulling the rigging for him, like any foolish ship rat. Just to obey his every command, just to have his startlingly dark eyes on me, watching me…the thought sent my heart racing. I could not keep my thoughts in check. He was amazingly handsome, though he had a few streaks of gray in his dark hair and beard. He was so lean and strong. And the man's hands. I had seen what he could do with those hands, and my mind was ever replaying those images, though I was the one he was—

"My Lady Princess! My Lady Princess, are you alright?" The high voice of the artist interrupted my thoughts.

I looked at him with wonder. Why was he stopping?

"What?" I demanded.

The man turned his wide eyes back toward the door and then again to me. "Are you feeling alright, Princess? Your cheeks suddenly flushed, and you seemed to be fainting. I was just wondering if the long standing was affecting you."

My cheeks did flush an even deeper scarlet then, as I could well see them in the mirror, but I shook my head vigorously. "No, no, I am quite alright. Pray, continue."

After an assessing look in my direction, he picked up his brush once more and I chided myself again and again for letting my fancies take me.

I sat on a stone bench in the shade of a young pine admiring the visage, a small folded paper in my hand. The note was from Katherine stating all was well, but that Robert of all people had come to visit in Chelsea and, not finding me at home, was heading toward Windsor. Robert. After everything, he was coming to see me now? I could not think of Robert. The wound of leaving me without so much as a farewell had my heart hardened toward him, but also nervous that he might demand I tell him of my power.

I looked at the neat script of my stepmother and thought of how wonderful the last few months had been with her. She was dear and sweet to me and encouraged me in my studies as well as in my hobbies. I continued to join her for prayers and sometimes scripture study.

I did wonder if she was still in love with Thomas and felt horrid knowing that he might ask for my hand at any time. I also dreaded what I might answer to that question. I was sickened at the thought, but I began to feel that I needed him. I needed him as I needed a drink of water after a long, hard ride, or as I needed breakfast in the morning. It was a desperate need, one that felt akin to life or death. I did not know if I even liked Thomas. He was bold and brass and a complete rogue, besides being selfish, heathenistic, and callous.

Nevertheless I knew, now that I was away from him, how badly I wanted him. I wanted him with the carnal part of myself that I tried to keep under control. When I was with him I thought I might go crazy with yearning that shot up in me like hot, liquid fire. I no longer had blood in my body, only fire coursing through my veins, giving the beast of desire within me power to smite me helpless. All I could do at these times was pray to God that he would intervene on my behalf. My thoughts were increasingly dishonorable I didn't know how much longer God would answer my call and give me strength. Then what would become of me?

Suddenly a voice I knew almost as well as my own whispered into my ear, and a lily the size of a plate was set in my lap by a hand I recognized. Robert must have chased down the courier, for the man had just placed this note in my hands. I knew it would not be long, with how Robert loved to gallop, but I was not expecting him so soon.

He looked tired and yet more beautiful than anything I had ever seen. All I needed were those deep, clear blue eyes filled with apology, as they were now, and I was weeping and hugging him. "Oh, Robert how I have missed you. Thank you for the lily. It smells wonderful. Lilies are one of my favorites," I said and touched my leaking eyes.

"I know. That it is why I brought it to you. As you can attest, I am not normally so thoughtful, but it was easy when there was a man selling them right at the gate." He smiled and wrapped my hand over his arm.

The gardens were beautiful, and I spent several hours walking them each day, so I knew where to lead him so we could be alone.

I stopped and looked into his eyes. "I have missed you

terribly, Robert, and I do not know that I will ever forgive you for leaving me the way you did."

"Well, what was all that blubbering for then? I usually do not let girls cry all over me for nothing. I thought for sure I was off the hook when you started sobbing the moment you saw me."

It looked as if today were one of his courtier days. I would get no serious answers from him now. Why had he come to me if not to have a serious conversation?

I pushed him away and scowled at him. "Well, Robert," I accentuated the name, showing him I saw that he would not be my Robin today. "If you did not come to make any apologies, and you have no explanations for your actions in February, then I am afraid we have nothing—"

"Explanations! Apologies!" His voice shattered the peaceful sounds of chirping birds and running water. "I do not think I am the one who has explanations and apologies to make, my Princess!"

I thought he had understood, that he was willing to…no, I don't know what I had thought, but obviously I was entirely wrong. He had been mad at me the whole time. He was just acting now, trying to manipulate me into telling him my secret.

Anger washed over me like the ocean tide. I did not understand why I did not just walk away from this infuriating boy. My blood seemed about to boil, and instinctively I called the power to me. I stood there with my nose in the air, arms folded beneath my breasts, and I almost flipped my skirts to walk away, however I caught a look in Robert's eye. It was only a flash, but they were emotions I knew well, for I knew Robert; awe, love, remorse.

Slowly the power purged my anger and I turned back to him.

His eyes were running slowly up and down my body, pausing at my arms, hands, neck, face—all the places where my skin was wrapped in the light of my power. He openly wore those emotions now and when our eyes met I saw something new.

Betrayal.

As quickly as I saw it, it was gone, and words were pouring mechanically out of his perfectly sullen lips. "Father said that Admiral Seymour has all but announced to the court that he will be asking the king for your hand. Since he is the brother of King Edward's mother and also the brother of the Lord Protector, I do not think he will be refused. Father wanted me to warn you that this would be a very bad match for you, and he pleads you to do whatever you can to stop it from happening."

He looked away for a moment, squinting into the afternoon sun. I saw how his dark hair shimmered with strands of red, the same colors as his long eyelashes which glittered feathery and full in the light. He was remarkably beautiful inside and out and I had hurt him deeply.

His voice cracked as he continued, and I did not think it was puberty breaking it because other emotions clouded his face. "I have not seen Father so concerned in a long while. He mentioned pleading on bended knee in front of the king himself, requesting him to refuse the suit." He turned back to me, a severe look in his eye. "He even suggested that I   " He turned away again. "It would not matter."

Clearing his throat, he took on a businesslike tone. "Regardless, I do have something more to add. Admiral Thomas was at your residence in Chelsea with the dowager queen, and I am very certain that, as I walked up, that I saw him streak past a window wearing only his small clothes. Not only that, I fear it took a very long time for the door to be answered and Katherine herself, who was quite out of breath, was the one that did so. She seemed all politeness. I asked if she needed any assistance, for she said that all the servants were away for a spring holiday of some sort. But she said 'No thank you'—with unnecessary vigor.

"This information connected with some other that I received yesterday from Lady Jane Grey leads me to believe that your stepmother and the Admiral are having an affair." He said it without batting an eye. "Yet he is telling everyone that he wants to marry you." A small consolatory smile graced his face and he added, "I am sorry to tell you all of this. It is obvious you can see the problem and are in shock. I just hope you realize that he is a trickster, Elizabeth; a rogue, and wholly unworthy of you…or the dowager queen." Breathing in heavily, he bowed and brushed a kiss on my hand. "I have delivered my message. I hope that it will help you decide, and to heal if you have been trespassed on." He still held my hand. His eyes went down to it as his thumb slowly brushed over my light-infused knuckles. Bowing down, he kissed it once more, though slowly this time, and afterward he would not meet my eyes. "If you will excuse me." With that he released me, turned on his heel, and walked quickly away.

I wanted to call after him. I wanted to scream his name, but I was in shock. His words ran through my head over and over again. "Your stepmother and the Admiral are having an affair." How could this be? I did not understand. I felt as if I now coveted something that I had not known I considered mine. Thomas was mine. I needed him. I wanted him. I would have him.

I could still see Robert as he walked away, and I knew that what was between him and me was what was real. My mind was mine enough to see that. Yet my body asked why I did not feel the overwhelming sexual draw to him that I felt toward Thomas? I loved Robert with all my heart. I would love to have him in that way, but I just could not. Perhaps that was the difference. I loved Robert. I cared about what happened to him. I did not want to take things, like fatherhood, away from him. I wanted him to be happy.

I did not feel that way toward Thomas. At that moment, all I wanted was to torture him, to make him feel the anguish of body I felt now as I believed that I would never have him. Most of all, I wanted to be that girl he tossed over a table and made love to, unconcerned with discretion and completely unattached. I felt the obsession take over my mind, and in that moment, I knew I had done this to myself. If only I would have been more vigilant in controlling my thoughts, for I could not see a way back now.

EPISODE 4

June 1547
Old manor in Chelsea, London

The truth was that, while I was gone, Katherine and Thomas were married in a secret ceremony. I had no idea what Edward and his council would make of that, but a very tiny, yet very loud part of my mind, hoped he would send them both to the Tower. Living with them was torment. I did not know what to do with the rage that seemed to fill me at every moment. I was sure my face would betray me as I watched them share a kiss over dinner or caress one another in the sitting room. I did notice that after these actions, Thomas' eyes would find mine and there was a boldness there that I detested.

I was of two minds about Katherine. I was so angry with her, yet I loved her, a conflict that caused me much anguish. She'd been so stoic and nurturing, but ill-fated with father. Now she seemed beyond happy and completely unconcerned with the gossip spreading about her. I did not like to hear the gossip, but again, a small voice in me said that it was completely warranted, for it had only been two months since Father's death.

However, my anger was a gentle simmer compared to how I felt when I learned that Edward himself had given them his blessing and that the council, and world, only just found out about the marriage.

I wanted revenge. I felt almost out of control about it. Having fits of crying and red-faced anger. Stomping around and yelling at most anyone. Kat said it was my age, adolescence and all, but that couldn't be it. It was Thomas. I wanted him, I thought I had him and now he was very violently ripped out of my daydreams and living under my same roof, making love to my step-mother.

Also, it seemed that Thomas' eyes were never far from me, and that in and of itself was enough to make me crazy. I was mad at him for all he done to me; how he had trespassed on my good will, made me love—or rather lust—after him in a way that I could not ignore, and then removed himself from my grasp. I tried to be cold, but a month and a half later, something changed with their marriage. I wasn't certain what, but I started seeing Thomas everywhere I went. At first it seemed happenstance, but then he began making a point of being where I was.

When he followed me out to the stables, he would stand and look at me, not saying a word the whole time I waited for my horse. Then he would take his horse out too, only he would ride behind me, never approaching.

It was unnerving.

He would walk around the gardens at the same time I would and admire the flowers, but it was as if I were the most beautiful one in the garden, for his eyes found me more than anything else.

Then I realized something. If I was looking at him every

time he happened to look over at me, was it he or I who was doing all the staring? I forced myself to not look at him. I considered it a battle of wills and my angry side won…most of the time.

It went on like this for months, and sometime around Christmas, Katherine asked me about it. "My dear Elizabeth, do you like the Admiral?" She glanced at me sullenly and then continued her needlework.

Do I like your husband? Let me see…I dream about him every night. Every time he walks into the room my heart begins to race. I fantasize about being in his bed and I hate every last bit of him for making me feel like a hussy that cannot control her thoughts as my Lord would have me do.

I did not want to admit even to my own self how much of my time on that prayer bench was spent thinking of Thomas. I was going to be struck down for my blasphemy.

I cleared my throat and ducked my head so that she would not see my blush for what it was. How could I answer? "I do not think I dislike him."

Katherine stopped her stitching to look at me again. "But you do not like him?" She sounded scandalized.

I was instantly angered by her tone. Why was she asking me this? I did not want to talk about it! "I do not even talk to the man. How do you like a man you do not talk to? Of course, I used to have many good talks with him but that was before you and he married. He is your husband. Why do you care how I do or do not feel about him?" My voice betrayed everything. I knew it did. Thankfully, Katherine was far too shocked that I would speak to her in such a manner to hear all I had betrayed.

"Goodness, all I wanted to know was why you do not speak to him." She had gone pale and rigid. The woman did not like conflict.

"I do not talk to him because I have nothing to say to him," I said with false sweetness that I hoped would cover up my anger.

"Well I do not want you to be put upon, but I think that there are a great many things you could talk about with him. He is very interesting." She looked at me with sincerity in her lovely face. "It is just that the Admiral has complained that he cannot be a proper stepfather to you if you will not talk with him or spend time with him. I think he is right. You have not had a father like most girls have, and so I thought that Thomas would be very good for you, but you cannot benefit from this congenial situation if you will not let him get close to you. When you have finished mourning your father, I hope that you will give Thomas a chance to help you have a more normal youth. He loves you already and is eager to guide you however he is able."

Those last words were his, I was sure, for their meaning was twofold.

"Thank you for telling me this, Katherine. I shall try to follow your wishes and become more friendly with the man. His heart, I am sure, is in the right place." I said the last with a tiny sneer I hoped she would not see.

From then on, I tried to treat him in the way I would anyone else. I tried. At supper he would make friendly conversation with me and I returned it with equal civility, but that and that alone was enough to start a whole new wave of sickening thoughts and schemes in my mind. I had to have him or get away from him, and yet I was still mad at him. The power this man had was equal to mine in every way, for I was completely under his control.

That gave me an idea. What if I were to use my power to make him crazy about me and only me, for I was sure that he was only playing right now. A man with his reputation could not be happy in a marriage with one woman. He needed the hunt, the game. I was sure of it. I had seen this at court and I knew that he was the worst one of them all. But I had never manipulated someone to love me or to have any kind of regard for anyone, and I wondered if it would work. It seemed completely wrong, yet I was tempted to try.

Over the next few days, it seemed he was growing tired of how slow his game was progressing with me and thus began to heighten the intensity. I soon understood his desperation, for Katherine announced she was with child, due in the late summer. She had been ill and only became more so, and I was quite sure that Thomas was not allowed to go to her as a husband for fear of the baby's health. As a result, he began to search me out, and though he would have very little to say when he found me, he would always find some excuse to touch me. It reminded me of when he courted me the summer before. Of course, we were limited to the indoors, for it was January, the deepest of the winter season, so I was many times cornered in a doorway or hallway, or in the library, for he knew I spent a lot of time there.

One day while in the library with Dr. Grindal, who was very involved in some book, Thomas entered and lingered near my side. I tried to ignore him, but his hand kept brushing mine.

I looked at him and then he would pretend to be ignoring me. How childish were these games that he played, and how strange it was that they drove me crazy.

I walked away from him and stood behind a tall book shelf that blocked out most of the rest of the room. I did not realize that I had put myself in a bad position until Thomas was behind me, hands around my waist, pushing his chest against my back, and breathing into my ear. "I think it is time to stop playing games, as enjoyable as they are. We must start putting some action into the play." And he ran the tip of his nose from my ear to my temple, his bottom lip skimming my cheekbone as he breathed heavily onto my skin.

Pushing against the shelf, I broke away and turned to face him. The haughty smile he had on his face and the lusty look in his eyes stopped me from slapping him right across the face. Instead I decided it was time that I play a game of my own, a game he did not know existed.

Surrounding myself with the power, I pulled courage around me like a cloak of supremacy.

Standing on tiptoe, I leaned as close to his ear as I could and said, "Your mind will think of me more often than you should, your body will react with pleasure at my coming, and you will want me and no other from this day forward." With that, I pushed the biggest ball of light I had ever used into Thomas.

And then I walked away.

Glancing back, I saw the hunger enter his eyes and felt the desire he had for me as I sauntered away from him. I smiled. Now we would see how he enjoyed being controlled.

For the rest of the winter, I was particularly careful to never be alone. Between Kat, Blanche, Katherine, and our newest guest, Lady Jane Grey, it was not a difficult task. I wanted to be in the open, yet completely inaccessible to him. I watched Thomas closely at dinner time and in the evenings when we sat around the fire. Several times he trapped me into playing a game of chess with him, and during said games, his whispered words told how he longed for me and implored to know why I was not going to the library anymore. I would ignore these comments completely and engage someone else nearby. I laughed with pleasure to myself as he got more fanatic day by day.

When spring arrived, I stayed in my room instead of spending time out of doors. When I did emerge from my rooms I was always in the company of someone and only then would I walk the grounds. I had no idea where I got the courage or the know-how to play this game with him. All I knew was that I was acting out as a powerful yet angry and spurned woman. I made the game up as I went along. I wanted to drive him wild, but it seemed that doing this only made me feel more so.

Before long, Thomas started showing up at my door in the morning and Kat naturally would let him in to sit and talk with us. Of course, he acted the perfect gentlemen and stepfather, even getting playful at times. Then one morning, he was feeling more deprived than usual and he chased me around the room when I told him I would not go for a ride with him. Kat came in to see what the ruckus was, and he began chasing her around the room too, as if he were playing a fun game with me instead of hunting me as his prey. At first, she was affronted, but after pushing him away, he began chasing me again and tickling me, and she laughed as if it were all very funny. He took her and tickled her a little and all I could think was that she was partly under his spell too, for why would she not think something strange of a man playing thus with a young lady? As things progressed and this chasing became common place—meaning Kat did not watch so closely—Thomas took it to the next step, sometimes he would slap my bottom and even throw me on the bed to tickle me.

Soon he was coming to my room almost every morning. I

would get up early to try and avoid him, but I could not, my studies suffered, and I would need to nap in the afternoon. Plus, where was I to go? I would be alone anywhere I wandered so early in the morning and that was exactly what Thomas wanted.

Soon Kat did not even bother to check when she heard a knock at my door. He'd worn her down and was now wearing me down. I did not stop him or inform anyone about him because, though I was petulant that he could not be mine, this new situation felt like he was mine and I was still eager to have him near me.

I was addicted to what my body felt like when he was close. Several times he came so early that he was still in his night shirt and I in mine. He was careful too, always making enough noise that Kat could hear everything—everything except what he whispered in my ear.

"I want you. I will have you, my rosebud. I think of only you."

EPISODE 5

April 1548
Old manor in Chelsea, London

My studies were done for the day and I wanted to be as far away from Thomas as possible, and so I sat on the ledge of the fountain in the lower garden where the branches of a great oak sheltered me from the house and from the afternoon sun.

I also chose this spot so that I could inconspicuously practice my manipulation of water. There was a small fish swimming near me, and with a thought and a bit of light I sent a current that took the fish away from the bit of algae it wanted. I smiled and stopped the fish again and again from its meal. It was an easy enough thing for me to do now that I knew I could do it. I just told the light to repel the water in this way or that and it would.

One momentous thing I discovered while practicing this was that I did not ever have to say my manipulations aloud. This made things much easier. I only had to grab the light first, think with intensity what I wanted, and then push the light away on my terms instead of letting it go by itself. From my reading of the journal, I was not sure that anyone before me had accomplished this. Also, I was uncertain whether anyone had had as many affinities as I, or as strong. I was almost certain I could see the future in my dreams, though this was a gift that seemed only on the verge of developing. I could control water and minds efficiently. Who knew what else I would be able to do?

"My sweet princess, there you are."

The unexpected noise shattered my reverie. My head turned as Thomas stepped from behind the nearby oak. I stood quickly, startled by his appearance. He walked confidently around to stand just feet away from me. He was wearing a cream doublet and hose to match. The doublet accentuated his narrow hips and broad shoulders, and the hose showed off his well-turned calf. His dangerously beautiful eyes watched me as I assessed him.

"I can see that you appreciate a fine formed man when you do not have so many people surrounding you. I enjoy your form too, or couldn't you tell by the way my hands linger over you in our fun little morning foreplay. But here I find you out of doors, far away from the house, and quite alone. It's as if my dreams are coming true. Could you finally be letting your guard down? Are you accepting my proposal?"

I cut in, determined not to let him have the upper hand. "You Sir, I would have accepted had you asked, but you did not and now you are my stepmother's husband, thus I am done with you," I said and smoothed my skirt over my hips. "I only humor looking at you and allowing you to visit to please Katherine. She asked me so nicely to accept your friendship. Still I have never said I enjoy the sight of you."

He laughed haughtily, his eyes twinkling as he stepped

closer to lay a hand on my upper arm, "Do not worry, my dear little princess, I like these games you play. I like them very much, No need to sell them to me so harshly." His hand went up and down my arm, causing a tingling to begin in my toes and move up my legs. "You did give something away you know. The fact that you want me. You thought I would ask for your hand. Whilst I have been playing house with Katherine, I have missed terribly our walks in the garden and our flirtations. Not that it has been all bad." He smiled wickedly and began to caress my arm more fully. "But Katherine does not have your freshness."

I pulled away from him, embarrassed I'd admitted what I had. Incensed and excited by his touch, I turned, putting one hand to my blushing cheek.

"Come now, don't be ashamed." Thomas cooed and sidled up behind me. I could feel his heat. "Here, I will admit something so that we are even." He moved even closer. I felt his breath on my neck as he whispered. "Did you know I asked your brother, my nephew, for your hand in marriage before I took good old Kate's?" He paused to let that sink in.

And sink in it did. My mind worked furiously on the words.

I knew I wasn't crazy. This wasn't Thomas's fault. It was Edward's! I turned toward him slowly, wide-eyed and breathing hard.

Thomas traced my jaw with his thumb, his dark irises following the motion. Then his gorgeous eyes found mine. Still whispering he said, "I was refused, and the only way I could think to stay near you was to marry Kate. Besides, I knew that she loved me and would treat me well. She is after all the dowager queen, and I must say a very good woman."

He made it all sound so reasonable. He made it sound like it was the only way I could have what I wanted, and I almost believed him. Parts of me did believe him and they warmed and hummed with his words and his look and his touch.

His hand cupped my shoulder, but he extended a long slender thumb to trace along my bare collarbone. It took all of my control not to melt in pleasure. I loved his hands. I loved them touching me.

What could I do? I watched his eyes and I knew that my face betrayed me, for he smiled and took me in his arms, pulling me into the dark shadows under a tree.

Pressing his mouth to my ear, he whispered, "Now my little rosebud, do you want what only I can give you? I want to hear you say that you want it. I know all you need, and I will give you more than you will be able to stand. All you must do is ask." His mouth closed around the lobe of my ear as he breathed haggard breaths and waited for me to speak.

Everything was happening so fast. I could barely understand what he was saying to me. What was he going to give me? What did he want me to say? I wasn't sure. All I knew was his mouth was touching my skin and his hands were clawing my back. I swallowed ready to say something, anything, but before words formed, Kat's voice came like an angel's carried on the breeze.

"Elizabeth, where are you?"

Thomas instantly let me go and, to my horror, stepped out from behind the tree. "She is here, Lady Katherine, safe as can be. I was just trying to get her to cool down. She has been sitting in the sun so long I fear she may be overheated."

He pulled me gently from behind the tree and I must have been red-faced, for Kat was instantly alarmed and rushed to my side. "Thank you, Admiral. I can see what you mean. You have not sat in the sun too long since you were a child, Elizabeth. What were you thinking? Let's get you to the house."

"May I be of assistance? Perhaps I should carry her?"

And with that, he swept me up in his arms without a problem, or consent for that matter.

As he carried me, I was very aware of his hand under my arm pressing very close to my breast. I wriggled, hoping to get away, but then he was talking. "I am just lucky to have happened upon her. I have two places on the grounds I walk to each day: this pond and the pergola on the other side of the house." He looked at me with significance. I of course knew the place that he spoke of and I took his meaning for what it was: an invitation. "I think with a little shade and cool water she will be fine."

"Yes Kat, I will be fine. In fact, I think I am fine enough now to walk," I said with a little aggravation coloring my voice.

But Thomas answered me without missing a beat. "Oh no, my Lady. I would not want you to exert yourself, not when you are overheated." And he gave my thigh, which was covered by my dress, a tight squeeze.

The next evening a devil must have possessed me, for I wandered through the garden as if under a spell. I did not think where my feet were taking me, but if my dreams were any indication, it was to Thomas and the under-boughs of that same oak tree.

He was there. His mood dark. He looked up as he saw me, his eyes narrowed. "I have been waiting here for a very long time." He rose and came toward me with purpose. I trembled. "I'm afraid you are in above your head, my little rose bud, for I am unaccustomed to waiting so long. I have had you fifty times in my mind whilst waiting and now," he'd reached me and took me by the wrist, pulling me toward the tree, "now, I will wait no longer."

Once under the great leaves, we were truly in the dark and before I knew what to do, Thomas had me against the oak truck. His mouth attacked my neck, biting, kissing, and licking me. Lifting me up and anchoring me between the rough bark of the tree and the strong length of his body, he made his way around my décolletage with his mouth and, though I was excited, I did not understand why he was spending so much time kissing that part of me. Still, I thought I enjoyed it. And even if I didn't, I needed this to happen. I had thought about this too much to stop it. Thus I did not care if I came out of it gnashed and bleeding. It was time.

After a few moments he looked up from the neck of my dress with fire in his eyes, desire like I had never seen before. A chill ran up my spine telling me this was not good. I was in too deep. I didn't know what to do. My body wanted Thomas, wanted this. But my heart and mind...they were screaming as well. Screaming to run.

"Say it." He said. "I want to hear the words out of these lips." His thumb appeared and pulled my bottom lip down. It popped back up to its regular position with a small clicking sound which made Thomas bite his own lip and breath heavily. "I can barely hold on here, Elizabeth. Do what I ask, or I will make you regret it." He growled in a way that I think he thought was charming. But it wasn't.

And I still didn't know what he wanted me to say.

I opened my mouth to say something, but nothing came to mind. Frustrated, I gritted out, "I'm sorry, Thomas, I just don't know what you want me to say."

He rolled his eyes at me. "Oh, stuff it. I'm over it." Then his lips were pressing against mine. I stood there—for he had put me down—stunned. I was having my first kiss and it was…awful and wet and no matter how much I intended to like it, I just didn't, not really. And then, Thomas forced his tongue into my mouth and flicked it around and around. Trying to play some sort of chasing game. I did not like the taste of him.

Still, I went along with it and got used to it after a second, but I was not impressed by it. I tried to get him to put his tongue back in his mouth, but he took that the wrong way.

His passion doubled, and his hands began ripping at the back of my black dress.

Rip it he did.

His exuberance was not wasted, for several minutes later I wondered if my fantasies were about to come true. I felt my body warm and relax. I felt myself settling into the rhythm of what he was doing with his mouth. But then he began fumbling for the bottom of my skirts.

Startled, I placed my hands on his chest, and pressed. He was a stone.

But then Katherine was there. Well not her just yet, but her voice calling out to Thomas. She had not seen us, she was still too far away, but there was no way to hide that we were under the oak in the darkness.

Thomas pulled away from me, wide-eyed. "Bollocks." He swore in a whisper and looked at me so forlornly I almost felt sorry for him. "We were about to get somewhere." He sighed. Then, to my dismay, he called out to her. Quietly he said to me, "Do as I say."

I nodded my head and he pushed me onto a low branch of the oak, then motioned me to climb higher, and I did. When Katherine came around to where she could see us, I was sitting securely a few branches above the ground, looking demure.

Katherine smiled when she saw Thomas and quickened her step.

"This fool girl of yours climbed this tree and now that it is twilight she is stuck up there. She is only now getting down to the lower branches, I happened by and she called out for help. The problem is her dress has gotten ripped and she is too shy to let me get her down for fear of exposure. Will you come help me talk her down?"

"Certainly, my love, but you startled me. I did not see you under there." She pushed her way under the low branches, looking up at me when her eyes had adjusted. "Oh, my dear, you are in a frightful state. Let's get you down."

So she proceeded to help me, and all the time I shot admiring glances at Thomas. He was superbly good at lying. I wondered when that had become something I admired.

I breathed a sigh of relief when we were finally out of the tree's grasp. Katherine looked at me questioningly and her arms cradled her small pregnant belly. "You look as if you were attacked by a wild animal, Elizabeth."

Thomas laughed and I blushed. "She could not have been, my love. A wild animal on the grounds? It is unheard of." He thought this very funny indeed and could not stop his laughing.

Katherine then looked at him questioningly. "Sir, you have not gotten in the wine, have you?"

He looked shocked. "No, my Lady. Not that I can recall, that is."

Katherine laughed and patted his cheek. "Things are so much more interesting when you have gotten into the wine." And the hussy winked and smiled devilishly. Why was she so flirtatious when she could not make good on it while in her condition?

I acted as if I had not seen any of it and starting walking

away from them, but I kept stumbling over a hanging bit of my dress.

Soon Thomas called out to me.

"Halt, my Lady Princess, and let us fix your gown so that you will not be falling all the way to the house."

I could not ignore him, so I stopped and turned. He had pulled out a small knife he must have kept in his boot and said, "Hold her, Katherine, for I fear she may jump and I will cut her instead of the dress."

Katherine stood close behind me, her swollen abdomen pressing into my back, and held me at my shoulders tightly. "Do not move. my dear. He is very skilled at this process, but I would not want to risk you getting hurt." Even that had a wicked ring to it and I looked down at Thomas who was kneeling at my feet. He flashed a surly smile at us.

Then all I heard was the ripping sound of material being severed.

Then I heard him laugh. "I cannot fix it. It will not go right. I just keep making it shorter and shorter. I am afraid that it is quite ruined, Elizabeth. At least you will not trip."

His speech was halted by Kat's approach. The sky was almost completely dark, but there was enough light to see the situation in its entirety. She saw Katherine holding my shoulders while Thomas had shreds of my gown in one hand and a knife in the other.

Alarm colored her face instantly. "What in the name of heaven is going on here?" she said and rushed toward me.

I looked down and saw my exposed legs and saw Thomas eyeing them appreciatively. Katherine, looking at Kat, laughed unconcernedly and began to explain. Thomas took advantage of their distraction and the dim light to run the hand with the knife gently across the back of my calf as he stood.

And it was then that two thoughts occurred to me. First, I liked that dangerous caress of my leg much more than all the kissing we had just done. Second, I was not prepared to be man-handled by him in front of his wife. It was too shameful.

This second thought had merit, and I left it to work on my conscience.

It didn't take long.

What was I thinking? Frolicking with a married man? Letting him kiss me and touch me?

Because of that, I stood in front of the people that loved me best with a ripped dress, showing off my legs.

I broke away from Katherine and, covering my face with my hands, fled past her toward the house.

May 1548
Old manor in Chelsea, London

I tried to avoid Thomas after that. I had tasted the fruit and it was not everything I dreamed. Still I could not stop thinking of it. It was as if I'd decided what Thomas should be like and longed for him to show me the man of my imaginings. So, I continued to hope.

I did not have to wait long for him to find a way to continue his pursuit. Kathrine fell ill, and Thomas convinced Kat that Katherine valued her as a companion and thus wished Kat would nurse her. The loving and kind soul that was Kat believed him and that left me many evenings and mornings alone in my chambers.

During such periods of unaccompaniment, Thomas snuck into my sleeping chamber. He paid me no respect by asking to engage me, he just took my acquiescence as a matter of course. Thus, I spent hours being petted and kissed and smothered by the lonely man.

In these moments when we could not speak for fear of

being overheard, we whispered, but Thomas never let me see the man he really was. He only ever focused on his passion and all comments were limited to that end.

One morning he prevailed upon me with more vigor; kissing me passionately did not suffice. He moved himself on top of me and my coverlet, then he pressed his body against me over and over, moaning softly between kisses.

His actions brought back that conversation I'd had with Blanche, about the relations between a man and woman and I wondered if that was where Thomas expected this to go. That of course was ridiculous. It had to be. But I worried that that was what he meant by 'having me'. And if it did, had he 'had' me and my coverlet, that morning? I pondered on it quite a bit because the description given me by Blanche did not line up, making me frustrated with confusion.

Still, I knew I was gaining something from my time with Thomas. I felt it. Something was happening to me. I felt that Thomas was teaching me in the art of love, a subject I was wholly ignorant on.

Besides in the garden, and that one morning in my bed, he led me through the processes gently. Teaching me what he liked, though he was not very concerned with what I liked. However, I did warm to his teaching and found that I had moments of passion as well.

That perhaps was the problem with the process. As I warmed to it, I desired things I did not understand and intrinsically knew were wrong. But the need grew. I learned what to do, how to move, and within a week of visits from Thomas in my bed, I felt stirrings of things deep inside me that frightened me.

This had begun as a seduction, then an obsession, then vindication, and now an education. One evening things came to a head. Thomas had me right where he wanted me, I was helpless and completely in his control. I knew he was about to take it to some new level, filled with things I could not imagine, when he pulled away from me and whispered, "Elizabeth, are you ready?"

I blinked away the fog of pleasure and asked, "Ready for what?"

He stopped breathing and just stared at me in the candlelight. It took a few lengthy moments before he released his breath and moved off of me.

"You really don't know, do you?"

"I don't know what?"

He stood. "If you do not know, I will not tell you. Ask a maid or a servant." He moved toward the door clearly frustrated, but he turned back with a few rushed steps, his face a mask of severity, and whispered harshly, "Find Isabel, or Emma, or Frances. They are all well versed." Then he practically stomped from the room.

Kat was back now and, though we knew how to be silent, Thomas did not come for several days.

In that time, I did as he commanded and talked to the maids. It was as I thought. The next step was what resulted in a child. That was what he was asking of me. As I listened to what the servants had to say about the matter, I felt very curious but frightened. I also saw that none of the girls had children, though they had firsthand experience. This all weighed heavily on my mind.

Still, I was not ready for that yet. And the fact that Thomas knew this and wished for me to get ready—that he did not rush ahead like he'd wanted to do in the garden— meant something to me. I felt my goals shift once more from the academic to personal. I did care about Thomas. I cared a lot.

So our time together changed again. I allowed him to progress things. Things that sent my heart racing.

Several times I did see a faint light in his eyes that told me he would not stop, and that was when I had to use my power against him. Thankfully it always worked. I wondered to myself if this was the exact thing my mother did to my father, and that made me sure that someday it would stop working and I would have to give in.

That time came on the first of May. I was finishing my studies and Dr. Grindal was leaving my antechamber. I'd had a hard time concentrating that day. Flashes of Thomas marred my every thought. Kat was spending the day going over the books with her husband and I was purposefully keeping to my room. Jane Gray—who was living with us to be tutored of Dr. Grindal—sat by me, working on her studies as well.

Occasionally she would ask me a question and I would answer her as thoroughly as I could. But soon her questions began to wear on my mind and I asked her if she would not go to Dr. Grindal for help, for I was having enough trouble with my own work. I think that I offended her for she gathered her things and left in a huff.

Finally there was peace to work on my translation. I did not clearly acknowledge the sounds of a door opening or the footsteps across the floor but when I looked up and saw Thomas' eyes, I knew that, ready or not, now was the time.

"Kate is fairly about to pop," Thomas growled, "and I am but a man. I hope, my lady, you are ready now for what must be done, for my patience is gone." Without any other interlude, he moved behind my chair, his beautiful hand swept my papers to the floor and roughly pulled me out of my seat, ripping at the laces on my corset. As he did, he kissed my neck and back passionately, and finally, he got the thing loose enough. He growled again as he turned me around and plopped me on my writing desk; gathering my skirts, he pushed his way between my legs and resumed kissing me everywhere.

While he did this, he whispered, "I shall make you blossom, my little rosebud. I know exactly what you need." He pulled his lips away from my chest to look up at me, and the desire I saw in his eyes could match none other than my own. "You can stop me if you wish, but you must say so now, for in a moment it will be too late and I will not stop until I am done."

My hands ran over his shoulders and up to his face, where I traced his lips with a fingertip. I now knew what he sought to hear. I had learned so much in our months together, so I said it. "I want you," I whispered as I looked into his eager eyes and then he was pulling at the laces of his codpiece.

It was that moment that Katherine walked through my door, a smile on her face—until she saw us.

I saw the scene slowly register in her face as she looked from the mess on the floor to Thomas' half undone codpiece, him standing between my legs and my dress up around my waist. She glanced at my loose corset, which exposed far more than any stepfather should see.

Once she had seen it all, she whipped around, her pregnant belly banging into the door as she hurried from the room, clutching at her abdomen.

Thomas looked at me and all my exposed parts, his eyes full of deep frustration. Not guilt or sorrow: frustration. He quickly backed away and went after her, retying his codpiece as he ran.

K atherine's eyes ran up and down me and I did not meet her stare. I was of course humiliated, but only because I was caught. What happened had built so gradually that any feelings of remorse had been easily set aside.

Katherine grudgingly recognized that Thomas was the pursuer in all of this, for she called me "an innocent youth only trying to do as she had bade me do." However, she did go on and on about how I had chosen badly, asking how I could receive attention from a married man and my stepfather. I had no answers for her. It would have been completely inappropriate for me to remind her that she'd married the biggest scoundrel ever to enter my father's court. Not even I would have expected him to keep his vows had I married him. Still, I did not fully understand how I'd talked myself into allowing it either.

She also insisted on knowing if I had succumbed.

"No, you saved me stepmother, for it would have happened that very moment had you not walked in." These were the only words I said in our interview. As Katherine continued to preach at me, I reviewed in my mind my actions and wondered at my stupidity. How did I think the situation would end? He was married, and to a woman I loved and respected. My only answer was that I hadn't thought of it. It was all about the game, the education, the vengeance.

Also, I realized what a sacrilegious girl I was, for I did not ever truly recognize the marriage. I had decided long ago that Thomas would be mine and that was where my mind had remained. I did not care about anything other than the way he made me feel and what he taught me and what I wanted. Selfish, stupid, lustful girl!

Only now could my mind see the potential consequences

to what Katherine called my fragile reputation. I felt acutely the cost of my actions as she told me I would be put out of her house. Sent to live without all that knew me and loved me.

When she was finished with me, I felt the long consuming madness of lust finally lose its control, and for the first time since meeting the man called Admiral Thomas Seymour over two years ago, I was in my own mind.

Before I left, I apologized profusely and expressed my love and gratitude to Katherine.

Also, in that moment, I vowed that I would never again use my power to induce love or passion, or any emotion such as these. They were too powerful, and as I looked at my own actions, I began to believe that God had naturally given mankind sufficient amounts of these emotions to cause problems enough to last a lifetime. I need not aggravate the matter.

EPISODE 7

June 1548
Cheshunt, Hertfordshire

Visiting Sir Anthony Denny and his wife, Joan Champernon Denny, was Kat's idea. Joan was Kat's sister and their manor in Cheshunt seemed the ideal place for me to ride out the tide of disgrace that resulted from my actions with Thomas. Denny was all a-dither about it and instantly began constructing a plan to halt the gossip, bless his practical heart!

Edward had heard of the debacle and sent me a letter of deep censure, which was exceptionally difficult for me, for it meant not only that I had displeased my king and brother, but that the scandal was out in the open. Any visitors the Denny's had seemed to look at me with disdain, princess or not, and I began to feel the injury in my heart.

I feared that I had become too vain a girl, for when I learned the mood of the people of my country and the atmosphere in court, I felt that all hated me and would like nothing better than to be done with me. It was in this moment that I realized that my actions had consequences that could be felt throughout the entire realm. I was the princess, and though I felt as if I lived a secluded life, I found that I was not alone with my sins. Everyone seemed aware of what I was doing.

What did they think of me? After several letters from court describing these exact sentiments, I felt so humiliated that I hid in my room for days. I wished I could march myself into court and use my power on the lot of them.

A further detriment to my mood was that only days after arriving, Doctor Grindal left us, for he had yet again contracted the plague and was very sick. I hoped that he would get better and that I could resume my studies, for I needed something to take my mind off my misery.

Before the second week in Cheshunt had ended, I received a different kind of visitor. I was in the sitting room on the front side of the house gazing out the window when a man on horseback appeared. It took me all of one minute to recognize the man's seat and I was running out of the house and down the lawn toward him.

Robert. It was Robert.

He had come to me, though I was censured. Though I was in the deepest abyss, he had come, and this time I would not be angry with him. This time I would throw myself at his mercy and beg him to be my friend and talk with me in the old way, so that I might heal somewhat from this cruel situation.

He did see me for he made his way toward me, and when he was close he leapt out of his saddle and came to me. Tears were streaming down my face and I could not catch my breath.

"Robert! Oh Robert!" I flung myself into his arms and my sobbing heightened as I smelled the earthy odor that I loved so well and felt his familiar arms encircling me and patting me in his special way. "Will you ever forgive me?" I asked, and looked into his face through my tears.

How could anyone be as beautiful as he was?

His face was gaunt and serious, but I saw love in his eyes and it gave me hope. When he spoke, his voice no longer held any of the boyish tambours I knew so well. It was a man's voice that came out. "Do I need to forgive you?"

My eyes left his and I looked at the ground unable to comprehend how he would react to the truth of the situation. What gossip had he heard? His deep voice again brought my head up.

"Tell me all that has transpired—the truth of it, Elizabeth." He whispered, as if to himself, "Though it may be painful for both of us."

After pulling him and his horse into the shade, I told him everything, every tiny horrid detail, except of course the part where I used my power against Thomas. I saw his face turn whiter and whiter with each explicit scene and his hands were in white-knuckled fists. I described how strange it all felt, like it was not me doing the actions. How I did not like it. How it was not all I thought it should be. Though my cheeks burned so hot with shame that I could not meet Robert's eyes for several long minutes, I told him of my obsession with Thomas and how it grew and changed. How educative it all was, but when I saw that he did not appreciate my need to educate myself this way, quickly I added how out of control I felt. How almost possessed I seemed to myself.

How could I help but tell him everything? It was so relieving to finally talk to someone about it. I felt liberated just saying the words and felt as if now that they were said I could absolutely leave them behind.

When I was finished Robert looked at me and spoke the first words he had since I started. "That is all?" I sensed a bit of relief in his attitude and it gave me hope. "He did not—you are still"—he cleared his throat and wiped his sweaty palms on his hose—"he did not violate you any further?"

I looked at him with shock. I had just told him! "No, Robert. No! We were caught."

"I can understand wanting to, Elizabeth. We are all human," he said, though he looked at me with a bit of something in his eye that told me he was not entirely sure what I was. "Do you think you are the only one who has been tempted with the carnal?" His cheeks flushed, and he said quietly, "Sometimes I feel like it is a raging river and I am thigh high in it. All I need do is take one step and I will be swept away and drowned, only the drowning would be pleasurable. It takes herculean strength to not take that step. I know, my Lady. I know." Now it was his turn to be embarrassed.

Partly to put him at ease and partly to let him know that once again we had thought of something in exactly the same terms, I took his hand and said in a thoughtful tone, "Precisely." When he looked at me, I smiled and nodded my head once with over-exuberance.

He smiled too. It was only a slight upturn of his perfectly proportioned lips, but a smile still. I had forgotten how ideal his face was and I could not take my eyes from him. He searched my face as well before becoming excessively serious.

"My brothers tell me to give in, Elizabeth. They say it is natural, but I do not believe it is so. I believe that we should do as God asks us and keep ourselves virtuous until we are married. That is what I intend on doing." Then his eyes asked me if I intended to do the same.

I wanted to answer him, but I did not know what I felt. I knew him to be right, but I wanted that river. Part of me wanted to be neck deep in it. I struggled but said nothing, only looked down at our intertwined hands and then back to his gloriously beautiful eyes.

He kept his eyes on mine and soon he took a deep breath in. I felt his fingers tighten around my small hand and suddenly my heart started thudding, blood rushing to my cheeks. Desire began to spread its bittersweet tentacles through my insides, yet there was something that felt very different. Instead of the hunger starting deep within me, it seemed to reach out from my heart, sweeping smoothly—not violently—along my veins, warming me like the rays of a beautiful, yearned-for sunrise.

The feeling did not abate. It only intensified, and I knew that if I did not look away from him that moment…but I did not look away and then Robert's hand was out of mine and it was on my face. Softly he brushed my cheek and pushed a wayward hair back. His lips moved as if to say something, yet his voice did not work and I could not stop myself from wondering how those lips would taste; how embracing him would feel, not as a friend but as a lover. As these thoughts came to me, I realized I was just a lustful girl. Or was it something other than lust this time? It felt very different.

It did not matter. What I needed was to get control of myself somehow. I would not push myself on a boy I cared so deeply about, for had he not just told me he wanted to be virtuous? Shame for my thoughts almost sent me into tears again.

Quickly I looked away. My eyes squeezed shut as my mind demanded that my body calm down. I forced myself to talk. "Robert, am I truly forgiven for so blatant a misstep? Can you still love me—as a sister, I mean?"

I stumbled over the words. Was it love that I had just now felt?

"I see nothing that I need to forgive. You are not betrothed to me and you cannot be faulted, no matter what my feelings are. You were facing the same temptations I fight every day. Perhaps I have been a tad more successful in the fight of late, but I do not know how I would have fared if in your situation." He took my hand again. "I am just so glad that nothing more took place, for I know your fears and I would not want you to face them without someone by your side that could help you get through them." He looked embarrassed.

Robert brought everything full circle with this speech. He was too good. I did not deserve him at all. He spoke so much like a man—the man that, I suppose, I had always known he would be. It was so strange to see him this way. "For how long are you here?"

"I could stay with father at Hampton. It is not that far, but I have not seen you in so long I hate the thought of being even that distance away. Do you think it would be improper if I petitioned Sir Anthony to stay a night or two here?"

"Oh Robert, I think that would be wonderful. Let us go ask him right this minute."

Sir Anthony knew Robert, but considering the circumstances, he was uncertain whether to allow him to stay until after Kat vouched for him.

"They are only dearest friends. I will stay by their side the entire visit. I promise you, my brother, nothing shameful will happen between these two."

Sir Anthony agreed to let him stay a few days, though he watched us with hesitation and anxiety in his eyes. Kat or Blanche stayed with us at all times, which I was glad of so that they could report on my good behavior to Sir Anthony. Hopefully he would in return report me to the King in a good light.

The feelings between Robert and I were the same, yet deeper, more intimate, and that changed the mood of our activities. Though we acted the part, I knew that we were no longer only friends. We rode horses and talked, but we no longer played as we always had.

When normally I would have asked Robert to race through the meadow and frighten larks, now we walked through the meadow and he would pick interesting leaves or small flowers to stick in my hair. Then he would say, "I love the colors of summer in your strawberry curls."

In the old times when we wanted a picnic, we would just take the food out of doors. Now we combed the grounds for the most beautiful spot and set it all up as if we were playing house.

We played chess, and instead of focusing on winning, Robert would be a gentleman and let me win more often than skill alone could procure. Secretly I did the same. It is amazing either one of us won with both of us trying to lose.

However, the biggest change of all was in the intense talking, playful bantering, and blatant flirting that had ever accompanied our friendship. Robert had always complimented me outrageously in front of other people, but now all that he said held a ring of truth and not the feel of a courtier. He had either perfected the craft or he was making love to me in earnest. I tried not to think of which it could be.

When it came time for him to leave, I snuggled myself into his neck and wept. I did not want him to go. I desired his company more than that of any other person I had ever known. The thought of facing the tide of rumors alone was very discomforting as well. I had all but forgotten them while he was here and now misery would be my companion, it seemed, until I was once again with him.

EPISODE 8

September 1548
Cheshunt, Hertfordshire

Only a few days into September, we received word that Doctor Grindal had died from the plague. It was also told us that my new tutor was to be the glorious Roger Ascham, who would join me soon. In the meantime, I was to receive some tutelage from Sir Denny himself. I would return to Hatfield in February, and Robert would be joining me again in my studies in March. He would bring his tutor, Doctor John Dee, who was very well spoken of.

Perhaps Edward did love me still, if this was his doing. This made my hopes heighten, for spring was not that far off and then Robert would be here. It was the first bit of goodness I had had in quite some time, though it did seem that Edward was purposely keeping me here in exile. A six-month punishment for kissing and flirting with a married man did seem rather harsh, I thought, but then I remembered Edward's stinging letter and reconsidered.

I suppose my punishment was just.

The very next day my happy mood was dashed yet again as I received the shocking news that my dear stepmother, the dowager queen, Katherine Parr, was a week dead. She had died from childbirth fever. Even more horrid, the day after this dreadful news arrived, we received an unwanted visitor.

I was walking past the small sitting room adjacent to the door when I heard Sir Anthony speaking in a tone I had never before heard from his mouth. I stopped at the door to listen and was shocked when I heard another voice that I would recognize anywhere.

It was Thomas.

"You are not her guardian, sir, and I can see her if I choose. Now summon her this instant." His voice was pompous and aggravated and instantly my mind found the memory of our last tryst. I began to breathe hard, like I was scared. My hands trembled, my head spun. Had the beast of lust I thought was slain returned? I did not know, but I did know that seeing Thomas was the last thing I wanted. Being near him would bring more pain than pleasure. Come to think on it, he really hadn't brought me any pleasure, only the censure of those I loved and guilt and shame and a knowledge of how *not* to use my power.

I heard words then that raced a tendril of dread up my back.

"I mean to have her as my wife, now that Katherine is dead. I went to the king this very day and put before him my suit. I have heard the most ghastly rumors, including one that she is pregnant with my child. Of course, they are all false— you yourself could testify to the fact—but I cannot help thinking how everything would be cleared up with our marriage. Besides, I love the girl. I cannot help myself. I do."

I was in shock. This statement completely knocked me off

balance. Thomas loved me? Could it be possible that this rogue of a man had finally found someone to calm him, and that woman was me? No, no that was not possible. The prospect of being his wife would be the absolute worst thing I could think of. How could I stop it from happening?

I had to think. I needed time to consider. To come up with a plan. I raced out of the house and to a small patch of trees near the road where a small stone bench nestled down in the bushes and where I could not be seen from the house.

The strangest thing filled my mind as I ran: Robert's face. His glorious, sunlit face. What would he think if I was forced to marry Thomas?

I flung that idea right out of my head, but part of it lingered, saying, *Robert would be devastated.* Why? *Why should Robert care whom I marry*, I asked the part of myself that seemed wiser than anything. *Because,* it answered, *Robert is the one that truly loves you.*

The idea didn't shock me, but I'd never allowed myself to think on it. Now that I had two loves to compare, I could see that Thomas had said he loved me, and as soon as he was free he came to me and wanted to ask me for my hand. But what had he done while he was married to another woman who thought he loved her? What had he done in court? I recalled how he'd worn me down and pressured me. That did not feel like love.

Robert loves you, my mind said again, and this time I repeated the words aloud: "Robert loves me." And then my mind was filled with flashes of Robert. I saw the smile on his face when he let me win a game of chess. The concentration he displayed when discussing our Lord. The freedom in his body when he rode his horse alongside me. The mischievous look in his eye when he flattered me. The truth his voice held as he spoke of caring for me, and the conscientious way he considered me. The quiet way he listened to me.

Then there was his beauty and the way he made my body feel. Loved and happy, yes, yet still there was desire. I only wanted to be with him, to touch his perfect face, to kiss him tenderly.

I thought of all the times he had been there for me, in school, in play, when I was sad, when I was happy. How loyal he was. I never had to use my power on him because he was always on my side.

I cared so much for Robert, if he was happy or sad. I cared if he thought badly of me. I thought of him always and missed him when he was gone.

Tears ran down my cheeks for I now knew that he was not the only one in love. I was in love with Robert. I had been all along.

And these feelings were nothing like what I'd felt with Thomas. No, I wanted Robert in the right way, the way that would insure happiness between two people for the span of a lifetime. I was not desperate at all; I was peaceful and blissful. I knew that if Robert asked me to marry him in that moment, I would have gladly said yes. If he asked me to bear him children, I would have cheerfully done it. I loved him more than I feared anything, and I would do all I could to make him happy. I smiled to myself through my tears, for what else could I do? I had found the one person I would love forever, and not only was he my best friend, but he had returned my love long before I was wise enough to see it.

No longer could Thomas hold sway in my heart—if I had ever had a place for him there. He did not love me. He wanted me, and though he'd wanted me before I'd manipulated him, the intensity of his ardor had to be a result of my trifling with his emotions. I wondered now if I could undo what I had done?

This brought my mind to an equally hard subject. I'd scarcely let myself think of how culpable I was in all of this. It was too painful, too shameful to think of it. I did not, while under Thomas's spell, want to admit that he'd not been as affected by me as I was by him. Now that I had my heart and mind in its proper place, I looked upon my actions with abhorrence and I looked upon my feelings with mystification. I would never be fooled by lust masquerading as love again. I knew the difference now.

I did realize that without this experience I might never had understood myself or this vein of my power, so my regret was tinged with scientific justification. And it had brought about something wonderful. Realization that I loved Robert Dudley.

I wanted to sing it to the world.

And I think the world would be happy for me.

I did not see Thomas before he left. I wanted to at least get close to him, so I could try to undo my spell over him, but Kat and Denny made sure that was impossible. Still in pursuit of marriage, Thomas immediately began writing Sir Thomas Parry, my cofferer, for details of my estates and inheritance. He was most confident that I would be happy to marry him and wrote a few lines to me stating his intentions.

My dearest Rosebud,

Though the last months have been difficult, I admit the

*only thing positive in all these circumstances is that I
will finally be able to make you mine. I know how
desperately we both want it to be so, thus I will start
the process of gaining your hand as soon as humanly
possible.*

With undying love,

*Admiral Thomas Seymour
1st Baron Seymour of Sudeley
Loyal servant to the King*

To this I did not reply. Kat was confused by the letter and
my reaction, but settled that it would not be so bad to be
married to the Admiral, and soon was convinced that I should
go through with it, if only to mend my reputation. Kat was
beguiled by Thomas. I understood the allure.

So I kept my tongue and my peace. I would save it for the
chance of coming face to face with the despicable man. I felt
I had worked out a way to undo what I had done and hoped I
had the chance to make it right. It was interesting to know
how long my influence lasted though.

And more interesting to me was how in the world my
mother lost control of my father. It didn't seem possible. The
regret I felt began to tax me. And I lay awake nights
wondering if I could release Thomas from the bond.

I received a letter at least once a week from him, as well
did Thomas Parry. Each letter to me professed his love and
asked why I had not written back. Each letter to Master Parry
asked of my fortune and how best to blend the two, his and
mine. Of course, he was very concerned with that facet.

Princess Elizabeth,

*It distresses me that I have not heard from you, I
wonder if you are receiving my letters. All I can say is
that I long to see you and touch you. Every feeling
demands that I will do both soon for it is the dearest
wish of my heart to be with you forever. Think back on
our times together and I know that you will also
realize how you long to be with me. Please send my
man with a reply, for I long to see your words
on paper.*

Yours etc.

After this letter, Kat insisted that I write the man back, for
the courier said he was directed not to leave without a reply.

Dear Admiral,

*Thank you for your letters and I hope that you are in
good health. It seems as if you know my heart better
than I. Though your proposals flatter me, I fear I
cannot do any such thing without the permission of
the council and the king.*

*Also, if you might oblige, kindly quell some of the
rumors about us, for you know most have not a scrap
of truth.*

*Sincerely,
Elizabeth*

The rumor that I was pregnant with Thomas' child was

most disconcerting and I wanted it stopped more than anything. Again, I wished there was some way I could use my power on many minds a great distance from me. It just would not be so. Therefore, I had to do what I could the usual way, and so I asked my companions if they would help me. Sir Anthony, Kat, and I each wrote to the king and to the Lord Protector, Edward Seymour, who was Thomas' brother, pleading with them to stop the gossip. However, weeks went by and they did nothing that we could tell of.

Kat and I thought for certain that Thomas would have talked to the council by now, but when communication between him and Thomas Parry continued through October and November, I began to wonder.

Then in the last week of November, I received two letters, one from Thomas and the other from Robert. This was the first I had heard from Robert since I decided that I was in love with him and I could not believe the excitement I felt while opening it.

My Princess and dearest Elizabeth,

I hope you are well and happy. I also hope that all your family is in good health. I miss you terribly and hope that I still hold a place in your heart.

I have some news from Father that is highly alarming. The Admiral has not asked the king for your hand, for the king has put it about that he would not sanction such a union, that you are in exile and will remain so until he is convinced you have been properly chastened.

However, Father has uncovered a plot orchestrated by

Admiral Seymour himself. He plans to wed you and to
wed the king to Lady Jane Grey. He will then have
authority over us all and he is prepared not only to
take down his own brother but to kidnap the king in
order to bring to pass his plans.

Father is taking measures to see that this does not
happen, and indeed I will say if things go as we all
hope he will have done you and the king a great
service indeed.

Do not show anyone this note and please burn it when
you have read it all.

I hope that I will see you soon, and again that you are
well and in better humor than your situation dictates.

Yours,
Robin

What was Thomas thinking? Kidnapping the king and
forcing him to marry when he was but ten? I suppose it was
not completely unheard of, but Thomas doing it? The man
must be mad. At that point I opened the other letter.

My dear sweet Rosebud,

I hope to taste of your sweetness in a very short time.
I have a plan to get all done and settled in a very
pleasing manner. You will be so proud to be my wife
and we will have the power to squash any rumors that
fly about us.

Remember what you said to me when we were last together? Those words repeat in my mind and spur me forward. It is for you that I become brave. It is for you that I stretch myself to greater heights.

Your loving,
Admiral

The man was certainly audacious. I could not believe him laying at my feet the responsibility of his actions. I was not the cause for any of it.

And then I thought of the way in which I had used my power on him.

Now that Katherine was out of his life, he had no more distractions and he could give himself wholly to my manipulation without even knowing that was what he was doing. Fear froze my bones. What if I was responsible? I tossed the parchment into the fire and set myself down to writing him a carefully worded letter.

Dear Admiral,

I hope that you are in good health. You must know that I will not do anything without the approval of the council, for our innocent foolishness has brought shame upon both our heads and I do not intend to repeat that shame or worsen it. I only wish to be a loyal subject. I hope that you will consider all you do carefully and not do anything out of the ordinary or anything that might put your person in danger.

I love my brother the king, and hope he is well. Since you have occasion to see him and I do not, I hope that

you would consider yourself one that would keep him
happy and safe, as a good uncle would. He does
deserve to have all good things for he is such a good
boy. Your brother has done an excellent job in
protecting him from anyone that would lead him
astray. I commend his good work and hope he would
prosecute anyone in defiance of this protection.

Elizabeth

That would have to do, for I could not say more. I only
hoped that he would get my meaning. Why, oh why, couldn't
I send my manipulations with my word in ink. This would all
be over if I could.

That night, I dreamt that I was before a livid Mary, her
skin all white and sickly, and her hair loose and stringy. The
signet ring of Princes encircled her first finger. She was
queen. She yelled madly at me and I cowered in ashamed
tears as she listed my sins, highlighting the long past debacle
with Thomas Seymour.

I knelt and begged her to forgive me as I kissed her ring,
pledging fealty to her and the crown.

I awoke knowing that one day that exact situation would
be upon me, and if I did not act in that exact way, I would die.
I shivered and gathered my sweaty sheets around me as I
repeated the dream to myself and considered the implications
this foretelling had for Edward.

I received many more love letters from Thomas before Christmas, each one more vile than the previous, yet none of them mentioned my warnings. Then in January, I received a very short note from Robert.

Elizabeth,

Watch, my friend, and be wary. Things are afoot that could do you harm. I miss you.

With concern,
Robin

His words left me feeling cold inside. My life had changed by the events that involved Thomas. I could feel the mood of those around me. I had hoped that no one else would be affected by the strange madness that had taken control of my body while living in my stepmother's house, but harm had been done and I felt that I would pay even more for my uncontrolled lust one way or another.

EPISODE 9

February 1549
Hatfield House, Hertfordshire

As I feared, Thomas either did not understand or he did not heed me, for in January, Robert's father, John Dudley, had gained enough support to imprison Thomas in the Tower and begin a trial, the charges being thus: embezzlement, theft, and treason.

I was told that my brother testified to the correctness of the charges and my world began to spin out of control.

Thomas's plot to marry me and kidnap the king was soon made known, and Kat and Thomas Parry were themselves detained by Sir Anthony Denny, Kat's own brother-in-law and our host. Of course, he was pushed into the situation when several armed men came knocking at his door. These rough men were sent to learn of my involvement in the plot, and taking Kat and Master Parry were their way of getting to the information.

New rumors were heard daily by the servants and read in letter and pamphlet form. I was in league with Thomas. I was trying to usurp the throne. I was with child. I murdered Katherine. I was evil. I was my mother's daughter. This last made me angrier than the others.

But it was the whole affair with Thomas which was the biggest thorn in my side, for no one even bothered to get my account of this or any matter. Or paid attention to the fact that I loved my brother and had never maneuvered politically, or that I was changed and trying. I was just a tarnished young woman, not any longer even a princess in their eyes.

Then the worst possible and unexpected thing happened. Lord Robert Tyrwhitt, the Master of the Horse while my father was yet alive, came to see me at Hatfield to interrogate me. I knew that the potential charges were great and that it could be my head on the chopping block if this man believed me to be a coconspirator against my brother the king.

He was a cold, cruel man, harsh in appearance, dress, and manner. He wanted me to be guilty. And this was who my brother sent.

When the appointed interview came, I was so flustered and nervous by his manner that I could not say a word to the man. I was so angered by his tone and his condescending address that my wits were completely taken from me. I stammered and wept as he accused, berated, and demanded, yet nothing was confessed and no sentence was delivered.

In desperation, I pulled my power to me, hoping that I would be able to make him go away. I pushed the words of my innocence at him. But for the first time, I saw the light go out as it touched the man. I tried again and again, but the light would not stay lit once it entered the man's space.

I was beside myself with trepidation. What had happened? How was I to get out of this without the help of my gifts?

After the interrogation, I wondered at my cowed behavior,

for now that the man had gone out of my sight and his accusing words repeated in my mind, I had a response to each. I berated myself harshly and wished he could have been fetched back at that moment when my rage could be used to my benefit.

But I would get my chance, for he interviewed me many times in the preceding weeks, and I was able to hold myself together on those occasions and answer him honestly. But I was never able to manipulate him with my power. And there was nothing to say except that I was not involved in the plot, nor had I accepted any marriage proposal. I had no proof but my own words.

We were at an impasse.

After getting nothing from me in these interviews, he stayed away for a fortnight. I used that time to determine what could possibly be happening with my gift. After easily manipulating several in my company, I came to the conclusion that Sir Robert Tyrwhitt must be so against me that his mind could not be touched.

When he came again, I was determined to control myself if only to see if I could get a little doubt in his mind and thus hopefully be able to use my gift. Besides, the man needed to be put in his place.

As I sat down across from him, I noticed that he seemed to be in better spirits as well. However, his first words cut my determination to dust.

"I have brought my wife to look after you until Lady Katherine can be returned. I am sure you will find her most pleasing, my Princess. She is at this moment settling her things in Lady Katherine's old chambers." He smiled and pulled some papers from his bag.

The shock of this information did not entirely tie my

tongue. I had enough wit to demand, "Where is Katherine Ashley and when will she be returned to me?"

Tyrwhitt straightened his rumpled doublet and said with a raised eyebrow, "It is I who will be asking the questions, my Princess. You must only worry about having answers this time." He always said "my Princess" with a sneer.

I glared at him haughtily and clenched my teeth together.

He must have understood that I would not be moved to speak until I knew the answer to my question, for soon he acquiesced in a matter-of-fact voice. "She and Thomas Parry are being held in the Tower, and they will not be returned until we are satisfied that they have committed no crimes."

I gasped. The Tower. How I feared that place, for no person left unscathed. Tears filled my eyes and I did not realize I was crying until Tyrwhitt handed me a handkerchief. He did not pause though, for he must take his advantages when he could. He took two pieces of parchment and held them up for me to see. They were filled with words, stamped at the bottom, and official looking. The one on top was in a hand I knew as well as my own.

"What is this?" I said through my tears. "Are they confessions? Did Kat confess?"

Tyrwhitt smiled at me as if he had won a great game. "Yes, they are confessions."

That made me cry even harder. "Is Kat still alive, you false wretch? She would have to be dead from torture if she truly confessed to any sort of involvement in this horrid plot."

That changed Tyrwhitt's smile and I took the papers from his hand. He snatched them back hastily and said, "I would have you tell me of all your involvement with Admiral Thomas Seymour over the last year, my Lady Princess." He tried to make his voice kindly, though all he managed to do was twist his mouth so that he looked like a stifled bear.

I sniffed at him, but I knew that I had to tell all I knew, for this situation had just gotten very serious for me. Kat was in the Tower, and for all I knew only I could save her. "I have only had letters from him since September. I have kept them all, but I do not believe it necessary for you to read them. All they say is how he loves me and wants to marry me. I am sure you know that I would not consent to anything without the council's approval. Even if I wanted to marry the blathering fool, I would not sink that low." I sniffed and wiped my nose with his handkerchief.

"You say that you do not want to marry the Admiral, yet you did have an affair with him this past year." He did not look ashamed at his words, only angry.

"I did not, not in the way everyone wants to make it out to be." I said with sincere shock. How dare this man say such a scandalous thing right in front of me. It would have been true had we not been caught, but the audacity of this man was beyond anything I had seen.

He shook the papers and yelled, "Katherine Ashley admits to seeing you romp with him in your bed and she also told us of a situation where she caught him cutting your dress off." A light shone in his eyes and I became certain that he was enjoying this. "Both she and Master Parry state that the Admiral planned to marry you and even asked after your accounts. Why would such a thing be done if there were no agreements of marriage?"

Poor Kat. What had they done to her to make her confess such useless yet personally disgraceful things? I lifted my head indignantly and said, "I do not have to confess to you or any other person the circumstances of my life. You are not here to question me about this matter. I do have one confession to make and it is on point: I had nothing to do with this plot against the king. I never would have involved myself in something such as this, especially not now when I am already exiled. Nothing could induce me to move against my beloved Edward. Nothing. Especially not something so silly as getting a husband. Furthermore, why would I go against the wishes of my beloved father? Sir, you accuse me of betraying two of the dearest men in the world. I would not do it!"

"What if the council were to give their consent to marry him?" he said gently.

"Then I suppose I would have to do whatever thing God put into my head at that time," I said shortly and with a grimace on my face.

"But you do not say you would not." He paused, seeming moved for a moment by my words but still convinced he had the right of it. "The point I am trying to make is whether you are in the Admiral's pocket so deeply that you have—perhaps unknowingly—aided or encouraged him to usurp the Lord Guardian and take control of the king. Your friends do not believe that you are impartial to the Admiral as you now claim." He looked at the confessions. "Lady Katherine in particular recounts several circumstances that show how in his power you were."

"'Were' is the correct word, my good sir. Were! Yet it has been some time now since I have overcome the follies of my earlier youth. I am certain that Kat also told of my reluctance to even reply to the Admiral's recent letters. She practically forced me to do it. She wanted me to marry him in order to clear my name. But I have proof enough that I have committed no sin. I am certain you have seen my letters to the Admiral. There is no affection in them. There is only acknowledgment and warning."

"Warning you say. Warning of what? Admit it girl, you knew of his plans and were party to them." Tyrwhitt was all in a rage now for he thought he had found the weak link in my story.

I gritted my teeth, but I could not stop the tears from flowing down my face. It was all so humiliating and evil for him to pounce on my every word and twist them to fit his own ends. And how dare he call me girl! Instinctively I called the power of the light to me and felt its sure presence, but I had to be so careful if I was to instill doubt in his mind.

The light brought peace. What would be would be, and if I were to be a servant of the Most High God, he would see me through this and much worse as he raised me to the place he needed me in.

I dried my eyes and looked calmly at my interrogator. "I am not the only person who was aware of the stupidity of Admiral Thomas Seymour. Who is the man that has brought him down?"

Tyrwhitt's eyes narrowed. "I have the feeling that you know who it was as well as I."

"Does not everyone now know? What I am saying is that it was not a very good secret that Thomas was in trouble. If you have read the two letters I sent him, you will understand instantly what I did about what I knew."

Awkwardly, the man pulled out of his bag the letters in question.

"Yes," I said as I eyed them dubiously. "It is the longer of the two. Read it out if you must, I will wait."

He did read it and I saw the understanding dawn on his face as now the context of the letter was clear to him. When he looked up at me I saw uncertainty in his eyes.

"I still believe that you and your friends have made a pact to tell the same story and that you were involved somehow," he said, but his voice did not contain the strength it had before.

"I am not interested in what you believe, sir. I am interested in the truth, as any child of God should be. As you can see, I told the Admiral that he was a fool and that I would do nothing without the council's permission, which I hoped he would never get. I had nothing to do with this plot. I barely have anything to do with the Admiral, except the role I play in his own mind." I decided now was the time to push my advantage. I gathered the light and said the words that I hoped would convince the man or rather motivate him to move on.

"Now go back to the court and tell them you found me innocent of any wrong doing." Then I quickly added before sending the light. "Also let them know that the rumors of pregnancy could not be true. For if it were so, I would have been in my birthing bed the first time you saw me." I shoved the light at him a little more violently than was necessary, but I was angry.

He needed no more than that. I saw the expression in his eyes change as he said, "I can see now that you were completely uninvolved. I am sorry to have wasted your time and I pray that you have not been offended by my words or manners." He smiled at me and rose. Then as quickly as he had arrived, he bowed his way out.

I sat in my chair for a long moment, wondering if I'd needed to use my power. I believed that perhaps I could have gotten my own self out of trouble. As these thoughts and ponderings came to me, I drew another line for myself. A line that involved using my power as only a last resort. God had given me a sharp mind and a mostly guileless attitude. I could prove myself without power. Especially when I was innocent.

Relieved as I was that the interrogation was over, I was soon cursing myself for not thinking to tell Sir Tyrwhitt to get Kat back for me, for now I had Lady Beth Tyrwhitt to deal with.

If Kat was the kindly butterfly that fluttered near my side, guiding me with quiet council, expressing love and befriending me in every situation, Lady Tyrwhitt was the watchdog always on duty, barking commands and growling at everything and everyone. She was a loathsome creature, always there in my ear, judging my every word and step, forcing me to spend all day in the schoolroom and all evening sewing. She was a mean gossip, taking every opportunity to slander Kat, denouncing her as unfit to be anyone's governess and even saying my ruin was the result of her ineffectual governing.

I despised the awful, sharp-nosed prattler more than I had despised anyone in my life. She was my true punishment for all my lustful fantasies, the worst punishment anyone could have pronounced.

The only good thing that came from Lady Tyrwhitt's presence was that I truly began to blossom under Doctor Ascham's style of tutelage. If I had seemed promising before, now, with so much of my day and effort extended to the books, I surpassed even his expectations.

I was further grateful to him for his hand in repairing my honor. He was a most discreet gossip and had many correspondents to whom his praise of me and my attitude did not go unaccounted.

When first at Cheshunt, Anthony Denny and Kat requested that I begin to repair my reputation by appearances, so I had taken to wearing the most plain and modest dresses with no jewelry except my mother's necklace, which mostly stayed hidden under high-necked frocks. My modest and virginal appearance was marked now by not only the friends of Dr. Ascham, but all those whom I saw. By the middle of February, I finally began to feel that I might be able to gain back my previous standing.

Only a few weeks later I received word that Thomas had been condemned and would be beheaded within the month. Shock and horror did not begin to describe the state I was in and there was no Kat to comfort me.

I wondered also who comforted Edward, for Thomas was his mother's brother. Killing one's uncle was not an easy task, I ventured, and I wished I could write to him and comfort him as inappropriate as that might seem.

Everything was happening so quickly and as the time grew closer and the reality of it all reached my heart, I fretted in earnest over Thomas. I did not want him to die, for if he was put to death it would be—in a very real way—my fault. His actions were a result of my manipulation. How could I know that he would stoop to such foolish actions? I could not.

Still, there was the helplessness of being able to do nothing to stop him. I'd used my gift so horridly that a fear of it began. That and a resolution to never act thus again.

When I thought of how this punishment might spread to that of Kat and Master Parry, I couldn't do anything but kneel at my prayer bench and beg God to spare them from the gallows. I wearied Sir Tyrwhitt and the Lord Protector with inquires and letters about them, but it seemed that they were quite forgotten for all of London was suddenly in turmoil. It appeared that the French were planning to come against us at

Boulogne-sur-Mer, and that they had also landed in Edin-burgh to help the Scottish fight us. Small rebellions were popping up all over the country, proving that the English were upset with their new king and his Lord Protector.

It did not take a genius to see where these troubles would take us. Unless Lord Edward Seymour could gather his forces, squash the rebellions, and keep control of my brother in the process, he was going to fall from the high position he now had, and I knew who would take his place.

EPISODE 10

March 1549
Hatfield House, Hertfordshire

Robert should have come to Hatfield by now for it was the middle of March and he was due at the beginning. His absence seemed to prove my theory that power at court was changing hands.

I waited for word from him, but instead only received word that Admiral Thomas Seymour was dead. He did not die easily, but the deed was done. I was surprised at the depth of my sorrow, but I could not show it, for Lady Tyrwhitt waited for my grief to overwhelm me and thus, in her eyes, condemn me. I kept it inside and analyzed it.

My conclusion was that I was not sadder for his death than any other person I knew well, but with his demise, my guilt and my fear increased exponentially, especially for Kat and Master Parry. If the Lord Protector and Edward could condemn and kill his own brother and uncle, would he stay his hand for two servants, whether they be innocent or not?

I begged Sir Robert Tyrwhitt, my jailer, to send for them

to return. Still he would not, and furthermore he seemed annoyed at my deep devotion to Kat. If the man knew anything about loving a person, he certainly had fooled me, for I saw him with his wife and the lack of affection was astounding.

Not that I could see a reason to be affectionate to the woman.

For several days, my thoughts turned often to Thomas. It was amazing the way his demise yet again cleared my mind. I did feel sorrow for him, but I also remembered the way his mouth had captured me, how his hands had caressed, and how his pompous air had drawn me to him. I vowed I would never again be seduced by dangerous, lustful men. I would be on my guard should I ever come face to face with one, for I now knew myself to be weak for a man with sweet breath, beautiful lips and hands, and roguish manners. Heaven help me, but I was, and now I could stay away.

"Thank you, Thomas Seymour, for teaching me such an important lesson, and may God have mercy on your soul," I whispered to myself before I drifted into sleep.

There I dreamt of my Robert. He was being crushed by something terribly heavy and I startled awake, barely able to find my breath and more worried for news of his whereabouts than ever before.

At the beginning of April, we received a letter informing us that Robert was training with the soldiers, for he was to help if needed with the civil unrest that seemed to be ravaging the countryside. With all the war that was about, there were not as many soldiers in

London as one would hope, thus many second and third sons were taking up the banner of England to help restore order.

Panic gripped my soul. I remembered my dream. What would I do if Robert was killed in battle without knowing my love for him? How could I live without him? It was not possible. I spent so much time at my prayer bench that I think even Lady Tyrwhitt was impressed. Whether she was or not, it seemed that she did treat me a bit more kindly.

At the end of April, Robert finally came.

While in the schoolroom one morning, I happened to see him and his horse charging down the lawn at a fast pace.

Hurriedly, I excused myself and was running to him before Lady Tyrwhitt could set aside her crocheting. I did not understand the woman's obsession with the needle.

It was still cold, but I did not even stop to pull on a shawl. I could not wait to see his face. I could not stand to know that he was coming to me and I was not going to him, so I ran. I could not think of his magnificent blue eyes without trembling and I could not imagine his quick smile without one of my own parting my lips. I did not care that I was not a girl any longer. Robin was here, and the faster I ran the quicker I could hold him and look into his face.

We met halfway down the lawn, my shoes and dress now wet with the dew that still clung to the cold, shade-covered grass. The dampness sent a chill down my back as I waited for Robert to dismount. He approached me slowly and his face held the beautiful smile I loved so much. His eyes studied me in a cautious manner. With a squeak of excitement, I threw myself at him and squeezed him so tightly that I was afraid I would hurt him.

He laughed and said, "It is good to see you too, my Princess."

I swooned a little at the smell of him: cold air, burning wood, and soap.

"Oh Robert, I am so happy to see you! You cannot understand how content I am right now, holding you in my arms." I realized what I was saying and how strange I must sound to him, as he did not yet know of my secret love. Instantly my cheeks flushed, and I pushed myself away from him, hoping I had not appeared a shameless hussy. Then I laughed nervously and quickly said, "How was that? As good as any courtier welcoming home her beloved soldier?"

His face went through several emotions, but his eyes never stopped evaluating me. Finally, he settled into his courtier manner and said, "Yes, my Lady. A welcome only a prince could expect of his princess." And he bowed slightly.

What in the world was that supposed to mean? I cursed my lack of self-control. I did not want him to turn into the courtier. I wanted him to be my Robin. When he rose and met my eyes, I finally saw what was there. He wanted to know how I fared now that the news of Thomas' death was known. He wanted to see how I was handling the tide of speculation surrounding me. I decided to put him at ease.

"Come now, Robert, you have not told me how wonderful I look, for I am sure you have heard that I only recently had a baby. The small child is inside, and Dr. Ascham watches her while I come and welcome you. He is marvelous with children." It did not take Robert but a moment to look relieved and to laugh heartily with me. I added for good measure, "I know that the death of the child's father was a shock for the whole country. However, I had been warned that it would happen, by the dearest and truest of friends, and have had plenty of time to gain the peace needed. I only pray that there is a place for the worst rogue of all history in the Kingdom of Heaven." I was making more light of the situation than I felt, just so Robert would not think I had feelings for Thomas still. Guilt pricked me as I did this.

"I am glad your wit has not been hampered by all of this and I am so glad to see you in such good spirits."

"You are here. How could I be anything but joyful? The world could be tumbling around me, but as long as I have my Robin to comfort me, I will smile and move forward." I meant these words, so fervently.

He laughed. "You must really be missing Kat." He misunderstood me, though he was right in a way. I did miss having a confidant. However, I let it pass and he continued. "I do bring some good news in that regard. She and Parry have been released, though they are not to return here."

To my shame I squealed again and wrapped my arms around him. "Truly, they are free? I do not even care if they cannot return if they will not die because of me! Oh Robert, I am so relieved," I gushed, not realizing until I was done that my lips had pressed against his bare neck as I spoke, and consequently a damp spot stood where the moisture from my mouth had rubbed onto his skin.

There was a moment of silence and I stayed in his arms, not wanting to show him how my cheeks burned. He was suddenly stiff and this time he gently pushed me away. As soon as I was out of his arms, his hand went to his neck, fingers touching the place my lips had been. His eyes changed in that moment and I saw something I recognized. Desire. Pure, unabashed desire. My cheeks continued to flush as I watched his moist fingertips curl into a fist and slowly move from his neck to his chest. It was then that I saw how he was breathing. His chest seemed to be heaving. I looked back to his eyes and had to quickly look away for I did not want to drown—not yet—and I knew that those blue pools of liquid desire would have me instantly should I let them.

"So," I said, desperately searching for something to say. "How was your—your training?" I still did not look at him. "Do you think you will be called to fight for God and country?" I frowned to myself and chanced a glance at him now.

Robert smiled at me, his face a picture of discipline and friendship, that smoldering desire completely gone. The admiration I had for him doubled. He was so good, so controlled, so beautiful. I felt my eyes exploring his face and my breath began to quicken. *No, no, no!* I told myself, just as Robert innocently took my hand and placed it over his arm.

"My Lady, you are freezing. Let's get you to the house and I will tell you all about my soldiering." He pulled off his riding cloak and set it on my shoulders. It was a bit muddy but very warm and it smelled of him. My heart sung with pleasure.

Once inside I asked, "Where are your servants?"

Robert cleared his throat and helped me lift his cloak off. "I rode ahead of them. I was eager to—to be done with traveling."

I smiled to myself. Robert could ride a horse all day, every day, for the rest of his life and be happy, so he did not want to admit that he was eager to see me. That was interesting. I led him over to the fire just as Lady Tyrwhitt came crashing into the sitting room.

"What on earth do you mean by—"

I cut her rampage short. "Lady Tyrwhitt, this is Robert Dudley. Robert, this is the Lady Tyrwhitt, Lord Robert Tyrwhitt's wife."

"We have met before," Robert said with a sweeping bow and a dazzling smile. "When I was ten, this lady was so kind as to paddle my bottom for stealing roses from her private garden for my mother. She taught me a valuable lesson about thievery. I might even have scars to remind me," he laughed congenially.

Her face was shocked for a moment, but she quickly covered it and said in her high voice, "Just as well. I hope you learned the lesson and have not had any more problems, for I would not have a problem turning you over my knee again if it were needed."

"I am sure that will not be necessary," Robert said in a tone that sounded oddly sweet, even coming from him. He did not like this woman either. A thought occurred to me, and without considering, I called my power to me. Stepping closer to Lady Tyrwhitt, I said, "Robert and I are only friends and I will be spending much of my free time with him. There will be no need to watch us so closely, for we play as innocently as children."

The light spun toward her and when she looked back at me, she nodded curtly and said, "Well I can see that you two have things to discuss. I will be over in the corner minding my needles." And with that, she promptly walked to the far edge of the room, plopped herself down in a chair, and began her concentrated sewing.

Still surrounded by light, I turned to Robert. It was then that I remembered that he could see the real me. His eyes were startled, and they ran up and down me like I was the most interesting thing he had ever seen. Hesitantly, he touched a golden, light-infused curl that had come loose at the nape of my neck. Tilting his head to the side for a better view, his fingers moved to my ear. Then he gently pressed his fingertips to my cheek.

His eyes never left what his fingers touched as he whispered, "You are so beautiful."

My heart raced, my blood pulsed, my cheeks flushed, and then I was releasing the light. He looked strange standing there with his head tilted, his hand still raised, and a look of wonder in his eyes. After a moment he dropped his hand and spoke.

"What—what are—"

I cut him off. "Have we not canvassed this subject?" I wanted desperately to tell him everything. He thought I was beautiful in my strange power and I could tell that it was not just curiosity that made him ask, but a desire to know me better and to understand me. But I just could not tell him. The words would not form. The thoughts would not organize. "I have already told you Robert, I cannot—not yet."

I saw disappointment flash in his eyes, yet it was gone with a blink. He cleared his throat, straightened his coat, and casually walked over to the fire, now speaking conversationally. "Father sent me to a camp that is set up just outside of London Township, and there we trained in the skills of warfare. The sword, bayonet, the pistol, and shotgun were all expounded. I saw Barnaby there. Can you believe it? Barnaby, after all this time. He looked well and asked after you, of course. I told him all I knew of you and he begged me to give you his greetings."

I smoothed my face and exhaled deeply before joining him in front of the fire. "Thank you," I said softly. Then I continued loudly, "So did you best him in all this martial? I know the two of you have always had a competition between you."

He laughed gaily. "Yes, well Barnaby has grown. He is a half-a-foot taller than me and he has long, gangly arms that strike as quick as vipers. Consequently, I did not best him with the sword, but I am a better shot than he. And of course, no one is quite my equal on the horse—excepting you, my Lady." He smiled brightly and motioned for me to sit with him next to the fire. "I am not certain what we will be called to do, but I hope that it will not take me away from my studies too long. It seems as if ages have passed since we last were in the schoolroom together. Do you know if Lady Jane will be joining us?"

Instantly, jealousy raged in me. Jane was a very pretty little thing and I did not want her around taking Robert's attention, not now that I felt so close to him, so in love with him. "I hope not," I said frankly. "She would just be one more person to tell tales about me." I added that last so that I would not sound so mean about Jane.

"But my Lady, you and she are friends, and if you are not planning on doing anything scandalous then why should it matter if she joins our party? If anything, she can serve as another witness to your purity." As always, Robert tore my excuses apart and forced me to analyze my true motives. Perhaps my mind was planning something scandalous— something that involved him. Flashes of best forgotten dreams came to my mind. Robert played a central role in every iniquitous scene. How I longed to have those images come true. Without thought, I closed my eyes and gave over, for just a moment, to the sensations that raced through me and then I felt Robert's warm hand touch my arm.

He had crossed the small space between our chairs and was saying, "Elizabeth, are you alright?"

Lady Tyrwhitt pushed herself between Robert and me and began assessing me.

"I am fine. Quite well. I just had some unsettling thoughts. That is all." My eyes flashed to Robert, saw the pain on his face, and I once again chided myself. Would I never gain control over my lustfulness? Lady Tyrwhitt poked at me in a competent way which only made my annoyance mount quicker. I called the light to me and told her, "I am fine. Let me be." However, before I pushed the light to her,

her hands left me, and she turned to go to her chair. Relieved that she simply listened, I turned to Robert.

As expected, his eyes were filled with wonder and amazement. "Do not take it away," he whispered almost pitifully. "I only want to look at you. I will not ask any questions. Only let me see you like this right now. Let me memorize you." Sure that I would do as he asked, he sat back down in his chair and did not take his eyes off of me. I felt them following my every move, my every breath.

I looked over at Lady Tyrwhitt, who was busy with her needles, and could not bring myself to return my eyes to Robert. We already had so much history between us, so many feelings, that almost any interaction could take us to the place we longed in our hearts to go. Awkward silences and flushed cheeks told the story without words. It was as if someone had dowsed the air between us with alcohol. All that was needed was a spark and everything would go up in flames.

I did not understand how we were to study and live together when the span of half an hour had brought us here. At this rate we would have to get married, and soon, before both of us made choices that we would never regret…until we were caught.

Thankfully it was then that Dr. Belmain, our new French tutor entered and asked if we were ready for French. I gratefully jumped to my feet and went to the door, calling behind me in French, "Robert, will you be joining us? You could use the practice." I shot a smile in the direction of his still-seated body but refused to find his eyes to see what reaction my taunt had caused.

I did hear a small chuckle.

EPISODE 11

June 1549
Hatfield House, Hertfordshire

L ife continued as it always had in the schoolroom, though I knew that Robert found Dr. Ascham very diverting in comparison to our previous tutors. Robert spurred me to do better, and I him. Master Belmain had us do some playacting, all in French, which was new and great fun. All would gather round and listen to me play the lute when Master Broushe's lessons commenced, and I was proud of the way Robert's eyes twinkled when I began singing. Master Ascham took a great liking to Robert, although he did not spend time teaching him.

Also, he and Robert's tutor got along famously.

Even Lady Tyrwhitt seemed to take a liking to Robert, once she saw that we were indeed great friends. Consequently, she let us sit and read, play chess, and ride alone together frequently, and we took every opportunity to do all the things she gave us freedom to do.

During most of our previous visits, conversations about

marriage flowed freely and frankly. However, Robert now only brought up the subject in passing, saying things such as, "When the war is over, I suppose it will be time to settle down. That is, if I do not get shot," or, "On my honor, I would do so, wife or no." Once, he said, "Fortunes being what they are, I hope to have a well-off bride, for I have nothing but a loving heart to offer and a promise of a governing office one day."

I could not understand his evasive measures until one evening when we rode to the crest of a wonderful hill that looked down on a valley of sprouting fields. It was beautiful and hot, and I was in a happy, chatty mood. Robert for some reason was not, and listened as I went on and on about horses and carriages, and even when I moved on to lace and hats.

When finally I did pause, Robert took on a rather formal tone and said, "My Lady Princess?"

I whacked him on the leg with my riding glove, "My Lady Princess?" I said in a mocking tone. "Where does this come from? You have called me Elizabeth when only my father or Kat would dare, and now you say my Lady Princess?"

"Elizabeth."

"Yes," I said as I scooped the pitch of my voice up and lengthened out the word.

"I know that you see what way the tide of politics is taking us."

"Yes, I do. I can see that your father is in position to take the power of the Lord Protector, if the current one does not gain a victory and soon."

Astonishment filled Robert's face. "Well thought out, my Lady. I can see that you keep a very close eye on the matters of men."

"Yes, of course I do. I am my father's daughter, am I not?" I said, pleased by his surprise.

"I am keenly aware that the position of the Dudley family is on the rise, for it might make a difference in my future." His checks blushed as he spoke these words.

What was he getting at? Robert never boasted—no more than other men. I could not see where he was taking this. "Yes?" I prompted with no pretense about the question.

He pulled on the reins of his horse and turned her toward me. "I was wondering if there could be some sort of—" He shook his head in disgust and murmured something to himself that sounded a great deal like a curse. When he looked up at me, his eyes were that smoldering liquid fire that tortured my dreams. He took a deep breath and burst out, "What I am wondering is if you have perhaps reconsidered your opinion toward the institution of marriage?"

I thought my heart was going to beat out of my chest. He had finally come to it. I pulled my horse around his and started walking her slowly. "I think that there may be one person in this world that I possibly could consider as a husband," I said carefully, looking at him askance. I was surprised my voice came out so even, considering the way I was breathing.

"Really? So, you have made a single allowance. Who is the lucky man? I hope for your sake that it was not Thomas Seymour." His brow furrowed.

"No! It certainly is not Thomas!" I said almost on top of his last words.

He stared at me and I laughed nervously while we looked at one another for a long moment. Finally, he continued, "Well that is a relief." He moved his horse closer to mine. "So, there is a man out there that may win your heart and have your hand?" His face seemed to be bursting with joy.

"I suppose. Though he would have to get permission from the council first, just as my father's will dictates," I answered a bit uncertainly.

"Yes, of course. Of course, he would." Now Robert was rubbing his hands together awkwardly. "Um, shall we find a nice place to sit and rest?"

"Certainly, it is rather hot," I commented and finally my heart began to slow. I felt hope that after all this time Robert and I might finally come to an understanding.

But once I found my seat, the conversation turned to other matters and did not lean toward matrimony again.

Over the next few weeks, many conversations of this tenor came and went. Robert was probing, and I understood why. He knew I once had said I would never marry or have children. I had in fact ruined our previous chances. If not for my idiocy, we would have gotten engaged at my father's wedding and could possibly be married by now.

So, to say the words he needed me to, to tell him I had truly and completely changed my mind, sparked my fear and my pride. Whenever the appropriate moment arrived, I felt myself shrink. I felt my bravery leave me weak-kneed. I could not allow myself to be the first to say the words.

He hinted all around but ultimately stayed silent on the subject, so I had to declare myself in other ways. When I looked at him, I tried to tell him with my eyes. As I spoke of how good he was, I hoped he'd hear my love. I proved it with affectionate touches to his hand and arm. I prayed the whole while that he understood me, for his sentiments were very clear to me by the same methods.

EPISODE 12

July 1549
Hatfield House, Hertfordshire

The first week of July, Robert received word that a man named Robert Kett had started a rebellion against the throne and that all able men were needed to crush it. It was the worst fear of us both, but not altogether unexpected. The country seemed to be in a slow burning riot after Thomas' death. Robert's father would lead part of the attack himself. Robert was called to join him immediately, and he faced the news bravely.

When it was finally time for our goodbyes, I stole him away to a quiet corner of the library and took his hands in mine. "I will pray every moment for your safety, but I still fear so much that you will not come back." I thought of the scary dream I'd had of him being crushed.

He folded my hands between his, brought them to his lips and kissed them as he had the first time I'd met him. Looking into my eyes he whispered, "I have something to come back to. Something I have waited my entire life for, it seems. That will drive me to return. It will give me courage and will make me smart."

Our gazes tangled and melted from the familiar way to a warmer, more meaningful insight. Robert took a step toward me. He stood over me like a beautiful creature of protection. How I loved him, his face, his hands, his eyes. Heat leaked from our gazes and moved downward, warming my whole body. Our breath came fast and blended in an anticipatory mingling. I stretched my mouth towards his, which waited, hopeful, eager.

He leaned toward me, but not toward my lips. He gently kissed my cheek, lingering there and whispering once more. "When I come back, there will be no more waiting. It will be time for clear speaking and clear thinking, and I will settle this thing between you and me. If I have to beg on my hands and knees, I will do what is required of me and all will be right."

I blushed but nodded as I moved away so I could look into his knowing eyes. I wanted to tell him how I loved him, how I could not wait to be his wife. I wanted to open my soul to him and let him see how it would kill me if he died in battle. But it all got caught in my throat, and before I knew it his soft lips brushed a kiss on my other cheek and he was out the door. Gone. My love was gone, and he took my heart with him. I prayed to God that he would return with it.

La Fin